The Union

By

Bruce Norman

ISBN 978-1-105-12279-8

Chapter One

An Interesting Life

Taking a deep breath, I sighed deeply and knocked. When the door opened, the sunlight streaming through the windows hurt my eyes but I could still see the same crappy room I had seen so many times before traveling around the country on business. They all looked so boringly similar with the same bland decor and the same cheesy watercolors looking down at the same beige bedspread. This room, however, was very different because there were two men standing in it.

"Come in, Mr. Quinn," the man said as he opened the door. It flashed across my mind that there should have been a tag line on those words like—*said the spider to the fly.* "I'm Bill Douglas with the FBI and this is Agent Felix Garcia with the Treasury Department. Please come in and sit down."

As I entered the room I nodded toward Garcia, but his coal black eyes just stared through a scowl as he sat down. I went over to the table by the window and pulled out the chair across from Garcia who sat there motionless. I smiled as I sat down crossing my legs and folding my arms across my chest. I was desperately trying to appear relaxed.

"What can I do for you fine gentlemen today?"

"You're looking at seven to ten years in federal prison for bribery and conspiracy," said Garcia as he pointed his finger at me.

"Believe me, we can help you with that," Douglas said as he sat down on the edge of the bed. "Just tell us what you know about Renato Costa, Sammy Merzone, the Massarro crime family, and their involvement with the Union."

Although I was physically in the room, my mind was thinking about everything that had happened. There was one thing I knew for a fact. If I continued to do 'little favors' for people, it wouldn't be long before I'd get my ass shot. I just wasn't sure if that would come at the hands of the Justice Department or the mob.

My name is Parker Quinn and five years ago, I was sitting in a beautiful office on the thirty-eighth floor of the newest building on Wall Street. By anybody's definition, I had it good. I had the expensive high backed leather chair, a huge oak desk, an Oriental rug, and all the other trappings of a successful Wall Street executive. What I didn't know at the time was that I was becoming the living embodiment of an old saying and a Chinese curse. "Be careful of what you wish for," and "May your life be interesting."

There I sat, lost in thought. I just went through a messy divorce and seventeen years of ninety minute commutes. It gave me a desire for a simpler life away from the crowds and the noise of the city. I was staring blankly at my desk when the intercom jolted me back to the present.

"Mr. Quinn. Jack Townsend is out here."

" Okay.......yeah,.... please Ann, send him in."

Townsend and I had been friends for many years, which was a bit strange because we were also fierce competitors in the investment management business.

"You look like crap, Quinn" Townsend said as he stood in front of my desk.

"Gee.......thanks, Jack."

"You alright?" Townsend asked as he sat down. "Look Quinn, I know the divorce ripped you up but you gotta move on, pal."

"Yeah, I know Jack. But honestly, it's more than that. I need to get out of the city and go someplace less.... well, less like this! I've had it. I need a change, Jack. If I don't get out of this fucking place, I'm gonna go crazy."

2

"Quinn, listen to me. You busted your ass to get where you are. You leave now and you're throwing all that away. Just hang in there. Pretty soon you'll feel a whole lot better, I promise you."

"Jack, I appreciate your concern. I really do. But when I look around, I don't particularly like what I see," I replied as I leaned back in my chair.

"Well, I think you're crazy but if I hear of anything, I'll let you know."

Two days later, Jack telephoned to say that he knew of a major firm in need of someone to go and straighten out a failing office in a 'lovely little city' of about 100,000 people. The pay wasn't great, but I knew I could build my own investment advisory business *and* get an override on the branch's production. More important was the fact that I could get out of this rat race of a city. So, all in all, I didn't think it was such a bad deal. The Lord may work in mysterious ways, but Chinese curses work in insidious ways because, and as quickly as that, I found myself diving head first into an 'interesting life'.

Three years later, I was fairly well established in my new life in the 'city'. I always laughed to myself when the locals talked about 'going to the city' as if it contained a million people and was the center of the universe. But it really was a nice place...at least from the outside. Now, my commute was only five minutes and I got to play golf twice a week. I went to some very nice restaurants and had a decent social life. Things were definitely looking up.

There were numerous opportunities for me to build my brokerage business. I found where all the old money in the city was buried, and by far the largest horde at nearly seven hundred million dollars, was the local labor union's pension fund. This was no ordinary labor union with a few thousand members. Quite the contrary, because *this* union had been started and carefully built over many years by a single Italian immigrant, into a forty thousand member powerhouse covering three states. Getting the Union's business would pay a small fortune in commissions. That Union was definitely at the top of my wish list but unfortunately at the top of the Union sat a very dangerous Renato Costa.

It was midmorning on a lazy Wednesday and I wasn't feeling particularly ambitious. It was one of those beautiful days when everything seems great because the weather was warm, the sun was out, and the leaves still had that bright green color that only happens in the early spring. When the phone rang, I didn't want to answer it for fear of losing the nice peaceful glow that engulfed me. Grudgingly, I slumped forward in my chair and my hand fell on the phone.

"Good Morning. This is Quinn."

"Quinny," the voice crooned. I knew immediately who it was because if 'Brooklyn accent' were ever represented in the dictionary, a picture of Nicky Tagliano would definitely accompany it. "It's Nicky."

"Hey. What's up?"

I met Nicky at a party about a year ago. He was like the brother I never had. There was just something about him that drew me like the moth to the flame. Nicky was known as the 'Puerto Rican'. He was not, however, Puerto Rican. He was Sicilian. He got tagged with the name because his naturally dark complexion always made him look as if he just came off the beach. By anyone's assessment, he was a handsome man and bore a striking resemblance to a young Jose Ferrer with black wavy hair going slightly gray at the temples and a salt and pepper moustache that lay trimly under an elegantly slender nose. I always wondered how Nicky was able to run a business and still have time to be *the* social butterfly of the city. I liked Nicky because he was the most naturally funny person I had ever met. When Nicky got into telling a story, he'd throw himself into it like a great stage actor and become a blur of waving arms and flashing eyes. Nicky once told me, that with my size and looks and with his charm, we could have all the women we could ever want.

"I got two guys for golf and I was wondering if you could get out this afternoon? Besides, I've got something I need to talk to you about."

I thought about it for a moment. It wasn't that I didn't want to go. Hell, it was gorgeous outside, but my conscience didn't want to allow me to leave work just to go play golf. But...Nicky *was* connected to the Union *and* his closest friend was the number two guy. Although Nicky was ever present at Union functions, he didn't actually work for the Union. In fact, for all his attempts to be the most stereotypical New York Italian on the planet, he was a successful pharmacist and owned three stores. I sensed that this might be an opportunity to get closer to the real action.

"Yeah, why not. I wasn't feeling all that inspired anyway," I said sighing in resignation. "What time?"

"Great! I'll meet you at the city course around 11:30. We can grab a sandwich before we go out."

"Sounds good."

I was looking forward to this. I loved golf. Nicky was certain to make me laugh, and who knew what devious little plot might be in the works.

Turning down the street toward the golf course, I was looking at the old maples that had grown so large that they formed a rich green tunnel. It made me smile as I thought how much nicer this was than the concrete jungle I spent so many years in. By the time I reached the course, Nicky was already taking his clubs out of his Corvette. There was only one reason Nicky had that Corvette. He looked damned good in it, and that's just what he wanted the ladies to see— him with that suave Latin look, the perfectly tailored clothes, and his shiny red Corvette. The hell of it was ...it worked! I could go into any crowded room and find Nicky's newest love. She was sure to have a petite face, raven hair, and a body so thin that it looked like it was made from pipe cleaners.

"Heyee.... my friend. How *you* doin'?" Nicky called to me as I pulled into the space next to him. The greeting was standard Nicky. The 'heyee' had to be slowly drawn from the throat. While the *How you doin'* came out to mean, How *you* doin'? Cause *I'm* doin' fine!

There were two objectives to Nicky Tagliano's golf game. First, was to shoot a low score and second, to harass the hell out of everybody around him. It was like playing golf with the Tasmanian Devil. Golf with him was three hours of one-liners and stories. He and I always had a good match, but there was no way I could match Nicky's mouth or his attire. People joked that Nicky needed a separate house just for his clothes. Being impeccably dressed in finely tailored clothes was, in Nicky's eyes, a basic human need.

"What's up?" I said as I hauled my golf clubs out of the trunk of the car. I didn't want to sound too eager, but the suspense had been eating at me.

"Let's grab a sandwich. I'll tell you later." Nicky's response left me with a slight twinge of regret that I might have appeared too eager.

"Not a problem."

It was only a short walk up to the starters shack/ sandwich shop/ golf shop/ all around hang out for all the old 'retired' Italian patrons. Inside, we met Gino Santori and Angelo Vito. Gino was a Business Agent for the Union and Angie was...well, Angie. He wasn't visibly employed, at least not that I could see, but he was a fixture at most of the Union functions. I was told that Angie took care of certain employer/employee problems—whatever the hell that meant. Being the size of a small building, he was apparently well suited for the job.

The golf bets were the standard buck a hole along with presses and double presses `and carry forwards as usual. It really wasn't the money that mattered. These guys would go to Vegas, drop ten grand, bang a couple of broads, and come home 'winners'. It was all about bragging rights at the local bar after the game that meant everything. You get to brag a little, cry a little over the shot that just missed, and congratulate someone over that beautiful shot on such and such a hole. No one ever lost any real money and Nicky would always have a few great stories that everyone had heard a hundred times before. Yes, life was good.

After Gino and Angie left the bar, Nicky leaned closer to me and in a low voice said, "Anthony needs a favor. Do you remember when you asked me to get that friend of yours in Jersey a job?" Nicky continued.

How could I forget? Good old Eddie Ryan, my friend from North Jersey. He called with a tale of woe about being unable to get work. In another moment of soft-heartedness, I said I might be able to help. So I called Nicky to see if he could talk to Anthony Traffarro. Traffarro was the number two man at the Union and for the last ten years was the power behind the Costa throne. I thought it might be possible that Traffarro knew someone who was hiring. Nicky called back and said that a guy in Jersey owed Traffarro a favor and could put Eddie on in the warehouse for a month and then get him on a truck. So, I got the favor for Eddie and then good old Eddie returned it by quitting after *one fucking day*! But now I was obligated and with these people, it was a matter of honor. Ask a favor, do a favor. My sense of eager anticipation plunged into a sense of dread. What the hell did I get myself into? To say that the Union had a bad reputation was a gross understatement. The Union had connections to the mob and there were more than a few bodies at the bottom of the river attributed to it.

"Anthony's wife needs a job," Nicky said flatly as he reached for his beer.

I felt a cascade of emotions. I was honored that Anthony Traffarro had asked me for any favor...required or otherwise. I also knew I was finally moving closer to the inner circle and to my ultimate objective of getting some of the commissions from that seven hundred million dollar business. *But what job? How the hell do you employ the wife of Anthony Traffarro? What does she do? Does she know anything? I'm in the fucking securities industry for Christ's sake. What the hell is everyone in the office going to think?*

"Sure," I said with a tone of assurance. "No problem."

Where the hell did that come from, I thought? No sooner had the words crossed my lips than I regretted saying them. Mr. 'Shoot from the hip' strikes again. It always amazes me how the human brain has the capacity to swirl wildly calculating an outcome while at the same time the mouth continues to bury you deeper in shit.

"Have her give me a call in the morning and I'll take care of it," I said, still maintaining the illusion of confidence.

It was 8:30 the next morning by the time I finally got settled in the office. The previous days' events had produced a poor nights' sleep because for all my attempts to think otherwise, I couldn't stop thinking about what could happen if I didn't employ Mrs. Traffarro. Even though I heard about the mob connection with the Union, I really didn't think I'd wind up as a dead body performing a lengthy examination of the local river bottom for something like this. On the contrary, I figured I would wind up in some gut wrenchingly embarrassing position that made me wince every time I thought about it. Thankfully, my agony was short lived because a little after 9:00, I received a call from Constance Traffarro.

"Mr. Quinn? This is Connie Traffarro. Nicky Tagliano told me to call you. He said you might have a job for me."

"Hi, Connie. How are you? Yes. I talked to Nicky yesterday and he said you were looking for something. When can you come down to the office so we can talk?"

"Well, I don't know what your schedule is, but how about in an hour?"

I told her an hour would be fine. Actually, it was great because it meant I could deal with this situation quickly and be done with it. Letting problems and issues sit around only made things worse. They tended to stink to high heaven after a few days. I prefer to anticipate the worst and hopefully be pleasantly surprised. Thankfully, when Connie arrived at my office that was exactly what happened.

Constance Traffarro was a very attractive, petite woman and probably forty-ish. She wore a beautifully tailored suit that spoke of a rather nice figure beneath it. I thought that had she not been married, I might have asked her for a date. I quickly decided to bury that thought when the other side of my brain reminded me that she was married to Anthony Traffarro. If I kept thinking like this, I might yet get that extended river bottom tour.

"Hi, Connie. Please come in and have a seat," I said as I rose to greet her.

"Thank you."

"So, Nicky tells me you're looking for work."

"Well, yes. You see my son has been in college for two years now and I've been bored stiff being home alone. This would be an opportunity to earn my own money, and that would mean I wouldn't have to ask Anthony every time I want to buy something. To be honest, he isn't at all pleased with me wanting to go to work. He thinks how would it look to have his wife working? People would think he couldn't support his family. But frankly, I don't really care what anyone thinks. I know I don't have a lot of experience but I promise you that I'll do a good job because I need to do this. Do you think you can find a place for me?"

I liked her immediately.

"Sure." My thoughts were coming out as words. "I'll tell you what. I can pay you twelve dollars an hour. You'll start out in operations catching up on some filing and then I want you to move to the wire to enter orders. After that I'll put you into the cashier's area. This way you'll be trained in all the operations areas and can take over when one of the girls is out sick or on vacation. After a little while we'll move that salary up."

I think Connie didn't have a clue what I was talking about, but it must have sounded good. A big smile came over her face as she rose to leave. She reached out to shake my hand.

"Thank you so much, Mr. Quinn. I'm looking forward to this and I know I won't disappoint you."

"I'm sure you'll do just fine, Connie," I replied. "And please, drop the mister. Everybody just calls me Quinn." I took a long look as she left his office. If there was one thing I could say about Traffarro, it was that he certainly had good taste in women.

On the drive back home, Connie's emotions were a swirling mix of excitement and anxiety. She hadn't gone to work in over twenty years. She wondered if she had what it takes. She didn't know anything about the brokerage business. Maybe this wasn't such a good idea after all. This seemed like such a good idea but now the reality of it all was setting in.

I told Cindy Carver, my operations manager, that I had hired a part-timer who would take some of the strain off of her and Beth. I wanted her trained in all areas of operations so that she could stand in during vacations or if someone was out sick. 'Hell, this actually *was* a good idea,' I thought. Now that I had the wife of the number two man at the Union working for me, it seemed probable that I'd be able to get closer to Anthony Traffarro. Maybe there was hope that I could get a piece of that pension business after all. I decided to call Nicky and tell him everything was taken care of.

"Hey, Nicky. It's Quinn. I met with Connie Traffarro and everything is set. She starts on Monday. Tell Anthony not to worry. I'll take good care of her."

"That's great, Quinny! I knew I could count on you. Anthony's been waiting for my call."

I had heard that Anthony Traffarro was the son of Sicilian immigrants. He grew up on the eastside in an all-Italian neighborhood. His formal education stopped at the tenth grade because that's when his real education began. He had always been a part of the action in the neighborhood. His father ran a poker room situated over the ambulance company he owned on the Eastside. When Anthony was eight years old, his father had him sit on the bottom step of the stairs leading up the side of the ambulance garage to the poker room. Traffarro always wanted to help his father and this job made him feel important. What he didn't realize was that most of the police were on his father's payroll and they knew which nights the games were held. He got to know everybody who was somebody and everybody who was going to be somebody: mob bosses, politicians, business leaders—*everybody*! Those were the connections that would make Traffarro great.

When Traffarro was sixteen, he started to drive a truck for one of the local trucking companies and naturally, all the employees were in Renato Costa's Union. Traffarro drove the truck during the day, worked some of his father's games at night, and every now and then did an ambulance pickup. By the time he was eighteen, he had more than enough money to buy his first car. It was a beautiful black Pontiac convertible with a black top and black leather interior and to this day, he got misty every time he thought of that car.

Traffarro always greeted people with a broad smile, a quick laugh, and a voice that had degraded into deep rasp. He told me it was the result of long nights drinking whiskey, running around with women, and an earnest attempt to keep at least one tobacco company profitable. Traffarro would smile when he talked about his 'misspent youth'.

Of course this city had laws just like every place else but it was the rules and traditions that really mattered. Violating one of the rules or breaking with tradition had consequences. This was often brought to light by Traffarro, who loved to tell stories about the old days. They all began with the same "you remember". My education started at the first Union party I attended..." Traffarro was standing with a group of friends when he began the lesson.

'You remember Larry Del Bono's joint over on Bleeker Street?" he began. He started telling one of a hundred stories using his best street voice. The ability to talk to anyone on their level was one of his many gifts. "I happened to be down at my father's ambulance garage, when Larry calls up looking for my old man. He tells me he's got this problem. It seems this big black guy comes into his joint all liquored up. The guy wasn't in the joint five minutes when he starts causin' all kinds of problems. *How the fuck* dis guy wound up in Larry's joint, I will never know. You know Larry. There's no way he's putting up with any crap. So he takes out that little bat he's got behind the bar and Bam!! Now the bum's layin' on the floor bleedin'. So somebody decided to have an ambulance come down and take da prick to the hospital before he really bloodies up da place. So naturally, I go down there and I swear, it took four of us to get this guy on the gurney and into the ambulance. This mother was *fucking huge*. I'm in the back and Vinny Longo's drivin'. So I say to the guy, "are you strapped down good and tight? I don't want you fallin' over or nothin' ya know." "Yeah," he says. I say, "are you sure you're strapped down *real* good?" "Yeah, man. I can't fuckin' move." "GOOD!" I say, and I start beatin' the crap out of the cocksucker. Vinny turns around and yells, "Anthony! What the fuck! For Christ's sake, what are ya doin' back there?" I told him, "I'm making sure this 'moolie' remembers which side of the fuckin' city he belongs on." Traffarro finished the story with a good laugh which was the signal for everyone else to laugh. As he slowly raised his glass to his lips, Traffarro looked at Quinn. The meaning didn't escape Quinn.

Anthony Traffarro was not an uneducated man. He had a doctorate in the ways of the street—*with honors.* There was a subtle detachment about him and was particularly adept at unraveling the convoluted schemes that swirled around him on a daily basis. He was a brilliant tactician and watched the people being shuffled around the chessboard of his world while he calculated the moves of the Unions' reigning king, Renato Costa. Costa had a nasty habit of twisting people's lives to keep them on edge. It was his way of letting everyone know who was in charge. This drove Traffarro crazy since he was trying to maintain some semblance of order in the union and figuring out what Costa was really up to was becoming increasingly difficult.

Traffarro was a man of stature. That is not to say that he was a big man. He was of average height and although the buttons on his shirt sometimes strained under the burden of an ample stomach, no one would have called him fat. His size seemed a compliment to his lifestyle. Always sharply dressed, he had that perfectly tailored look. His pants flowed down from that somewhat excessive waist in a symphony of pleats and creases that did not *dare* move out of place. He was almost fifty by the time I met him and his thinning hair had started to show the signs of the gray that goes with the age. A pencil-thin moustache sat above a casual smile. Here was a man that was respected not only for his position in the Union, but for his character. Everyone knew that Anthony Traffarro was a man of his word and could be counted on when things get tough.

It's been two months since Connie started work in the office and things seemed to be going well for her. She fits in well with everyone in the office and I was happy with the work she was doing. She and I had become fond of each other. I'm a fairly easy-going guy and I think that made her feel comfortable. She asked me if I would come out to dinner with Anthony and her, as well as Nicky and his wife.

"Sure," I replied. "When and where?"

"How about Terrabella's Restaurant on Bleeker...Saturday night, about seven?"

"Sounds great. I'll be there."

She was quick to add. "I don't know if there is someone you want to bring along, but feel free."

I had been involved with a few women, but nothing lasted very long and now was one of those gap periods. I wasn't a bar hopper and that left the number of encounters to a precious few. Nicky and some of his friends, who now comprised the bulk of my circle of friends, were constantly trying to fix me up. Suzanne Romano flashed into my mind as I thought of the string of gems these guys kept throwing my way. I recall one particular afternoon when I was having a few drinks after golf with Nicky and the guys.

"Quinny. I'm telling you, you'll love this girl," Nicky began. "She's Jimmy Romano's ex and she's loaded. She lives over on Park Drive in that big house on the corner of Maple. I think she was a dancer or hooker or something like that. Believe me Quinny, she'll fuck your brains out" said Nicky, in who's mind those were top qualifications.

Angie Vito was quick to add, "Quinn, she'll buy you a fuckin' watch."

"Really, who could pass up such a deal?" I said with a careful touch of sarcasm.

Two days later, I met Ms. Romano at Bobby Risolli's Ristorante d'Napoli, a nice little Italian restaurant on the Eastside. When I arrived, she was already seated at a table in what seemed to be the darkest corner of the restaurant. She was a very attractive blue-eyed blond and showed her money in the jewelry and the obviously expensive dress she wore. It was cut low and revealed just enough of what I was sure were a pair of truly exquisite breasts. This was a nice complement to her trim body. *Maybe the Puerto Rican got it right this time*, I thought. It was such a pleasant surprise that I was actually a little nervous. I introduced myself and started some light conversation and then it happened. She spoke! It wasn't that her voice was so raspy or chirpy. It was that she was completely devoid of a single intelligent thought. I actually could not carry on a conversation with this woman. I was pretty damned sure this was going to be the longest hour of my life. As we were leaving the restaurant I could see she wanted to take this liaison further, but how could I make love to a woman I couldn't even talk to? The evil side of my brain was saying, *forget about it Quinn. Open your eyes and take a good long look at that body.* Yeah, the bad brain did have a point. She really looked hot and had the kind of reputation that would make any man happy. Thankfully, I managed to catch myself before the good side of my brain lapsed into a coma for a couple of hours. In the end, it was a courteous goodbye that ended the tension along with a "We'll have to get together again."

I didn't want to be a fifth wheel at this dinner, but I also didn't want to give the impression that there was someone serious in my life. This was an important dinner and I didn't want anyone to get the wrong idea by showing up with someone like the slinky Ms. Romano. Yet as I approached the restaurant, I was mildly uncomfortable about being alone. I saw Nicky's Corvette in front of the restaurant but Traffarro's black Cadillac was nowhere in sight. *This was probably good,* I thought. It would give me a chance to get acquainted with Nicky's wife before Traffarro arrived.

Walking through the door, I saw Nicky at the end of the bar with his wife. She was definitely a Nicky girl: pretty petite face, big mane of black hair, and a pipe cleaner body with two perky little breasts. Yup...vintage Nicky! She was a bright, well educated school teacher who was a good conversationalist—that is, whenever Nicky was quiet long enough to allow her talk.

"Heyee! Quinny" Nicky shouted as soon as I entered the room. "How you doin'?"

"Good. How 'bout you?" I said walking over to the bar. Then I turned to address Nicky's wife.

"Hello. I'm Parker Quinn. It's a pleasure to meet you."

"Yes, Mr. Quinn. It's a pleasure to meet you, too. I'm Lorie Tagliano. How are you?" she said as she extended her hand.

I gently took her hand as she presented me with a lovely smile. Somehow, behind that smile, I sensed a certain chill. It's the feeling you get when you look into someone's eyes and realize that either they don't want to be there or they simply resent your very existence.

"Please, call me Quinn. Everybody else does." I continued. "I think my mother named me Parker because she was sure nobody could come up with a nickname from it. It's been just plain old Quinn since I was a kid."

Out of the corner of my eye, I saw Nicky turn towards the entrance and enthusiastically announce that Anthony and Connie had just come in. He quickly got up and went over to greet them.

"Heyee. Anthony. How you doin'?" Nicky greeted them in his standard fashion.

As Nicky shook Anthony's hand, he put his left arm over Anthony's shoulder to give him a warm hug and a respectful kiss on the cheek. Connie was next for the same treatment, after which they proceeded to the bar to greet me and Lorie.

"Hi, Quinny," Connie said in a singsong teasing voice. She knew Nicky called me that and that I didn't particularly like it, but tolerated it. Besides, Nicky had that kind of a personality that wouldn't allow you to stay mad at him for very long, at least not during these times.

We stayed at the bar for a cocktail while Traffarro had his usual club soda. He gave up drinking years back. Someone said there had been an incident that caused some embarrassment at a Union meeting. It seemed that Traffarro had a few too many drinks and had gotten into a minor brawl with a shop steward. Costa had called him into his office the next day to tell him that as much as he loved him, if he ever "pulled that shit again," he'd throw him out of the Union. Traffarro pledged to Costa that he would never take another drink and if there was one thing Anthony Traffarro had, it was discipline.

This evening was no different than any other for Anthony Traffarro. There wasn't a restaurant or bar he could go into without half a dozen people coming up to him for a warm greeting or a hushed conversation. Tonight was particularly active. The conversations were either casual and filled with humor, or instructional and peppered with facts brought from his broad mental database. I heard enough laughter and hushed voices to figure that for tonight, there was plenty of both. After about half an hour and one more round of drinks later, we all sat down.

The evening passed quickly. They always did when Nicky was at the table and on a roll. He had an amazing capacity to make everyone have a good time. At one point, Nicky had Traffarro laughing so hard he could hardly catch his breath. Even Nicky's wife warmed to the occasion.

"Hey, T. Tell Quinny about that meeting you and the old man had at Longview Drugs," Nicky requested, using his nickname for Traffarro. To really understand the flavor of this nickname, you have to understand the subtle nuances of how this neighborhood treated the name Anthony. First, it was pronounced "ant-knee". However, there weren't too many people who actually got called by their real name of Anthony. As you might suspect, the obvious nick name was Tony, but in this city it was often broken down into a simple 'T'.

"Oh, Jeez! What a time **that** was," Traffarro replied. "But before I forget, Quinn, I want to thank you for taking such good care of Connie. You know..... teaching her all about your business and all."

"Really Anthony, it's my pleasure. She's doing a great job."

Over that few months, Connie and I had grown close. We both respected each other's position, and developed something of a sibling like relationship and formed a bond of mutual trust. Connie had long since stopped being nervous in her new environment and had rekindled the fiery spirit she said she thought she had lost.

"Yeah, but Quinn. What the fuck did you do to her?" Traffarro asked in feigned seriousness. "She's got a mouth on her now that..." Traffarro couldn't finish his sentence before Connie cut in.

"No, Anthony. I always had this mouth. You just never let me use it," she snapped back in mock indignation.

I was getting a little uncomfortable. I wasn't sure if Traffarro was really upset or just kidding. Fortunately, I got my answer quickly.

"Oooohh! Listen to her," Nicky moaned. "Quinny, what have you done?"

"Who me?"

Traffarro slapped both his hands down on the table as he broke into fits of laughter. "Oh, God! Christ Quinn, the look on your face."

I continued to mug it up, protesting my innocence until everyone finally settled down. I was becoming much more comfortable with my new friends and was pretty good at these little word wars.

"Come on T. Tell Quinn about Longview," Nicky said as he egged Traffarro on.

"Okay! Okay! Well, we had been out on strike for maybe nine or ten months," Traffarro began. "What the members wanted in the new contract was ridiculous. They were pissed off at Longview for God knows how long and they just wanted to stick it to 'em. Of course the management basically took a 'fuck them attitude'. We had guys bustin' up trucks and all kinds of crap. They were yelling at people from the picket line and generally it was a very bad situation," Traffarro said as he waved his hands around in true Italian fashion. "Reno and I were supposed to go down to the warehouse and try to reason with these maniacs and bring them their strike pay," he said referring to Costa by the nickname he had picked up many years ago. "When we get there, there's a bunch of guys beatin' the shit out of some guy's car. We go into the warehouse and there has *got* to be two hundred screaming guys passing a bottle around. They had this long banquet table. So we go over and sit down and we made damned sure we put that table between us and that fucking mob. I lean over to Reno and whisper to him 'Where's the strike money'? So, he tells me, I was supposed to bring it. Like the old man would ever let anyone carry thirty grand of *his* fuckin' money. Danny Fitz, the other Business Agent was there, so I ask Danny if *he's* got it. 'Fuck no,' Danny whispers. No? I says. About this time, I'm really getting nervous because these guys look like they wanna kill somebody. So I turn to the old man and ask him what the fuck is he gonna do? 'Don't worry', he says. '*I'll* take care of it.' So the little shit stands up on his chair. You know Reno", Traffarro said as he turned his head back and forth looking at everyone. "What's he, five foot and a little bit and a fuckin' hundred pounds? So there he is on his chair, waving his arms and yelling for everyone to keep quiet. Finally, after a few minutes, everyone settled down. So he yells out 'You fuckin' people wouldn't know a good deal if it hit you in the fuckin' head! I'm not giving you another fuckin' dime until you settle this strike!' There's dead silence. Reno gets down from the chair and calmly walks out the fucking door leaving me and Danny there to face these maniacs. I turn to Danny and tell him to give me his gun. 'Why?' he says to me. *Why*? I yell. Because these fuckin' guys are gonna kill us, that's why! Just as he hands me the gun, the place goes nuts. Two hundred fuckin' guys start to charge Danny and me. I fire three shots from that fuckin' cannon Danny carries around and the place goes quiet again. So *I* get up on a chair and yell—Look at you! You've all gone fuckin' crazy! You guys have been on strike so long you forgot what the fuck you're workin' for. Ya got families for Christ sake! I know this strike pay ain't payin' the bills. Reno's right. Settle it! Danny looks up at me like he can't believe what I just said. So I motion to him that we had better get the fuck outta there before we get killed. Two days later we're sitting with the old man at the bargaining table and the strike ends," Traffarro ended, raising his hand in the traditional *I swear..... hand to God* motion.

While I sat there in disbelief, everyone else was nodding their head in silent affirmation that indeed, it had happened just that way.

As the evening was drifting to a close over repeated cups of espresso, I noticed Traffarro reach over and slowly grab Nicky's arm and pull him close. I wasn't able to hear the short conversation, but I did catch Nicky's confirmation that he would meet Traffarro in the morning at Nino's Coffee Shop.

Chapter Two
The Really Big Favor

It was eight the next morning by the time Nicky walked into Nino's. As he opened the door a little bell jingled to announce the new customer. Nicky immediately looked for Traffarro at his usual location in the back. He saw Traffarro sitting with his back to the wall so that he could see everyone as they came in. This had been the mandatory position for Traffarro since he was a young man. He never sat with his back to the door believing that doing so was a very good way to get a nasty surprise. Traffarro lowered his newspaper as Nicky approached.

"Hey T. What's up?" Nicky said in a subdued voice. He knew there was a time for fun and there was a time for business, and this was going to be a business meeting. Traffarro had that look on his face. He had seen it several times before and it usually preceded a conversation that wasn't going to be pleasant.

"The Feds are really turning up the heat on Reno."

"T", Nicky said as he brought his hands up and together in a pleading gesture. "They've been after the old man for twenty five years and they still don't have anything on him. The guy must have spent a million dollars to keep his scrawny ass out of the can. He's like fuckin' Teflon." The 'Teflon' term was being used quite frequently around this time. The infamous John Gotti managed, numerous times, to keep himself out of prison and earned the name "The Teflon Don". In this city, watching John Gotti on television, triumphantly walk out of a Federal Court as a free man was cause for celebration. It would be drinks all around in the bars frequented by this crowd, as they watched him on television. Just like baseball or football...it was their spectator sport!

"Yeah, well...that was then and this is now," responded Traffarro. "They got a new Federal Prosecutor in this district now and this guy's looking to make his bones by puttin' the old man away and breaking the Union. The guy is obsessed. It's like the only thing important in his life is to see Reno in the can. The Feds did it to the International and now this prick wants to put the heat on the local."

"I knew about the International, but when the hell did this all happen to the local?"

Nicky had been with Traffarro for many years and looked upon himself as Traffarro's right hand man and knowing what was going on was all part of the job. It was embarrassing that he hadn't heard about this.

"This new prosecutor came in six months ago and ever since he got here, everything's gone to shit. About a month ago, I got a call from Pete Murray. You remember Pete. He used to run the local office that Sammy worked in," Traffarro said, referring to Sammy Merzone who handled all the brokerage business for the Union's pension funds and was paying kickbacks to Costa. "Pete got moved up to some regional position but he and I still keep in touch. He told me that the Feds subpoenaed Sammy's transaction records and a lot of his client files. He thinks his company is gonna get rid of Charlie Vero and Sammy. That means Sammy has to find himself new home and I sure as hell don't want that moron goin' some place we don't have any control over." Traffarro was a man who believed that planning ahead was a good way to stay out in front of Costa...not to mention staying alive.

Charlie Vero was the branch manager of the local brokerage office where Sammy Merzone worked as a stockbroker. He was put in an impossible position early in his term as manager. It was part of

Vero's job to review all the activity in the client accounts at the office. He had complained about some of the things he saw going on in Merzone's business dealings, but the company they worked for was making a fortune from Merzone's commissions. The last thing they wanted was to kill the golden goose. So, they told Vero to stay out of Merzone's business. After all, they told him, he didn't have to worry because they were assuming full responsibility.

"Just leave Sammy alone and worry about the rest of the office", Vero was told. The company's plan had been to keep this going as long as they could. Maybe they'd get lucky and neither the regulatory agencies nor the Justice Department would find out and if they weren't that lucky, so what. Now the day of reckoning finally arrived. They would just throw out a few sacrificial lambs to the regulatory wolves and be on their merry way. It was standard procedure on Wall Street. The company would have to pay a fine but it would only be a fraction of what they collected in fees. Of course they had to get rid of Vero and Merzone, but who cared? The company had made their money. Life goes on.

"Jesus Christ!" Nicky exclaimed. "What the fuck do we do now?"

"Quinn seems like a nice guy."

"Quinn? Yeah, I guess he is," responded Nicky with a perplexed look. *What did Quinn have to do with any of this*, he thought.

"You trust him?"

"You want Quinn to take in Sammy and Charlie," said Nicky, now getting a sense of where this was going.

"What I want to know is if you *trust him!*" said Traffarro emphatically, now showing his irritation...and no, not Charlie. Charlie's too fuckin' unpredictable," he said with a dismissive wave of his hand. "Charlie tried to move Sammy out by going to Reno. He figured he could sweeten whatever Sammy was paying the old man and grab a couple million in revenue for himself. What he didn't realize was that, as big a prick as Reno is, he was still loyal to Sammy. Reno knew Sammy didn't have the balls to screw him and besides, Reno never trusted Charlie anyway."

"Look T, I've known this guy for over a year now. We've played golf, hung around, and even chased some broads together. When I asked him to find a job for Connie, he knew he had an obligation and he did the right thing. And, let me say this, he treats her good because she's Connie not because she's your wife and that makes her feel needed. This guy is stand up. I trust him more than most of the fuckin' assholes around here."

Traffarro sat there for a moment sipping his coffee. He was a little amused by the heat he sensed in Nicky's voice and pleased that he had judged Quinn correctly. He lowered his cup and carefully placed it on the saucer.

"Good! If we can convince Quinn to take Sammy in *and* if Quinn's as stand up as you say, then we can keep tabs on that part of this mess. I want you to call Quinn and see if he can meet us for lunch."

"Sure. When and where?"

"Terrabella's. Tell him to be there around one o'clock. No. Ask him if he can be there. I don't want Quinn to think we're trying to push him around. I've got a meeting this morning with some of the business agents, but I should be able to get there by then," instructed Traffarro.

When I got Nicky's call, I was buried in work. I was looking at one of those very long days and figured I'd be tied up until well into the evening, but Nicky made it sound important, so I decided to make the time to go. Things were going well in the office and I was also starting to sense that I was slowly being pulled into a higher level of involvement with Traffarro and the Union. I thought it wouldn't be much longer before I'd get a piece of the pension fund's business.

The Eastside was a close knit Italian community where gossiping was a favored sport and hanging around Nicky had meant that I was seeing a lot more of it. Of course, I stood out there like a pink tutu at a Goth concert. So it was no surprise when someone as un-Italian as me started to appear at a few of the local hot spots, that some questions were raised. In fact, the first time I walked into Terrabella's, half the people ran out the back. It seemed that in my suit and tie I bore a strong resemblance to your typical FBI agent and many of Terrabella's patrons were not on friendly terms with *that* group. When my actual associations were ultimately revealed, I gained some level of respect. As I walked into Terrabella's I was surprised to be greeted by the owner's daughter as if I was an old friend.

"Hi. How are you?" Gina Terrabella sang with enthusiasm.

"Good. Thank you," I replied mildly surprised. "I've got two more people coming, so if someone comes in asking for Parker Quinn, would you show them over to my table?"

"No problem, Mr. Quinn. I know who you are. Is Nicky coming?"

"Yes, he is."

Okay. So now my curiosity was definitely peeked. Sure, I had been in there a few times but she acted like I was a regular.

"It's Gina isn't it?" I asked. I figured if I was being treated like a regular, I might as well act like one.

"Yup"

"Well, Gina, if we're going to be friends, please forget the Mr. Quinn. It's just Quinn".

"Got it. I think you'll want to sit in the bar area. It's nice and quiet there."

She turned and started to lead me into a small private bar and I followed without hesitation. *Why not*, I thought. *She seems to know more about what's going on than I do*. She brought me to a small round table in a corner. It was covered in a red and white checkered tablecloth on which rested a slender green vase with a few fresh flowers and a small red vase with a candle in it. Dark paneled walls and flagstone floors exuded an air of old world charm. For all the regulars, this was very warm and homey. I, however, was no regular and the history of the place along with the mystery of Nicky's call made me uneasy. I sat positioned with my back to the corner so I faced the doorway and could see Nicky and Anthony when they arrived.

"Would you like a drink while you wait?" she asked.

"I'll have a glass of club soda with lemon, please." I didn't know what proper protocol was, but I knew I'd be safe with club soda because that was what Traffarro drank. Besides, I wasn't sure whether Nicky and Traffarro would be late and too many cocktails now might allow my mouth to get me in trouble later.

"I'll bring you some garlic pizza too, so you'll have something to nibble on while you wait," she offered with a smile.

She soon returned with finger sized slices of pizza, which seemed to consist of mozzarella cheese, oregano, oil, and garlic. I reached for a piece. It smelled so good. When I bit into it, the crust crunched and the soft warm goodness flooded my mouth. "Oh, my God! This is so good". *Great! Just what I needed, a new food addiction.*

"I thought you'd like it. Garlic pizza is one of our specialties. I know Nicky loves it."

A few minutes and half the pizza later, Nicky walked in with Traffarro. They were both dressed as if they just stepped out of a magazine. Look, I'm no slacker, but these guys knew how to spend money.

"Hey, Quinn. How's things?" Nicky opened first. I noticed that his tone was remarkably subdued. *What happened to the heyeeeee and the Quinny,* I thought?

"I'm good Nicky. Hey Anthony, it's good to see you again," I said in a respectful tone.

After a few minutes of social chatter, Traffarro got down to business. I'm sure he knew what he was about to ask me was important and he wanted me to know as much of the background as necessary. Traffarro seemed to want to bring me up to speed slowly. Maybe it didn't make good sense to hit me with all this too quickly. He told me about the history of the Union, Costa, and about himself. How over the past decade, the old man had become an embarrassment to certain people. They felt that it was bad enough that he was running around with whores, but he had purchased a house for a big black woman just down the hill from his own home so that he could look down from his terrace and keep an eye on her. He would go to Union banquets and sit at the head table with his 'black whale' at his side. Traffarro continued on about the fact that the old man thought all the Union's money was his. He didn't go into the fact that the 'certain people' he had referred to were the mob nor how important the Union was to them. I guess scaring the crap out of me wasn't a good idea.

"This son of a bitch lives like he's the fucking King of Siam," he went on. "The Feds don't have to dig to find shit on this prick. He lays it out all over the place. Does he quietly go around and do his business without making waves? Oh, hell no!...and fuckin' Sammy!...that fucking pimp!" Traffarro continued with contempt and getting more animated with each new word. "I swear, that stupid son of a bitch was vaccinated with a fuckin' phonograph needle. He's all the time talking about the money he's got to pay the old man and every detail of every deal he's done with him. If that wasn't bad enough, one time, that idiot yells this shit to me across the fucking airport, for Christ's sake! Did you get that Quinn? The...fucking...airport," he said throwing his arms wide as if to show the breadth of the airport. "It couldn't be any easier for the Feds if

Sammy took out an ad in the fucking newspaper," Traffarro continued by explaining what was going to happen with Sammy at his firm.

"Quinn, I need your help," Traffarro said. "I want to clean up this Union, but if I have to worry about what Sammy is doing, it's going to make things that much more difficult. I need somebody to keep an eye on this asshole and that big fucking mouth of his."

"You want me to hire this guy?"

"Yes," came Traffarro's simple response as he sat back in his chair.

I brought both hands to my face and rubbed my eyes and face slowly. I finally lowered my hands and tilted my head back casting a look at the ceiling not believing what I had just heard. I just groaned a soft "Aaaahhhh!"

I saw Traffarro look at Nicky with mixed anger and disappointment. Nicky just raised his hand as if to say 'Wait, be patient.'

"Anthony," I began. "This guy sounds like trouble. And, even if I wanted to hire him, I'd have to take it to the top. He's got too many strings attached. I'd have to hard sell him to the powers that be. I can't guarantee that I can even *get* him hired. And, if I do get him hired, how the hell am I supposed to know what he's doing day to day?"

"Quinn, listen to me," Traffarro began in a soft calming voice. "I'm asking this as a personal favor to me. I'm not asking you to guarantee anything other than your best effort. And, as far as knowing what Sammy is doing, believe me, you'll know. You're a likable guy and I know Sammy. That moron will tell you *everything* he's doing because he's too fuckin' stupid to know any better". His voice had grown quite loud by now and he quickly scanned the room to see if anyone had heard him. "Trust me! You'll pray to God you could just...shut...him...up!" Traffarro said in a final halting voice of complete exasperation.

Anthony Traffarro was not in the habit of asking for personal favors, particularly from relative strangers. I sat quietly for what seemed like forever, but perhaps was only a moment. I mean I liked Nicky, and I liked Anthony, too, but this was serious shit! Sure, I wanted to get in on the action, but I never counted on being involved in anything like this. It seemed like a 'noble' cause. Clean up a Union. Wow! These were the heroic things that everyone dreams of, but...could I make this all work without getting trampled in the process? I knew the mob was involved. The Union, the regulators and the Feds were all running around in my head as I tried to figure out how bad things could really get. Yeah...I could see it now. There I would be, standing against the wall and each one of the previously mentioned groups would line up and shoot my ass off. *Oh my!... What fun!!* was my deeply sarcastic thought.

"Okay, Anthony, I'll do the best I can," I said not believing that my mouth was once again getting me into a situation that in the back of my brain, I knew was going to get messy.

Traffarro seemed relieved. He looked at Nicky, who gave him that *I knew my man would come through* look.

"Thanks Quinn. I genuinely appreciate your help," Traffarro offered, casually picking up a menu. "Now let's eat."

"Great," said Nicky, rubbing his hands together in satisfaction over the result of the conversation. Nicky had been a help to Traffarro before, but bringing me to the table at this crucial time was the most he had ever done. My friendship had become a valuable tool for Nicky. In his mind, it helped make him invaluable to Traffarro and *that* was a position that he coveted.

"You want me to call Sammy today or tomorrow?" I asked.

Traffarro never even looked up from the menu as he said casually, "No, don't worry. He'll call you."

While driving back to the office, I thought about what was happening. I wanted to get close to the Union to be able to have a shot at getting some of their business. *Things seem to be going in the right direction*, I thought as I tried to rationalize my most recent actions. Granted, Sammy would be the guy getting the commissions but with my override on all the business, I'd do just fine. What I would soon realize was that I had stepped into quicksand and was sinking quickly into a very dangerous situation. Some of these guys were known to kill people.

Chapter Three
How the Game is Played

Renato Costa may have been homely as a young man, but by the time he had passed his sixtieth birthday he was a troll. A little man with a large broad hooked nose that could not be balanced by his sagging dull eyes or those thin pale lips slicing across a drawn face. His Dumbo ears could find no cover in the thin scraggily hair. If that twisted hair had once been like prisoners forever trapped on his head, it now looked like there had been mass executions with only a few withered survivors remaining. The hair was dyed many times and was so black, dull, and lifeless that it looked like it was colored with cheap shoe polish. The brilliant mind for organization had become treacherous and reveled in keeping people on edge and in constant turmoil. Money and absolute power had corrupted him absolutely. The character that had been admired for its strength, was now twisted into a cruel disposition. To call Renato Costa a greedy lecherous old man was to insult greedy lecherous old men.

Costa lived in a pretentious five thousand square foot house, located on the side of a hill. It was in the best section of town and the neighborhood was populated with doctors, lawyers and the prominent citizens of the community, who had homes of equal or greater size. None of his neighbors were happy that Costa lived there and viewed his presence the way you might feel if your neighbor's property was covered in weeds, uncut grass, and a broken down old car in the driveway. Driving past the house made them cringe with disgust.

The basement area had been converted into a separate residence for Renato Jr. who everyone called Sonny, along with his wife and children. Of course, this meant that Sonny had never lived anywhere but with his parents. That was exactly the way Costa liked things...under his complete control. Sonny had followed his fathers' orders his entire life. He was the Union's attorney, which meant taking orders from Costa was still a daily ritual. Costa was rich, powerful, and had originally gotten his son a job with the Unions' outside legal counsel. Five years later, when Sonny got married, he was given his own legal practice specializing in labor law, and of course his biggest client was the Union.

Sonny was a bright and decent man, who was a loyal husband and dedicated father. He loved and respected his father but those feelings were also blanketed in a heavy layer of fear. They engaged in many heated arguments regarding Union activities and Sonny knew they went way over the legal line. He desperately tried to balance his dedication to his father with a well-deserved respect for the powerful United States Justice Department. The family survived many long and expensive court battles with the government, but now his father had become more arrogant and brazen. Sonny knew it was just a matter of time before this carnival that was his life would fall apart.

Sammy Merzone, on the other hand, was not all that bright. Traffarro said many times that, "Sammy couldn't spell CAT if you spotted him CA_." Sammy went to college in the city, but how he had managed to graduate was the subject of some speculation. The fact that one of the dormitories was named Renato Costa Hall might have been a contributing factor. Upon his graduation, Costa had insisted that Sammy enter the investment business, and in this case, there was no doubt in anyone's mind that someone else had taken the licensing examination for Sammy. However, brains were not a required ingredient in Costa's plan. Soon after Sammy completed his required training, Costa held a large banquet in Sammy's honor and under each plate were new account forms. In his first year,

Sammy became one of the highest producing brokers at the firm. Sammy's lack of brilliance was necessary for Costa, but to insure that Sammy didn't screw things up, Costa "suggested" that Sammy's older brother Ralph, join him as a partner. Unlike Sammy, Ralph was clever and conniving with as much touching sentimentality as a rabid dog.

It was the perfect arrangement. Ralph could stay in the office while Sammy became the middle man for Costa, acting as a buffer between Costa and illegal money deals; as a personal pimp, and as a dedicated gopher for the most inane jobs at the most ridiculous hours. By the time Sammy's 'career' had reached its fifth year, he was *the* highest producing broker in the firm. The professional money managers, who handled the actual management of the pension's money, directed *all* the Union's brokerage business to Sammy's office. Sammy joked that, "He was the highest paid entertainer in America."

Sammy was a fairly attractive if not somewhat effeminate man of average height and build. Like so many other people in these circles, he spent a fortune on clothes and jewelry. A thin clean-shaven face and hair that was combed straight back gave him a touch of elegance. He was not a ladies' man, but he learned to surround himself with some friends who were. Sammy had the money and they had a rough suave demeanor.

Costa had created the perfect plan. Here was someone over whom he had total control, doing all the messy jobs that he either didn't want to do, or would have exposed him to people and relationships that the Government would have jumped on. Sammy was ignorant, obligated, obedient, and oblivious to the perilous position he assumed.

By the time I became involved, Costa was earning in excess of a quarter million dollars a year from his various Union positions for over a decade. However, the kickbacks, bribes, and other unreported benefits, added another half million or more dollars. He had as many as six months' worth of his payroll checks in his office drawer at any one time. Costa had little need for money because he never spent any. His wallet usually contained a couple of dollars and a driver's license which was perfectly understandable since he never paid for *anything*. Why should he? That was what Sammy was for. It was a standard joke that if Renato Costa ever brought out his wallet, moths would fly out. The good news in all of this was that it produced an unexpected benefit for Sammy. Since the old man never paid for anything, he didn't know what anything cost. Even better news was that he didn't have any idea how much Sammy was making each year. On the downside, lunches for six or seven people with three or four take-outs from fine restaurants and lavish dinners every day were costing Sammy a fortune. When gifts for women, trips, and other assorted items were included, he was shelling out over two hundred thousand a year. That was the cost of doing business! It was also a frequent topic of conversation regardless to whom he was speaking or where. Airports! Restaurants! It didn't matter because he was oblivious, and that made Traffarro very nervous. Sammy's monthly cash stuffed envelopes were small by comparison. Small because Costa hadn't the faintest idea that this 'fool' was making nearly two million dollars a year. But, this wasn't good enough for Sammy. He constantly schemed to find ways to make up for the money that Costa cost him.

One of the most profitable schemes the Merzone brothers came up with involved the hot 'New Issues' market. It was during one of those crazy times in the markets when any company that had anything remotely to do with technology could call up one of the major brokerage firms and ask them if they would bring the company public. If you were lucky enough to get your hands on any of this stock at the original offering price, you stood to make a lot of money. Many of the companies that offered stock to the public, saw the share price go up two, three or four times on the very first day of trading. The problem was that everyone wanted in on the action and brokers would save these little gems for their best clients. Now Sammy may not have been all that bright but his brother certainly was. The investment managers that managed the pension fund's money received a very large amount of fee income. They also had billions of dollars of other pension money that was traded on a daily basis and that trade volume was a powerful tool which could be used to influence the brokerage firms that received those trades. Ralph simply told Sammy to call the various investment managers and 'tell them' to get other brokerage firms to allow 'special clients' in on the hot new issues. These special clients were friends of the Merzone brothers. Sammy would give his friends the money to buy the new issues and after the money doubled, tripled or more, they would sell the shares for a huge profit. The 'special clients' would return most of the money to Sammy and keep a percentage for themselves that they referred to as 'the vig'. Everyone was happy, and Sammy and his brother were making a fortune.

Several years ago, Costa called Sammy into his office. It was a dismal place. Costa had purchased one of the old brownstone mansions in the city and converted it into the Union's headquarters. It was a huge, hulking Victorian structure with slate roofs and towers on each of its four corners. Everything in it was over thirty years old, the furniture, the phone system, the file cabinets, and even the fading paint on the walls. The place smelled as musty as the old man himself. He used the large living room as his office, while he stuffed the Business Agents two to a room, in the bedrooms upstairs. The old man sat behind a huge, dark oak desk facing the door. His back was to a large window that extended twelve feet upward meeting a ceiling that was water stained by an angry storm many years before. Costa's small stature made him look like a child pretending to be working at his father's big desk. The dark paneled walls gazed down on a room sparsely populated by the old man's desk, two wooden chairs and an old leather sofa. When Sammy walked in, he went straight to one of the chairs in front of the desk and sat down.

"I have a request from our friend down south," Costa began, referring to the mob boss.

Sammy always got a twinge of anxiety when he heard these kinds of opening statements. Not because he sensed any danger, but because in the past, it had sometimes cost him some serious money.

"What's he want?"

"Capital Development needs a twelve million dollar loan from the pension fund for a hotel they're building," Costa continued, referring to a mob owned company. "I want you to look at this Proposal Statement and figure out what's in it for me."

They had played this game before. The pensions fund would make a loan to Capital Development who would actually build a new hotel or office building. The materials for the buildings were shipped by union truckers to the site for the union workers to use. The bills were padded by the supplier because he would still make his profit and could count on a good night's sleep rather than having a nasty accident on the way home from the office. Once he got paid, the mob would stop by and pick up their end of the deal. The general contractor had to kickback to the mob if he wanted the work to get done without a strike or repeated delays on the job. This average twelve million dollar deal could be worth about five hundred thousand to the mob.

Sammy's heart soared. He had seen a number of these deals before, and although he never had a clue what all that legal crap meant, he had long since learned what the 'juice' was on these deals. He just asked the guy at Capital. The standard finder's fee was two points. He might not have been bright, but he was quick when it came to *his* money. He took the offering document from

Costa and leafed through a few pages, while at the same time putting on his most intelligent expression. When Sammy used the 'intelligent look' outside of this office, people found it quite amusing. They all knew Sammy had the intellectual capacity of your garden variety brick.

"It's the standard deal, Reno. Half a point! That's an easy sixty grand," he said in his best matter of fact voice, laying the document down on Costa's desk.

"Good! You arrange for one of your people to act as an agent on this, and get me my money. You can take care of your guy."

"Reno, that's a lot of fuckin' money," Sammy moaned in protest. Knowing it would cost him the taxes owed on the fee income *and* an incentive for his friend.

"I know, but I'll make sure you get something extra in the next deal. Right now I need that money for something."

Sammy knew he'd never see any benefit from Costa in the form of 'something extra', but who cared? He was elated and not the least bit worried that Costa would find out what his cut would be. He knew Costa hated any legal documents. The language made his head swim. That's what his son and Sammy were for. Sonny and Sammy had grown up together and Sonny knew how expensive his father could be. Besides, for all the bullshit that Sammy had to put up with, Sonny figured Sammy had more than earned it.

The Union Pension Fund was a cash generating machine for Costa and the mob. They had the pension fund invest in a company called Maytag Finance. It made short term business loans to various companies owned by the mob. Maytag would make the loan and the shell companies would pay it back in six months or so with drug money. These guys had a real sense of humor because they thought it was appropriate to name the company Maytag since that was the best machine for doing laundry. They would run fifty million dollars of dirty money though Maytag earning five million a year in the process.

Sammy slowly walked to the door, looking like a poor beaten dog while carefully controlling his enthusiasm and quickly calculated his end of the deal. Let's see, he thought. I should wind up with about a hundred grand. I'll give my guy twenty-five and— *Bam*! Seventy five grand for yours truly! *That*, he thought, will buy a lot of fuckin' lunches. Before Sammy could close the door he heard the old man shout, "One more thing!" Now *this* he knew was going to cost him.

"Come in here and close the door. Why don't you call Carlo and Vinny, and we'll all go up to the Shoreline for some dinner...and tell them to bring some of those girls along, too!" he said as if he was ordering from a menu.

The Shoreline Bar and Grill sat on the Eastern Shore of one of the State's largest lakes and in the heart of one of the most popular vacation areas. Costa had the foresight to buy a thousand feet of lake front property many years ago and long before the area became a Mecca for sun worshipers and boaters. The 'camp' as it was called, started out as a modest structure and had been added on to as the old man's fortunes grew. It was now a stunning stone and glass structure with a boathouse, dock, tennis courts, beautiful gardens, and lush green lawns. Ever the entrepreneur, Costa constructed the Shoreline at the far end of his property when it became obvious that the number of tourists arriving each summer would make this a popular spot. The food was excellent, the drinks were large, and the atmosphere was warm and inviting. He gave the restaurant to his son as a wedding present and Sonny's wife managed it during the season. There was never any consideration given as to whether the restaurant would be profitable or not. The place was a license to print money, or steal it. During the season, Costa arranged to have most of the Union's meetings held at the Shoreline with cocktails and dinner afterwards. The padded bills were sent to the Union for payment and since the old man approved all of the expense accounts, there was never a problem. All of the trustee meetings for the various pension and welfare funds were held at the restaurant. However, the Union didn't get billed for all the events. On a regular basis, the six money managers would each host a meeting and be required to pay the tab for the food, beverages and a hefty room use fee. It made no difference whether they attended or *even knew about it*. These were extraordinary events. Sammy would invite his friends and their female entourage. Some of the boys in the mob would 'just happen' to be in the area. The Business Agents and their 'friends' would usually show up and having fifty to sixty people at one of these bashes was not out of the ordinary. Neither were the five to six thousand dollar tabs.

By the time Sammy, Vinny, and two young ladies arrived at the restaurant, the sun was just setting. It was a warm late spring evening with a soft breeze casually drifting across the lake. They went into the bar area to wait for Carlo and his guests. Costa had arrived at the camp several hours earlier and was waiting for the mood to strike him before he walked the short distance to the Shoreline. Sammy looked up when he heard the laughter pour through the front door and saw Carlo arrive with two striking raven-haired young women wearing just enough clothes to state their intended purpose. After two or three drinks and some raucous conversation, the old man emerged from the kitchen where he often went to review the night's receipts like a king in his counting room.

"Let's go to the room in back and eat," Costa said as he walked past the lively group. "I'm hungry."

Costa sat at the head of the table with the ladies seated next to him down each side. Having Sammy and his friends at the table was like having your own private floorshow and as far as Costa was concerned, the women at the table were part of the menu. Bottles of wine were brought out and more drink orders were taken. Costa motioned to the waiter.

"Tony, bring out a big platter of hot antipasto so we can pick on it while we wait for the dinners," Costa said.

The meal was sumptuous and included lobsters, steak, and three types of veal. During the conversation the old man would take little naps. No one paid any attention because they became used to it. What they couldn't figure out was how he could be asleep and wake up to participate in the conversation as if he had been listening intently the whole time. This happened at dinner, at lunch, and even during business meetings. It was an old habit developed during his early Union years when he worked constantly.

Just as the pastries were being brought out, Sammy leaned over to one of Carlo's raven-haired beauties and told her that Costa wanted to see her for a minute. She turned to the old man who motioned her to follow him. Costa had obviously made his dessert selection.

"Come on Honey," he casually requested. "I'd like to talk to you for a minute in the next room."

She followed him into a dimly lit empty dining room. She was just a few feet into the room when Costa turned to face her. He brought one hand up to softly caress her face as he said, "You look beautiful tonight. I'm so glad you came." While he was looking longingly into her eyes, he undid his pants and let them fall around his ankles. What God had deprived Costa in looks, he more that made up for in other areas. "I know you could take care of this little matter," he said as he pressed down on her shoulder.

"That's not a little matter," she cooed as she willingly complied. It was her cost to run with this crowd.

Chapter Four

Let's move Sammy

Two weeks passed since I met with Nicky and Anthony Traffarro. Nicky and I played golf with the boys again and all Nicky would say was that Traffarro was taking care of setting Sammy up to come work for me. Traffarro met with Costa and explained what was about to happen to Merzone and his present job. He told him he met someone in town who was running another brokerage operation. Someone he felt could be trusted to do the right thing and who wouldn't get in the way. Costa was pissed that the Feds were causing problems, but he appreciated Traffarro's initiative in seeking out a solution.

"This Quinn, what's he to you, Anthony?" Costa asked. Over the years Costa learned to see every angle of every deal. He trusted no one, and even though he knew Traffarro from the time he was a child, he was suspicious that maybe Traffarro had something going with me.

"I did the guy a favor. Nicky knew this guy for a while and he approached me with the request. I got a friend of Quinn's a job. Then, when Connie was breaking my balls about going back to work, I had Nicky contact this guy Quinn. He knew he owed me and he did the right thing when he hired her. He's treated her good and we've had dinner a few times since then. You know, just casual stuff. The man's got a good sense of honor, Reno. I think he'll do just fine. Besides, now that all this shit's hit the fan, I don't know what other firm will take Sammy. Quinn's got the second biggest company in the city. The others are just too small."

"What about his company?" Costa asked. "You think they'll take Sammy?"

"I don't know Reno, but I gotta say, this guy's our best shot," Traffarro replied. He was getting a little irritated with the old man. Traffarro had more than just lost respect for this man. He viewed him as dangerous because of his reckless behavior and lack of attention to the needs of the members. In fact, at this point, Costa could give two shits about the members. But Traffarro never forgot that Costa still had 'a nasty bite'. He knew it would make things a hell of a lot more difficult if Costa became suspicious and threw him out of the Union. And...this was a *very* suspicious man.

"Okay. I'll speak to Sammy. You just be damned sure your guy *keeps* doing the right thing," Costa said, pointing a threatening finger at Traffarro.

A few days later, I got a call from Danforth Faulkner, the president of the firm. He wanted to see me in his office the next day. *What the hell is this all about*, I thought? I could count on the fingers of one hand the number of times I had ever spoken to Faulkner much less received a call from him. It was a short flight and a long taxi ride to get to the company's head quarters, and by 11:00 in the morning I found myself walking through the huge double doors to Faulkner's office. It was breathtaking. Located on the top floor with walls of windows on two sides, the office had a commanding view of the city. I was surprised to see Richard Dennison at the meeting. Dennison was the head of operations and the firm's number two man. He was also their number one trouble-shooter and that gave me one of those uncomfortable little twinges in my stomach.

"Come on in, Parker," Faulkner began. "I'm so glad to see you again. Dick and I were just commenting on what a fine job you've done out there. Please, sit down," Faulkner said, sweeping his hand in the direction of the chairs in front of his desk.

Faulkner waited for me to sit in one of the high-backed leather chairs before he resumed. With Faulkner sitting behind that huge desk and me settled down in this enormous chair, I felt like I did when I was a kid and got called to the Principals office.

"Parker, I'm sure you've heard of Sammy Merzone," he said. I answered in the affirmative. "Well, it seems that things have gotten a little messy at his present company," Faulkner continued. "Dick here will fill you in on all the details later, but suffice it to say that I'm guessing that Mr. Merzone walks a very fine line between what is and is not proper in our business. Have you heard of anything illegal going on in Mr. Merzone's business? I mean after all, you're in the same city with this man. I would imagine it could be the topic of conversation around town. You've also got that woman who's the wife of one of the Union officials. Do you ever get a chance to speak to him?"

My mind was racing. How the hell did Faulkner know about Merzone, and if he knew about Merzone, what else did he know? I wasn't sure what to do. If I revealed everything I knew, it might kill this deal. On the other hand, if Faulkner *was* well informed and I looked like I was deliberately hiding something, I could find myself on the street looking for a job just like Merzone. I realized that as difficult and dangerous as this situation was, it was the best thing that could have happened. After all, it was *their* idea and I thought that fact might provide me with some cover down the road if things ever went south. If I brought this deal to them, *I'd* have to assume all the responsibility. Under these circumstances, I could claim I was dragged into a bad situation by another greedy firm.

The fact was I'm sitting in this office because Costa didn't trust this situation to anyone on a local level and had instructed Merzone to call the President of the company. He knew that when Merzone told Faulkner who he was and how much business he was doing with the Union along with how poorly he had been treated, that it would be probable that Faulkner would add him to his company. Costa knew these people well and always counted on them caving into their most basic instincts. Greed!

"I've heard about Merzone's problem," I said. "To be honest, I wasn't really sure this was something we should get involved in." I knew I was pressing my luck, but I relied on their greed to push this through. "Of course, I'm not privy to all the details about Merzone, but I've heard a few rumors here and there." I figured that the mention of rumors would be the best approach because I could easily discount them if I was pressed. "I've also been to dinner with Constance Traffarro and her husband. Although it was purely a social occasion and we never really spoke about the Union. What is it you had in mind?"

"We've offered Mr. Merzone a very attractive compensation package. He's considering it, and I'm sure he will be back to us shortly," said Faulkner, full of confidence. "Assuming that he takes the deal, we want to pay you a little incentive bonus of an additional three percent of his gross revenue. That's another $60,000 a year in override if he keeps producing the way he has."

"But!" Dennison chimed in. "We want you to keep a very close eye on this guy. We don't want this to blow up in our face like it did at the other firm. That's why we're going to pay you something extra." The truth was that Dennison wanted evidence that the firm had made an extra effort to monitor the situation and if it went bad, they would point their finger at me. It was a neat little catch all offense called 'Failure to Supervise' and was a favorite of the regulatory agencies.

"You've done a fine job with that office and we respect your position. But, you have to admit that this could be a very profitable opportunity." *Profitable for whom?* I thought. If they weren't going to make a small fortune off of Merzone's commission business, they wouldn't touch this guy with a ten-foot pole. Frankly, when it got down to it, I have to confess to a touch of greed myself and besides, this was getting to be too much fun. Dancing with the devil does have its moments as long as you don't get burned in the process.

"Of course, of course," I said with feigned resignation. "I'm certainly not going to stand in the way of progress. I assume someone will call me and let me know what the outcome of Merzone's decision is. By the way, if he does come on board, we'll need more space. There's a nice office across the lobby from us that ought to make this even more attractive to him."

"Whatever you think is necessary, Parker," Faulkner said with a Cheshire Cat grin. "You know we're behind you one hundred percent." *Yeah, right,* I thought. *These bastards would be behind me alright...behind pushing me out the door at the first sign of trouble.*

Faulkner's secretary came in to say that there was an important message for me. It seemed that Merzone had called my office looking for me and wanted to stop by to see what the accommodations were like.

"I'll call him as soon as I leave here," I said. "Don't worry gentlemen. I'll convince him." I was absolutely confident in that statement because I knew that Merzone didn't really have any other options and that Traffarro would make sure he got a shove in the right direction.

"We knew we could count on you," Faulkner said beaming with the anticipation of a nice piece of revenue.

I did my part and Nicky and Traffarro should have no complaints. When I thought about it, I felt I should feel happy and relieved. However, what I was feeling was not what I would call happy and I as sure as hell was not relieved.

I arranged to meet Merzone the next morning and much to my surprise Merzone showed up right on time. After some initial chitchat in my office, I took Merzone across the lobby to the proposed space. It was one of the nicest set-ups in the city and when

Sammy Merzone saw it, he was overjoyed. His former offices were nice but strictly sterile corporate issue in their design. These on the other hand, were something else altogether and Merzone knew it would impress everyone who came to see him. I knew Sammy was hooked.

"So Sammy, what do you think?" I asked. I knew Merzone would go for the deal because I could almost see the drool sliding down his chin. Merzone didn't seem to be that difficult to deal with. In the past, I had met quite a few very large producers and almost to a man they were arrogant pains in the ass but this man appeared simple and straight forward and not a bad sort at all.

"Does the furniture come with the offices?" Merzone asked.

"Absolutely!" I responded. "It'll take me about a week to get all the electronics hooked up and of course and we'll have to put in a phone system that's compatible with ours so our receptionist can cover your calls if yours is tied up. If there is anything else you need, like filing cabinets or whatever let me know and I'll see that you get it."

"Well, I've got one girl that has been with me for years. I would like to bring her along too.

"No problem," I said quickly, patting Merzone on the shoulder for reassurance. "We needed to hire somebody anyway to cover the extra work."

"My friend Carlo Bonaface has a girlfriend that needs a job," Merzone said as they walked toward the exit. "Any problem with getting her in here? You don't have to pay her a lot. Carlo takes care of her pretty good. He just doesn't want her hanging around all day."

"No. I don't see why that would be a problem. Anything else?" I asked, wondering what in God's name he would ask for next. I was starting to feel like the government. If this kept up, pretty soon a quarter of the city's workforce would be on my payroll.

"This is great, Quinn. Just let me know when I can start to move my stuff in. Oh, by the way," Merzone added as he stopped in the hall to make his point. "We're having a party out at the Shoreline Friday night. The Board of Trustees is holding meetings during the day and there'll be a lot of people there you should meet. You know where it is, don't you? Everybody will be there around 7:00 P.M. Why don't you come? It'll give you a chance to meet everybody," Merzone said with just a touch of insistence.

"Sure, I'll try to make it." I felt as though I was being carried downstream by a flood. It wasn't that long ago I was trying to figure out how I could get close to the Union and now I stood hip deep in it. It certainly looks as though I pulled it off.

I called Traffarro immediately after Merzone left. I knew Traffarro would be happy with the news and when I finally got him on the phone, I told him about the party Friday night and my thought that it might be a good idea if I went. Traffarro agreed, but he wanted to meet me on Friday morning at the coffee shop to explain what was going on. Of course I agreed knowing I'd feel more comfortable if I knew the lay of the land.

Bright and early Friday morning I arrived at the coffee shop and found Nicky and Traffarro seated at a rear table. They both rose from their seats when they saw me come in and greeted me with a warm welcome.

"Heyee, Quinny. How you doin'?" Nicky said as he gave me a hug and a kiss on the cheek. This was a first for me and I was flattered because I had seen people do the same thing to Traffarro. I knew it was a sign of respect and I was getting the feeling that in some strange way, I had been promoted.

"Nice job with Sammy, Quinn," Nicky continued, reaching over and slapping me on the arm. "I told Anthony you could pull this off."

"He's right, Quinn," Traffarro said. "You did a good job. Let me explain why I wanted to see you. The Feds, as you know, are causing problems for Sammy because they want to get Costa. He's managed to avoid going to the can for twenty years, but this time it's different. This prosecutor the Feds have in now has got a hard-on for the old man. I don't know what this guy's problem is but he acts like there is nothing else in the world but nailing the old man and this Union. They went after Sammy hoping to put him out of business and take away some of the old man's strength by hurting his finances, but they sure as hell didn't count on you getting him hired."

"So now what does that mean?" I said a little irritated. "Now, I'm under investigation?"

"Let's just say you'll now have more pictures taken of you than when you were a kid," Traffarro replied with a little laugh. "Look Quinn, they don't want you. They want the old man. Just don't do anything stupid and you'll be fine." Somehow I didn't find Traffarro's words all that comforting.

"There are a lot of people who want the old man out, and I don't mean just the government. He's become a liability that we can't afford to have. I've been working to get him out for years, but don't kid yourself, that old bastard is still sharp. If I could move him out and take over, this Union could be great again. The members could get a fair shake and have somebody who believed in them, instead of someone who's always wondering how he's going to steal his next buck. The old man used to be a man of principle, but not anymore. Your job is to keep an eye on Sammy. Tell me what they're up to and for God's sake Quinn, don't get sucked into any of his weird schemes. He's gonna go to jail and I'd prefer not to see you in there with him"

"No shit, Anthony. That wasn't my first choice either," I said. "How much real danger is there? I mean, well—. Well, okay look. I hear Costa's really tight with the mob. If he or Sammy gets suspicious, am I going to wind up taking a dirt nap?"

"Nah. That shouldn't be a problem." Traffarro responded calmly and sipped his coffee.

"*Shouldn't* be a problem?" I yelped. "That doesn't make me feel all warm and fuzzy all over, Anthony."

"The very people you're worried about are some of the same people that want him out. I told you, he's bad for business. The old man would probably get whacked before you would anyway," Traffarro said dismissing the thought with a wave of his hand. "I'm in touch with certain people who let me know what's going on. If anyone wanted to make you disappear, I'd know about it immediately. I'm telling you Quinn; you don't have to worry."

The only word that I could seem to get out was, "Okay" and it came out rather slowly.

"Nicky and I will be there tonight. So, if you have any questions, just quietly ask either one of us. Look Quinn, you'll be fine. Trust me." The words hadn't left Traffarro's mouth before I thought of the old Jewish joke about the man who had his headstone read 'Trust Me'.

Chapter Five
Meeting More Players

By the time I got to the Shoreline, the parking lot was packed. I drove around once but finally had to pull up to the front and have the valet park the car. When I opened the door, the level of noise from the crowd inside hit me like a body block. Handing the keys to the valet, I walked toward the open double doors and stood in the entrance for a moment and surveyed the noisy crowd. It was one of those moments when you take a mental deep breath before you charge into what is sure to be a nerve racking situation. I made my way through the crowd smiling and nodding a hello to all those who simply turned and stared at this new face. I soon noticed Nicky at the end of the bar entertaining a small group of men with what I was sure was his latest story. After he finished and the group broke into laughter, Nicky noticed me and motioned for me to come over. I obliged Nicky's wave and walked to the group. As soon as I got there, Nicky threw his arm around my shoulders and enthusiastically introduced me to the group. He began by explaining that I was the guy who 'saved Sammy's ass'. I was pleasantly surprised by the warm welcome. One man in the group was the biggest human being I'd ever laid eyes on. He had to be at least six foot six and weigh three hundred and fifty pounds if he weighed an ounce. When we shook hands, my hand disappeared into this guy's massive paw. I just hoped the deer-in-the-headlights look that was plastered across my face wouldn't be noticed. Standing next to the behemoth was a slightly reduced version that turned out to be his son. I just met Napoleon Brufalo and his son Napoleon, Jr., affectionately referred to as Big Nappi and Little Nappi, a proud duo who were enforcers for the mob. *Dirt nap specialists I'm sure*, I thought in a moment of sarcasm. *How proud the giant must have felt that his son was following in his footsteps.*

Mingling was my business, but tonight I felt a little uncomfortable. Being cautious in new situations is my nature but with this crew I knew I better be especially careful. Nicky ventured off into another story and I decided that wandering around for a while surveying the crowd would be a good way to get a feel for this crowd. After a few minutes of drifting through this Italian ocean, I noticed a man in his late forties standing by himself. He had such a lost look about him that I felt somewhat sympathetic. *This guy looks like I feel*, I thought *and besides, I can't just keep drifting around this place all night.* Approaching the man, I was taken by the fact that he reminded me of an older cherub from the Italian section of heaven.

"Hey, my name is Parker Quinn, but everyone just calls me Quinn," I said extending my hand. I was hoping the choice of words would make it sound like I actually belonged here.

"Hey, I'm Mike Fazio. I'm one of the portfolio managers for the Pension Fund and the Health and Welfare Fund. I haven't seen you at one of these things before," he said in a pleasant welcoming voice. Fazio was a managing director at one of the largest firms specializing in the management of union pension funds and had been around union types his whole career. He knew to be suspicious of new faces. Experience taught him that you better know who the real players are if you want to stay out of trouble and retain the business.

"Well, to be honest, this is the first one I've been to. My firm just hired Sammy Merzone. Quite a crowd we have here."

"You're telling me?" was the emphatic response. "I've got to pay for all this. I heard about Sammy's problem. Whatever prompted your company to hire him?"

"Anthony Traffarro introduced me to the situation."

"You know Anthony?" Fazio asked before he took a sip of his cocktail. It was a rhetorical question more designed to continue the conversation than elicit any actual information. He knew all about the situation because it meant he would have to direct his firm's trades to a new company.

"Yeah, his wife works for me. We've been out to dinner a few times along with Nicky Tagliano," I said. I was sure we were now in a probative dance trying to find out where the other one stood.

"Anthony and I are fairly close. We've had numerous discussions about the pension funds," Fazio said as he continued with more empty conversation and his exploration of this new acquaintance.

My guess was that he wasn't really sure at what level I would be playing and Fazio wanted to check with Traffarro first. For the time being, he must have had enough of this verbal dance. "It looks like we're going in for dinner. Maybe you and I will be able to talk some other time," Fazio offered, as he flashed me an empty smile and walked away.

I walked into the large dining room and saw Nicky seated at a long banquet table. There was an empty chair next to Nicky and I had done enough mingling. It was time to relax in a more familiar setting. I also thought Nicky could give me some background on a few of the players. As I approached my newfound haven, I noticed two men in the corner of the room in what appeared to be a heated argument. Nicky was in a deep conversation with the attractive brunette seated next to him. I put my hand on Nicky's shoulder as I pulled out the chair to sit down.

"Hey, Quinny," Nicky said as he felt my hand came to rest on his shoulder. "This is Maryann. Maryann say hello to my good friend, Quinn."

After pleasantries were exchanged I asked Nicky about the scene taking place in the corner. "That's Reno Costa and Charlie Burrows," Nicky said in a matter of fact tone. "You never met Reno did you, Quinn?"

"No, not yet"

"I'll introduce you later," Nicky continued. "Charlie Burrows is Reno's small company guy on the fund and my guess is that Charlie isn't doing what he's been told," Nicky said leaning closer to me for privacy. "Let me explain. You see, the pension fund has eighteen locals in three states all contributing into it. That way there's some efficiency in size but the truth is it makes it easier for the old man to control the money. There are eight trustees on the board, four from the Union and four from the employers. Now, the Union guys do whatever Reno wants so there's no problem there, but...the potential problems come from the employer side. Way back, Reno decided that all motions would be passed with a simple majority. He made it so at least one small company had to have representation on the fund board. That way the large companies couldn't control the board. It's a good plan because the board chairman always chose the guy from the small company and of course, the chairman has always been the old man."

"That doesn't sound like it would be good for that guy's health," I said, continuing to watch Costa shake his finger in Burrows's face.

"Nah. Charlie might have some labor problems if he doesn't do what Reno wants. That's all," Nicky replied, reaching for his cocktail. "Besides, Charlie's gonna be replaced in the next election anyway. The old man doesn't like any problems so he'll just find somebody easier to control."

A moment later, I saw Costa and Burrows part company and Costa took his seat at the head of the table.

"Come on," Nicky said as he grabbed Quinn's arm. "I want you to meet Reno."

When we arrived at the end of the table, Costa was whispering into the ear of the young lady seated on his right. Nicky waited a moment until Costa sat back.

"Reno, this is Parker Quinn. He's the guy who took care of Sammy. He runs the office here in the city."

"Hey. Look, thanks for helping Sammy, Parker. I was a little worried about my boy. Sammy told me about his new offices. It sounds like you did a good job," Costa said, surveying me carefully. Sammy Merzone was far too valuable to Costa to let anybody interfere with his money machine.

"Well, Mr. Costa, we're glad to have him," I said knowing full well it was hardly the truth. "By the way, please just call me Quinn. That's the way it's been ever since I was a kid."

"Okay, Quinn. The International is having a Taft-Hartley conference for all the various pension funds from around the country in two weeks in Hawaii. It would be a good idea for you to come. It'll give you an opportunity to get to know Sammy and some of the other people here a little better," said Costa in a friendly but somewhat instructive tone. Costa was a suspicious man and I doubt he was convinced that Traffarro and I didn't have something going on behind his back. My guess is that this trip would be a good opportunity for Costa to get a better read on me.

I told him I would certainly try to attend. I was getting inside the action now and this trip could help to solidify my position. It might have made a difference if I had known that not everyone attending the meeting in Hawaii would live to tell about it.

Chapter Six
Murder in Paradise

It wasn't too difficult to convince me to go to Hawaii. I loved that place with its sunny days and warm balmy nights. When I opened the taxi door at the entrance to the Hilton on Waikiki Beach, a warm breeze gently caressed my face and I could feel myself starting to relax. I had no idea what was in store for me, but somehow, at this moment, I just didn't give a shit. It seemed like decades since I had taken a vacation and even if this was a working vacation, I was determined to make the most of it. This could be a pleasant change of pace. I walked across the lobby area with its marble floors and plush leather sofas, in search of the front desk. I was bone tired and was looking forward to getting up to my room. I got out of bed sixteen hours ago and cramming this body into those little airline seats had left me sore and completely done in. There was no doubt that an hour or so of rest was definitely in order. Unfortunately, no sooner had I turned to head to the room, than I saw Nicky heading in my direction.

"Heyee...Quinny, you made it," Nicky said enthusiastically as he greeted me with a big smile. "Anthony's plane doesn't get here for a couple of hours. Reno got here yesterday and he brought that big black buffalo with him. I can't believe him. You watch, he'll be with her for a week and nothin' will happen, then one day he'll come down looking like he fell down a fuckin' flight of stairs."

"Why is that?" I asked.

"Easy. He and the blimp will get into a fight and she'll kick the shit out of him," Nicky replied as we moved away from the check-in area. I couldn't believe what I was hearing. How could one of the more powerful men in the country get beat up by anybody...except maybe the mob of course? Nicky assured me that this wouldn't be the first time it's happened.

"One night about two years ago, Sammy gets a call at 2:00 in the morning," Nicky went on. "Reno tells Sammy to get in his car and meet him in front of Terrabella's and that he'll be waiting in his car. Even for a dumb shit like fuckin' Sammy, this sounded strange. So Sammy drives downtown and sees the old man's car parked all by itself on the street about half a block away from the restaurant. He goes up to the car and knocks on the window, but no answer. So, he opens the door and inside is the old man. His fuckin' face is all beat to shit, split lip, one eye swollen shut and he's got this fuckin' knot on his forehead the size of a fuckin' pineapple. His one sleeve is torn off and hangin' down around his wrist and his fuckin' collar is so ripped up that it's sticking straight out the back of his neck like some fuckin' sail."

All the time Nicky is telling the story, his hands and arms are waving frantically arround his body, not only giving drama to his description, but once again making it so funny that I was starting to laugh at a story that Nicky didn't think was too funny.

"So Sammy asks him who the fuckin' guys were that mugged him. I mean, he's thinking that this was a guy who had people whacked for Christ's sake. The old man says don't worry about it and that Sammy should drive to the all-night drugstore to get some stuff to patch him up. Sammy thinks the old man is pazzo and he wants to take him to the hospital, but the old man tells him to do what he says and take him back to the Union building so he can repair some of the fuckin' damage and spend the rest of the night there. After he gets Reno back to the building, the old man tells Sammy that it was that bitch Louise, that beat the shit outta him. The very next day, Reno's telling everyone that he tripped over a table in the dark. Quinn...come on...I saw the fuckin' guy the next day. He looked like somebody threw him through a meat grinder. Now who the fuck's gonna believe that he fell over a table? And this is the guy who runs this Union? Please, gimme a fuckin' break!

I didn't think it was appropriate to laugh, but I couldn't help himself. Nicky was always so animated when he told a story, that everyone laughed. You just couldn't help it. If Nicky Tagliano got up on stage and told the story of how the world was going to end in five minutes, everyone in the room would meet their maker laughing their asses off.

Nicky was quick to change course, "The old man is having a late dinner party tonight for about two dozen people and he told me to tell you to come. It's at 9:00. Meet me here at...aaaah, screw it," Nicky said as he happened to glance across the lobby. "Some of the boys are meeting in the bar now. Why don't you come over there with me and have a few drinks . Then we'll go up stairs and change and go together." Nicky motioned to the bell hop to take my bag to his room. There was little I could do except agree and just like that, my little nap was history.

I followed Nicky into the bar like a little duck behind its mother. After my eyes got adjusted to the dark room, I noticed six men standing at the end of the bar. I knew this was the group they were looking for because I immediately recognized the mob's version of the Twin Towers—Big Nappi Brufalo and Little Nappi. Nicky was reintroducing me to the group when Big Nappi placed his big mit on my shoulder. His hand felt like it weighed forty pounds.

"Hey. How ya doin'," Brufalo said in a voice that was somewhere between a long rolling thunder and a deep belch. "You know when you walked into the shoreline the other night, I thought you was a fuckin' Fed. I thought I was gonna have to pop fuckin' Nicky here for lettin' you in. We checked you out and you're okay. But I gotta tell you Quinn. You *gotta* do somethin' about the fuckin' way you look. Lookin' like a fuckin' Fed like you do...you're gonna give somebody a fuckin' heart attack or somethin'." He said this without the slightest bit of humor and I didn't know what to say until a moment later when everybody started laughing including Brufalo. Brufalo's laugh was just a series of 'Huh, Huh, Huhs' that sounded more like sacks of flour hitting the floor.

Being around Nicky long enough, I knew some of the phrases this Italian crowd used. "Well Nappi, every good Italian sandwich needs a little 'mayonaisse'," I said in self deprecation. Everyone let out a soft little 'ooohh' and began to laugh. The Italians used to refer to blacks as moolenans or 'moolies' which actually meant eggplant. The obvious comparison was to the dark skinned vegetable and the darkness of the African race. Mayonaisse, on the other hand, was a reference to the lighter skins of those not from the Southern Mediteranean region. Believe me, neither term was a compliment.

Dinner that night was uneventful but it seemed never ending. It was after 1:00 in the morning by the time I got out of there which meant that I'd been up for thirty-six hours and some sleep was definitely called for. Nicky made plans to meet at 9:30 the next morning while Traffarro had seminars and meetings to attend for most of the day. It would actually be a vacation day and I was planning to head for the beach, but by the time breakfast was over, I found myself sitting in a hotel van headed for Diamond Head. Nicky had the 'great idea' to see the view from the top. I was still dragging from the events of the previous day but figured it would be a nice relaxed ride and I would get to see some more of the island. However, not much time passed before the van pulled off to the side of the road and everyone got out. I just looked around. What the hell was going on? I didn't have a clue where we were but I sure as hell knew where we weren't, and that was on the *top* of Diamond Head.

As the van pulled away, I asked Nicky in a slow voice, "Nicky. Where the hell are we?"

"What do you mean where are we?" Nicky responded with some disbelief. "We're at Diamond Head."

"Nicky. Diamond Head is up there," I said pointing to the distant peak. *"We're down here."*

"Yeah, I know. We're gonna walk."

"Walk?" I cried. "Do you know how far that is?"

"Yeah. 1780 stairs. I saw it in a travel guide in the room this morning. Pretty neat, huh?" replied Nicky as I cast my eyes skyward with the 'why me?' look. I couldn't get out another word before Nicky turned and started his great adventure. Now I consider myself to be in fairly good shape, but walking up Diamond Head in wing-tips I knew was going to take its toll. Not to mention the fact that I didn't relish looking at Kicky's butt all the way to the top. When we finally arrived, I collapsed against the concrete bunker that was built during the war and looked out over Waikiki. If this had been some type of torture I was definitley ready to talk. The view would have been much more enjoyable if it wasn't for the constant throbbling in my poor feet and the thought that we were going to have to walk back down. *I should have that fuckin' Nicky send up a helicopter and airlift me out of here,* I thought as another pain shot up my leg.

I spent the better part of what had been left of the afternoon in my room soaking in a hot tub in hopes of relieving the pain in my feet and legs. *Some vacation,* I thought. *Not only is this work, its painful work. At this rate, I'll be lucky to make it back in one piece.*

That night, I arrived at the banquet about forty-five minutes late. It was being hosted by one of the unfortunate money managers. There had to be three hundred people in the room. An enormous ice sculpture dominated the center of the room and each large round table was covered in a black tablecloth with a huge floral arrangement in the center. The decorations were said to have cost over five grand. *Once again,* I thought *that Costa certainly knows how to spend other people's money.* There was no doubt in my mind that this was going to cost some poor bastard a small fortune. Walking toward the bar, I noticed Big Nappi Brufalo either talking to the corner of the room or to somebody completely hidden by the huge man's body. I slowly pushed my way through the crowd and when I finally reached the bar I ordered a drink. As I picked up the glass, I happened to catch a glimpse of the other man in the corner. It was Charlie Burrows. His face looked white as a sheet. I was taking a sip of my cocktail when I felt a hand on my shoulder. When I turned, I saw it was Traffarro with a big grin on his face.

"Hey, Quinn. I'm sorry I've missed you so far. I've been meeting with the old man and going to these fucking seminars. God forbid the old man would want us to have a good time on these trips. He made it so if we miss two of them the Union won't pay for our trip," Traffarro said in obvious frustration. "What you been up to?"

"Did you know that Nicky's into fuckin' mountain climbing?" I said with a little laugh. "I think I'm two inches shorter from the beating my legs took today."

"Yeah, I heard about that," Traffarro laughed. "What a fucking idiot. He thinks he's still twenty years old."

"Anthony? What's with Charlie Burrows? He's had Big Nappi in his face for ten minutes. He's not looking too good," I said as I pointed toward the corner.

"Yeah, well...most people that Nappi talks to like that don't usually feel too good," Traffarro explained as he slowly grabbed my pointing finger and pulled it down. Traffarro knew that pointing out these types of scenes wasn't good for your health. It identified you as a witness. "Charlie's a '*testa dura*'. You know—a hard head. I think the old man wants Nappi to talk some sense into him. I saved you a seat at my table with the idiot mountain climber and me," added Traffarro quickly changing the subject and gently pushed me in the direction of the table.

I arrived at the table and Nicky was already telling his version of the look on my face when I found out I was going to have to climb to the top of Diamond Head.

"Hey, Quinn. You recovered yet?" Nicky asked with a laugh. All I could do was flash a mock smile and groan. This set the tone for the rest of the evening and the only time anyone had a moment to eat was between bouts of laughter. The stories ran from one to another.

"I'm coming out of the hotel late this afternoon," Nicky began. "When I see this big black limo pull up in front of the hotel. I figure it might by a movie star, so I decide to wait and see who it is. The door opens and who should step out but the old man. He's got on the most God awful bright Hawaiian shirt I ever saw. He looked like a little stick all covered in fuckin' orchids. Anyway, he gets out and turns around and starts pulling like a son of a bitch on what looked to me like a fucking over-stuffed chair...and the fucking chair has the same colors on it as the old man. Finally, the old man stops pullin' and what comes out but that fucking black whale. He went out and bought a shirt for himself and a fucking moo-moo tent for the whale—*in matching patterns.* They looked like some crazy walking garden for Christ's sake. Can you believe this fuckin' guy went all over town with her looking like that? Un...fucking...believable!"

"No Nicky. You're unbelievable," said Traffarro as he took his turn. "Do you remember about three years ago when we had that meeting in Bermuda?" Nicky was quick to jump in and try to change the subject because he knew where this was going. "Shut up, Nicky," said Traffarro in jest. "We're at this beautiful hotel by the ocean. I think it was the Westin. Anyway, Nicky goes to the bar after the banquet and meets this attractive young girl. It gets to be about 3:00 in the morning, and he asks her if she'd like to take a walk outside. 'Sure' she says. So they walk out into the night and wind up on the ninth green of the fucking golf course. My man here starts to put the moves on her and she gets all hot and everything. Bada-bing! Nicky starts bangin' her on the green. Her fuckin' head is poundin' against the flagstick and when they get done, they both fall asleep right there on the green, both of them naked as jay birds. The next morning Nicky hears people cheering from the fucking hotel balconies and some guy out in the fairway yelling to get off the green so he can play through." At this point Traffarro was laughing so hard he had tears coming down his cheeks.

It was a hundred laughs later before I finally decided to pack it in for the night and take the long way back to the room. The hotel had a walkway that ran along the beach and the solitude of a nice walk in the moonlight was in order after an evening of endless conversation. The breeze danced in off the ocean in little gusts that ruffled my hair. I stood leaning against a railing that kept drunken guests from falling off the sidewalk and onto the beach, and gazed longingly off across the Pacific. *What would it be like*, I thought *to get in a sailboat and set off for foreign shores with no strings or commitments to worry about?* I felt like I could stand there forever listening to the palm fronds clattering out a melody in the warm breeze that brushed across my face. There weren't too many times that I had the opportunity just to be at peace with the world.

The next morning, when I got up my head was pounding. *Way too much of a good time,* I thought. I dragged myself into the bathroom and started the shower and got a pot of coffee going from the set-up the hotel provided. I was certain Nicky would be having breakfast in the usual place and I shook at the thought of what Nicky might have cooked up for today's activities. I cranked open the windows to let the warm Pacific Ocean breeze revive me. It struck me that this might be the perfect day for just lying on the beach and recapturing a little of the peace I felt the night before.

After my morning routine, I gathered up some strength and left the room to attack another day. The ride down in the elevator was spent with a little planning for the day but when the elevator doors opened, I noticed a large group of people in the lobby. There were police cars parked outside the hotel with their lights flashing and cops all over the lobby talking to various people from the Union. *What the hell is going on here?* I thought. *Not another Nicky golf-green incident.* My head gave me a jolt of pain as if to punish me for the thought. Walking toward the crowd, I saw Nicky talking to a police officer. I figured I'd better walk over and find out what trouble my friend had gotten into this time.

"Hey, Nicky. What's all this about?" I asked cutting the policeman off in mid sentence.

"They found Charlie Burrows on the beach. He's dead," Nicky said with shocked look.

"And you are?" The officer said with obvious annoyance at having his interview with Nicky interrupted.

"I'm Parker Quinn. I manage a brokerage office and some of these gentlemen are clients."

"You knew the deceased?" the office asked.

"No, not really. I knew he was a trustee on one of the Union's funds but I never actually met the man. My company has a new relationship with the Fund, so there were quite a few people that I hadn't met." I glanced over at Nicky and could see him giving me a strange look. I wasn't sure what it meant, but I assumed it was a sign to keep my mouth shut.

"Did you see anything unusual last night?"

"No." My response was brief and to the point. I was starting to agree with Nicky. The less said the better. This was unfamiliar territory for me and I knew if I wasn't careful things could get very nasty in a hurry. I couldn't keep my mind from racing back to the conversation that Big Nappi had with Burrows in the corner of the dining room. *Burrows looked like he had just seen a ghost and maybe that ghost was his*, I thought. I had seen enough movies to know that testifying against the mob was not good for one's health. I had no desire to do a Godfather movie rerun and star as 'Luca Brazi sleeps with the fishes'.

It wasn't long before the police officer was convinced that neither Nicky nor I had anything meaningful to contribute or at least nothing that we were willing to volunteer. After the cop left, I was about to say something when Nicky put up his hand in a motion to keep silent.

"Not here, Quinn. Way too many ears," Nicky advised. "Let's go into the bar. It's closed now and quiet."

I walked with Nicky across the lobby with neither of us saying a word. When we were inside the bar, we sat in a booth in the back. A waiter behind the bar was setting it up for the afternoon. He looked over at us, but before I could say anything Nicky explained that we just needed a quiet place for a moment.

"Nicky, what the hell happened?" I asked.

"Really Quinn, I don't know," Nicky said as he leaned back in the leather chair and lit a cigarette. "All I know is, they found Charlie on the beach and he apparently drowned. He still had his tuxedo on from the night before. They said there were no signs of foul play. I mean it's not like anybody shot him or anything like that, but who the fuck knows?" he said shrugging his shoulders. "Maybe he got drunk and decided to take a swim."

"With all his clothes on, for Christ's sake?"

"I don't know. Maybe," Nicky said as he calmly took a drag on his cigarette. "Hey, I got drunk and fell asleep on a fucking golf course with a naked woman. Who the hell knows what Charlie would do?"

"Where's Big Nappi?" I asked.

"He and Little Nappi left on the first flight this morning. I saw them leaving the hotel a couple of hours ago."

At this point, I wasn't sure I wanted to know any more. The "don't worry Quinn" that Traffarro had offered was looking pretty thin. I had no doubt that Burrows had been murdered and that Big Nappi and company were neck deep in it. After all, it *was* his job. It crossed my mind that good old Charlie was probably gasping for air at the very moment I was enjoying the night air after the banquet. The thought gave me a chill. I also had the very strong feeling that if anyone thought I was spying for Traffarro, I might meet the same fate. Sure cleaning up the Union was an honorable and noble thing and all, but I now realized I hadn't truly considered the fact that I might die trying.

The investigation into the death of Charlie Burrows lasted several weeks. The police took the names and addresses of all the people who attended the party the previous night. What they got were all the names of everyone other than those of the mob's two mountainous hit men. Ultimately, the County Coroner ruled it to be 'Death by Drowning' because they could find no evidence of foul play. The fact that Charlie Burrows was a trustee on a pension fund worth hundreds of millions of dollars and the fact that the fund was under investigation by the Government for links to organized crime caused the police to suspect that Burrows's death was anything *but* an accident. Proving it however, was another thing. Burrows's position on the pension fund board was filled in two days by an appointment made by Costa. The Board met two weeks later and voted the approval of the twelve million dollar loan to the Capital Development Company for the construction of a hotel.

The flight back seemed short. I had plenty of time to reflect on the events of the past several days and it made the trip go by quickly. I wondered what Costa had threatened Burrows with to get him to sit on that pension board and what the hell was Burrows up to that they thought they had to kill him? Choosing your battles carefully is one of my cardinal rules. Burrows must have made one hell of a bad choice. What was so important to Charlie Burrows that he was willing to die for it?

Chapter Seven

Christmas with Friends

Arriving back in the city after enjoying the warm sunshine and tropical breezes was always a let down for men. Exiting the terminal, I got smacked in the face with a message from a cold wind. *Winter...crap,* I thought. There hadn't been much time to spend with either Merzone or Costa while we were in Hawaii. Aside from a few brief conversations, they were too busy meeting and talking to mobs of people to spend time with me. Getting back to the office helped make things feel normal again. Well, as normal as things would ever be with the Merzone brothers working there. The fact was that Sammy was gone most of the time and his brother Ralph did most of the day to day work. Ralph was a royal pain in the ass. It was Sammy who had all the connections and made things happen, but it was Ralph who had the attitude. It was his arrogant above it all manner that really pissed me off. More than once, I found myself biting my lip during encounters with Ralph. He acted as though the only reason for the existence of this office was to serve Sammy and Ralph Merzone and that attitude of superiority made the veins on my neck bulge. At times when I was speaking to Ralph, I could picture my hands around Ralph's scrawny neck choking the last bit of life out of him.

The Christmas season was near and Nicky asked me to attend his company's Christmas party. Thankfully, I managed to find another commitment. I usually didn't get to see my kids until the summer. For whatever reason, it just seemed to work out that way. They had lives of their own and their schedules never managed to coordinate with mine. Normally, I would have spent Christmas alone watching football games and trying to forget how alone I felt, but not this year. Connie Traffarro had invited me to their house for Christmas day. I think she knew I would be alone and despite my weak protests, she nagged me into going.

The Traffarro's lived in a very nice stone ranch style house. It was fairly large and sat on a good sized lot with a fair number of huge oak trees. The house was located in the better part of the city and just below the hillside community that contained Costa's home. When I arrived at Traffarro's house I saw that the small pine trees in the front of it were covered with little white lights. It was so festive that I actually felt at home. Connie was always as nice as could be and my relationship with Anthony had warmed considerably. I knew that even though Connie had found her voice in her marriage with Anthony, there would be no way I would be spending Christmas with the Traffarro's if Anthony didn't want me.

When the door opened, I could hear the chatter inside. Connie greeted me with a big hug and a kiss on the cheek and led me through several rooms to the family room at the rear of the house. A fire was roaring in the huge fireplace at one end and twelve or more people with cocktails, laughing and having a good time basked in its glow. The house was full of holiday decorations. They had a big Christmas tree in the living room covered in red bows and flickering lights. The mantle over the fireplace was covered in garland and had beautiful antique lanterns at each end. The scene was straight out of Good Housekeeping.

"Everybody! This is Parker Quinn. He's my boss where I work," Connie said as she announced his arrival. "Please call him Quinn...everybody else does."

Traffarro was the first to greet me and approached with a big smile. He extended his hand and when I reached out to shake it; Traffarro pulled me close and gave me a big hug.

"I'm glad you decided to come," he said with warmth normally reserved for family. "Christmas is no time for a friend to spend alone."

"A friend?" Now there was a term that I hadn't heard all that often, certainly not on Wall Street. On Wall Street, people just come and go. Everybody came in from the suburbs in the morning, spent their day working and went home at night. They moved from job to job or got promoted to another department and friends in that environment were not really friends. They were acquaintances. People simply moved into and out of your life and temporarily filled some basic human need for social interaction. There was never any deep expectation of a lasting bond regardless of how much everyone swore that they would keep in touch. Their bond was only as strong as their email or an eight-hour day. But, in this neighborhood, there was a cultural history centuries old that was so deep and strong that it made these people friends even before they met each other. Their heritage was a common bond and although the newer generations could fight it on the periphery, they would never change what was in their blood. My clients were nearly all Italian. My friends were all Italian and the friendship and culture of these people warmed my heart.

I was introduced to all the cousins, aunts and uncles, brothers and sisters. They all made me feel like I belonged. Although I couldn't pass for an Italian even in the dark of a moonless night, I think they could instinctively sense a decent character and that I shared their principles. It wasn't my fault that God Almighty had chosen to have me born something less than an Italian. Being here was like having a front row seat at the best Broadway show. The stories all had a wonderful purpose. They brought back memories of departed friends and family so they could laugh at their foolish acts or admire the deeds that upheld their old traditions. Throughout the afternoon and on into the night the stories came and went, separated by laughter, knowing nods and a constant motion of the hands. Glasses of wine and tiny cups of espresso along with more different types of beautiful fresh Italian pastries and food than I ever thought existed were lovingly offered on into the evening. It was one of the best Christmases ever. One of the things that I had so desperately wanted was to belong. I wanted that extended family that was missing throughout my life. As I looked around the room, I realized that if my soul was looking for a place to belong, I had finally found it with these 'friends'.

I was scheduled to meet Nicky and Traffarro the next day at Salvatore's Restaurant. It was the quintessential neighborhood 'joint'. I passed the place many times driving through the Eastside but for some reason it never seemed like the kind of place that would be patronized by outsiders. It was a plain one-story building sitting unpretentiously on the corner of the block. There was a large 'Salvatore's' sign that sat unlit on the front edge of the roof and a parking lot starting on the left side of the building and winding around to the back with just enough lights in it to keep someone from walking headlong into one of the cars. Although the front door was clearly marked, I noticed that most of the patrons seemed to prefer the back door. It was well known that the FBI had a camera positioned on the telephone pole across the street taking pictures of everyone entering and leaving the restaurant.

The Salvatore of Salvatore's Restaurant was Salvatore Traffarro III, son of Salvatore Traffarro, Jr. who was Anthony's cousin. Everyone, not so surprisingly, referred to him as 'Junior'. Junior also ran the largest bookmaking operation in the state. He purchased the restaurant for his son Salvatore the Third, who they called 'Trips,' as a graduation present when he finished high school. Much to Junior's credit, he managed to keep the place running while his son was trying 'to find himself' by bedding down ever raven-haired beauty on the Eastside. Junior tolerated this since it had become somewhat of a family tradition. Junior was referred to as 'The Father of Our Country' because over the years he had sired enough illegitimate offspring to populate a small city and being a man of honor, paid out enough self-imposed child support each month to retire the national debt in a few years. The food was traditional Southern Italian and Sicilian originally prepared by Junior's mother who, at Junior's insistence, reluctantly gave up her chef's job after six months. He loved his mother dearly, but her daily 'advice' on how to run the restaurant was driving him crazy. There was no chance the menu would ever change because 'Ma' was always sneaking into the kitchen to 'instruct' whomever Junior hired to cook. This usually resulted in a verbal free for all two or three times a week, which the regular patrons enjoyed as much as the food.

Except for the new Cadillac every year, Junior was not a visibly rich man, even though he brought in a small fortune every year from his book. He lived in a modest apartment and drove a truck for one of the local Union shops for just as many days as it took to be laid off and collect unemployment each year. This provided him with great medical benefits and a solid pension for his old age. These were the kinds of items not normally associated with bookmaking. The truth was that this provided him with a 'visible means of support' and that was something that he knew the IRS *definitely* didn't associated with bookmaking.

Junior operated by an entirely different calendar than the rest of the world. The days were counted by how many it would be before he would be laid off or by how many it would be before he had to go back to work. His seasons were not the standard summer, fall, winter, and spring, but those of baseball, basketball, and football. Forget about hockey. No one in this city gave a crap about hockey. The holidays weren't Christmas, New Year's and the Fourth of July, but College Bowl time, March Madness, and the World Series. Junior's goal wasn't the 'big score'. He was in it to win every day on his piece of the action. Junior was the 'house,' and the house always won.

He was a generous man who shared his winnings. Junior Traffarro helped more people in the neighborhood each year than any charity. Thousands were spent every year helping friends out of tight spots. He never loaned anyone any money. It wasn't good for business, but he gave freely. Gambling debts were not hard for Junior to collect. The people of the neighborhood truly loved this man and more importantly they respected him. People paid Junior Traffarro because it was the right thing to do and in not doing so, they would lose the respect of their friends and neighbors.

I arrived at Salvatore's at 12:45 for my 1:00 meeting with Traffarro and Nicky. The parking lot was nearly full except for a few spaces near the street and Salvatore's front door. I had on a dark blue suit with a dark blue wool topcoat to protect myself from the cold winter's wind and aviator sunglasses for the bright sun. I strode up the few front stairs and through the tiny vestibule, opened the front door and walked into the dining room. It took a few moments for my eyes to adjust to the soft light of the interior so I waited a moment just inside the door. I noticed that the chatter inside the restaurant subsided quickly to a palpable silence. The dining room was nearly full and the bar at the rear of the building had fifteen or eighteen people seated or standing around it. The bartender was standing facing the front door and drying a glass with a towel. As I started towards the bar, the bartender raised his head and uttered just a single word.

"Shit!" the bartender said with obvious surprise from his frozen position. A moment later, the people at the bar turned to see a tall darkly clad figure heading in their direction. It was inevitable that the next response was almost unanimous. They jumped up from their seats and headed out the back door. Junior was just attempting to enter through the same door when the small mob reached it and nearly knocked him over.

"*Jesus Christ!*" Junior cried. "What the hell happened?"

When Junior finally got inside, he noticed me standing at the bar. He waited a moment to gather his thoughts and then walked up to me. The bartender continued to stand stone still with the towel and glass motionless in his hand as Junior approached the stranger.

"I'm Junior Traffarro. Can I help you?" asked Junior.

"I guess so," I said. I couldn't for the life of me figure out what just happened. "My name is Quinn and I'm here to meet Anthony Traffarro and Nicky Tagliano. I'm a little early, so I thought I'd have a drink. Is everything alright?" I said, looking around at the half empty restaurant.

Junior started to laugh so hard that he wrapped his arms around himself to hold his sides. He fell against the bar gasping for breath. Finally, he was able to get out a few words to the people still standing and staring in amazement at the scene before them.

"This is Quinn. My cousin Anthony's friend," Junior said as he gasped out the explanation. "He wants to know if everything is all right."

Junior motioned me towards a seat at the bar. "I'm sorry, but you gotta understand," Junior explained to me. "You don't exactly look like the average guy who comes in here. When these idiots saw you come in with that dark suit and those sunglasses, they figured you was FBI." He paused for a moment and reach for a napkin from the bar. "Oh, God," he moaned as he wiped the tears from his eyes. "I swear to God, I don't know when I laughed so hard. Carmine, give this man whatever he wants and it's on the house."

"I'm sorry I caused any problem, Mr. Traffarro," I offered as an apology.

"No, no. No problem at all. Really!" Junior replied. "And please call me Junior. I'm Anthony's cousin and he *has* mentioned your name. But, I gotta tell you. You gotta do something about the way you look. You're gonna give someone around here a fuckin' heart attack or something. Maybe you could call before you come down, that way I could warn these guys."

"Yeeeeaaaaah...well, I've heard that before."

"No, I'm just kidding. You're fine. Besides, when the story about what happened here today gets around, you won't be able to go anywhere around here without people knowing who you are. Trust me!" Junior said with one last chuckle. "So, my cousin's meetin' you here today?" He didn't wait for my response before adding. "Good. I got a few things I need to talk to him about. I hear you're helping him out with that goof Sammy and the old man."

No sooner had the last word left Junior's lips, than the front door opened and in walked Sammy Merzone with Costa and the usual entourage. They liked to make the rounds of some of the neighborhood places so they could be seen and today they had chosen the very spot that Traffarro selected for this meeting.

"Oh, shit! This ain't good," Junior said as Costa and his crew walked in. "Wait here Quinn. I gotta call my cousin. He's not gonna wanna be seen here with you while the old man's hangin' around." Junior left quietly to go use his car phone and I sat nervously at the bar wondering how the hell I was going to explain being at Salvatore's. I didn't have long to think because a minute later, Sammy came over to say hello.

"Hey, Quinn. I never expected to see you in this place," said Merzone obviously wondering how I wound up in this joint.

"Yeah...well...you know...I like to try different places in the city, Sammy. How else are you going to find where the best food is if you don't explore? I've been by this place a few times and I always meant to stop. I guess today was the day. What's up?" I asked trying to quickly change the subject.

"I'm havin' lunch with Reno and some friends," Sammy replied apparently accepting my explanation. "The old man's costing me a fucking fortune."

"Really?" I responded with mock surprise. Traffarro wasn't kidding when he said that Merzone would talk about anything anywhere.

"Yeah. Hey why don't you join us for lunch? We'll show you what real food tastes like."

I wasn't going to object too much. It probably was a good idea to get to know Costa better. I grabbed my drink from the bar and followed Sammy over to Costa's table. I said hello to Costa and was introduced to the rest of the group. Sammy explained my presence and how they had to show me what real food tasted like. Costa barely acknowledged me.

"This is Carlo Bonaface," Merzone said. "Cheri's Carlo's girlfriend." Cheri Simmons was the young woman that Sammy wanted me to hire as a favor. I had come to realize that she wasn't the brightest bulb in the box, but since she was working in Merzone's area, I really didn't care.

"Yeah. Hey, thanks for hirin' Cheri. She was getting' to be a real pain in the ass what with her hangin' around all the time. It's a lot better now that she's got somethin' to do during the day," Carlo said.

"So Reno, how's things going over at the Union?" I asked in what I hoped would be a way to open a conversation with Costa.

Costa just looked at me for a moment before he said, "Fine. How's things going in your office?"

Maybe it wouldn't have bothered me so much if it wasn't for the fact that Costa was hunched over the table staring at a piece of bread. *Being ignored is one thing, but finding a piece of bread more interesting than someone's conversation is really an insult,* I thought. My comfort level was going downhill fast. It was obvious by Costa's tone of voice that he felt I was prying into things that were none of my business and Costa was not a person who made idle conversation. "Good. You know, Sammy seems to be settling in very well and all," I said in an attempt to get out from under my error.

"Yeah, so I hear." Costa's reply was of the type and tone that led me to believe that this was going to be a long awkward lunch. Thankfully, the waiter came over and rescued me from myself. Seven lunches were ordered for the people at the table and four to go. These would be for Costa's sister Mary and her chosen few from the clerical staff back at the Union offices. Costa hardly spoke and everyone else talked as if I wasn't there. I think he was making it clear that I was not welcome. I finally resolved to eat lunch quickly and leave under the pretext of having pressing issues back at the office.

When I got into my car and reflected upon the events of the past hour, I shuddered. Thankfully, Traffarro never showed up at the restaurant, which I attributed to Junior's quick response to Costa's arrival. Costa treated me like a leper and Sammy and his friends were never going to be the source of stimulating conversation. I knew I was lucky that Costa's arrival hadn't occurred while Nicky, Traffarro, and I were having a cozy little lunch. I would need all the luck I could find because things were starting heating up.

Chapter Eight

The Invitation

Time passed and spring finally arrived with its warm breezes, green leaves and flowers. I had been to numerous meetings, dinners, social events, and every other form of gathering where business, broads, and booze were talked about, played with and consumed. I was around so much that even Costa was speaking to me. The old man wasn't saying anything important, but at least the agony of one-word sentences and long periods of silence seemed to be a thing of the past. What Costa lacked in flow of information Merzone made up for in spades. On a quiet Wednesday morning, I was sitting in my office when Merzone walked in and sat down.

"Quinn, I've got something going that you're really gonna to like," Merzone began.

"Really. What may I ask is that?" I replied. I couldn't possibly imagine anything that Merzone was into that would interest me, but I had to admit that my curiosity was peaked.

"Well, you know how much the old man costs me each month. I mean take this month for example. It's Louise's birthday, so the old man wants me to buy her this necklace. That black bitch cost me forty-eight hundred dollars, and with the dinners and everything else, I paid out nearly thirty grand this month," said Sammy as he rambled on.

I couldn't believe what he was hearing. If Costa knew that Merzone was telling the whole world about their arrangement, he'd have killed him. It had to be beyond Costa's comprehension that anyone could possibly be this stupid. I stopped my thought process for a moment to chastise myself. I really liked Sammy as a human being. Hell, Sammy would give you the shirt off his back if you asked for it, and there wasn't a mean bone in the man's body. But, my God! How is it possible that anyone connected to the mob could be this naïve?

"Anyway, I got this deal worked out with this money manager in Los Angeles," Sammy continued. "You know how hot the New Issue market's been for the last year? Well, when I told him about Reno and the expenses, he told me that I could cover them by placing New Issues with people I knew. Those things come out at fifteen dollars and go to fifty the same day for Christ's sake. My guy tells the brokerage firm's gotta set aside ten to fifteen thousand shares for me or he won't run his stock and bond trades through them. The brokers don't care 'cause they gotta sell this shit to someone anyway. I buy a couple thousand shares in the old man's account and sell it out the same day. He thinks I'm a genius. Then, since we're in the business and it's against the law for us to buy any New Issues in our own accounts, I buy them in some of my friend's accounts. I put up the money for the purchase and we split the profit. I'm making thirty or forty grand a month. So, I thought that since you been so nice and all, why not give you a shot at makin' a few bucks. All you gotta do is get a couple of friends to do the same thing. You can make five to ten grand a month easy."

I leaned forward and put my elbows on the desk and buried my face in my hands. I just sat there in total disbelief. As I thought about this scheme, I swore I could hear the cell door slam behind me. Now, what the hell was I going to do? I was already well aware of what Sammy was doing. The very fact that Sammy told me about this game when coupled with the fact that it was as illegal as hell made me a part of it. If I didn't report it to the firm's Compliance Department I was screwed. If I did, they would nail Sammy and I was screwed. Basically, either way, I was screwed. The idiot sitting in front of me had just punched my ticket to jail time and a huge fine.

"Sammy, you know of course that this is as illegal as hell, don't you?" I said peering out over the top of my hands.

"Sure, but how are they ever gonna find out? It's not like I send these guys a bill or something, or there's all kinds of memos floating around. Nobody's ever gonna find out," Sammy replied, leaning back in his chair and dismissing the notion of being caught with a wave of his hand. "It's really a sweet deal, Quinn. Why don't you try it? I'll even lend you the money if you're short."

"I really appreciate the opportunity Sammy, but I don't think my stomach's as strong as yours," I replied, leaning back slowly until I collapsed against the back of my chair. "Besides, I don't want to cut into your action."

"Nah, it's not a problem. There are plenty of shares for you to get cut in," Sammy argued.

"Well, I'll tell you what. Why don't you let me think about it and I'll let you know," I suggested as I desperately tried to end the conversation.

"Okay. Oh, I meant to tell you. There's going to be a meeting tomorrow morning around 10:00. There are some people that would like to meet you. You gonna be free?" Sammy asked.

"Yeah, I don't see a problem." I responded, slightly perplexed. "Who are these people?"

"Rocco Massarro and a few of his guys." Sammy answered as he was getting up to leave.

"As in Rocco Massarro the mob guy?" I stammered in disbelief.

"Yup," Merzone said with a good-bye wave as he left my office.

I watched Merzone leave my office then leaned my head back and cast an empty stare at the ceiling. *This is fucking wonderful*, I thought in a flash of complete sarcasm. *What is this guy trying to do to me?* Then it hit me. Maybe Merzone wasn't as stupid as everyone made him out to be. He'd been running his mouth for months and I had enough information to bury Merzone, Costa, and a lot of other people. Maybe it just hit Merzone that I wasn't a true part of his crowd. Was it possible that Costa or Merzone knew of my relationship with Traffarro? They certainly knew the Justice Department was after them and Merzone had just been forced out of his job because of the pressure. Everyone knew that Traffarro would be next in line to take over the Union if anything happened to the old man and it was Traffarro that had suggested that Merzone go with my company. Costa hadn't held on to his power by making stupid mistakes and he had his fair share of spies around the city and in the Union. If Costa suspected that Traffarro was trying to muscle him out with my help, he might have asked Merzone if he had mentioned anything about their 'arrangement' to me. Even if Merzone told Costa that he hadn't said anything, Costa was smart enough to know that I had access to all the transaction records for the Union, for Costa and for anyone else who conducted business in that office. My thoughts were off to the races. All Costa would have to do was to have Merzone go to me and ask if I wanted some of the action. If I said yes then I'm involved, and as likely to go to prison as anyone else if the shit hit the fan. If I said no, I'm still involved unless I tell the authorities. So the real risk is that I would turn in Merzone. However, it was Merzone, not me, who was bringing in the real money to the company and Wall Street doesn't throw out their money machines.

"Shit! Shit! Shit!" I just sat there mulling over the possibilities, none of which I concluded, were looking too good. Why would the head of a mob family from the southern part of the state want to meet me? This was the same guy that Big Nappi Brufalo worked for. What did Sammy mean when he said 'and a few of his guys'? Maybe I was wrong about Costa's plan, maybe they figured it would be a lot neater if I just disappeared.

"Double shit!" I said. I thought I had better call Traffarro. There was also no way I could explain this over the phone even if Traffarro would let me. Traffarro told me that the FBI tapped the phones at the Union as well as his home phone, Costa, and Merzone's phones. No one *ever* said anything meaningful on the phone. There were times when it got so cryptic I could barely figure out what Traffarro was trying to say. I suggested that Traffarro meet me for lunch at Salvatore's and after some mild insistence, Traffarro said he would rearrange his schedule and meet me at 1:00.

When I arrived at Salvatore's the place was packed as usual and Junior was behind the bar. "Christ, Junior, it's nice to see you doing an honest day's work," was my joking hello.

"Fuck you, Quinn," replied Junior in mock anger. "It's not like sittin' behind that desk of yours playing on the phone all day. It's also nice that you come around here enough now that my customers don't jump out the fuckin' windows no more."

"Thanks, Junior. It's nice to see you too," said I in protest. Junior and I always tried to get into a verbal sparring match whenever possible. Junior walked over and shook my hand and at the same time gave me a playful slap in the face.

"How ya doin', Quinn? Ya look good. You waitin' for Anthony?" Junior inquired.

"Yeah, but it doesn't look like you have any tables available," I said, as I peered into the dining room.

"No problem! Some of these assholes have been here two fuckin' hours. Anthony comes, I'll throw 'em out," said Junior as he offered his simple solution.

It was just a few minutes later that Traffarro walked through the back door. As he made his way towards me, he had to stop several times to say hello to various people. He finally reached me and shook my hand while Junior served a customer a drink.

"Hey, Cuz'. How ya doin'?" said Traffarro as he greeted Junior. "Is your mother in the kitchen? I'll go back and say hello."

"No, thank God and it's been peaceful here all day," replied Junior with a noticeable sigh of relief. "Wait a minute Anthony and I'll get you and Quinn a table."

Junior walked around to the back of the dining room and from around the corner we could hear him say, "Get the fuck outta my restaurant you two! You been hangin' around here all morning. I need this table for people who actually help pay for this fuckin' joint." As Junior made his way back to the bar he stopped at every table were there were any women and apologized for his language. He explained to each one that he had to keep the riffraff out. The scene hadn't really insulted anyone, and even the two men who were now leaving were laughing. This was just Junior and it was all part of the restaurant's 'ambiance'. When he finally got back behind the bar he came over to Traffarro and Quinn and said, "Ya know, ya try to be a nice guy and they take advantage of you. Wait just a minute 'til Jimmy cleans off the table."

"God! I love you Junior," I said only half-jokingly. "You're such a class act."

Junior shrugged his shoulders as he turned away and muttered something about "What else could I do?"

When Traffarro and I finally got seated, I told Traffarro about my conversation with Merzone that morning. I gave him my analysis of the possible reason for the dialog and how I wondered if Traffarro thought I was right. Traffarro kept injecting phases such as "you've got to be kidding", and "I don't believe this". These were not the responses that I was really hoping for. I held the faint hope that Traffarro might be aware of what was going on and that he might be able to give me reassurances that it really didn't mean anything. Maybe, Traffarro thought my imagination was getting the best of me or possibly that he didn't believe that there was any problem. Unfortunately, that was not the case.

"They got money coming in like a fuckin' fire hose and it's not enough." Traffarro said as he placed his two hands together as if he were going to pray and slowly shook them up and down. "It's not enough they have the FBI, the Justice Department, the Department of Labor, and Christ knows whoever else on their ass. Now they've got to get the Securities and Exchange Commission involved. Who the hell is next? The fucking *Russians*! These guys have more money than God knows what and they're so greedy they've gotta have more. The Union members always knew the old man was skimming from the Union but they didn't care because they were better off with him than without him. There was a time when he actually listened to their problems and tried to help. But now? Fuck no! He wouldn't listen to anyone if Christ came down from the cross."

There was no doubt in my mind that Traffarro was surprised and upset. Traffarro didn't let things bother him, at least not as far as I could ever tell. He always seemed to have the opposition's moves mapped out well in advance, but this time I could tell it was different.

"What do you think I should do?" I asked.

"Nothing," said Traffarro as he made a short sweep of his hand through the air. "You're sure your records are okay? There's nothing in this New Issue business that can come back to you?"

"The records are fine. They're all automated anyway with copies at the branch office *and* at the main office. My responsibility is to monitor trading patterns and wave the red flag if anything looks wrong and on the surface, nothing does. There's no law that says that a broker can't give some of his clients' preference on New Issues. What it clearly states is that he can't participate in a client's gains or losses. However, when some idiot comes in and tells you they're breaking the fucking law, it's the manager's responsibility to report the violation."

"Was anyone around when this moron told you about this?" Traffarro asked.

"No. It's his word against mine." It wasn't a position that I liked being in. What was worrying me was that it might be an indication that Costa knew that Traffarro was working to take over the Union. I was also concerned about the meeting with Massarro. It seemed to me, that mob bosses were not in the habit of traveling fifty miles to see some branch manager at a brokerage firm. Especially not seventy-five year old mob bosses.

"Then I wouldn't worry about it," Traffarro said.

"Okay. What about the meeting with Massarro?" I asked.

"I'll be honest. I haven't got a fucking clue about that one," Traffarro responded.

"Anthony, I have to say that I'm—oh, just a little fucking uncomfortable about that!" I said most emphatically. "I really don't want to take swimming lessons like Charlie Burrows with Big Nappi as the teacher. He's got a very bad record on student survival."

Traffarro leaned back in his chair and laughed. "Christ, Quinn! Thank God, you haven't lost your sense of humor. Damn, I needed that. Things have definitely gotten a bit tense around here."

"You're telling me?" I said.

"Look," Traffarro began. "Nobody's gonna meet you at a public place and then kill you. The Feds will have more pictures of you at that meeting than you could ever imagine, believe me. But I'm really curious about what an old 'Moustache Pete' like Massarro is up to.

I was starting to get my arms around this whole thing. It was becoming clear to me exactly what my role in this was. Traffarro was ready to take over the Union and clean it up as best he could and he needed me on the inside to funnel information. All Traffarro had to do was sit and wait, and that was something he was very good at. He wouldn't have to run against Costa because he would simply be filling the vacancy when Costa was jailed. What I kept coming back to, and the one thing that made me very uncomfortable was, that I was at the epicenter of this whole mess. All of the dirty laundry of Merzone and his friends had been laid out before me during months of parties and meetings, and I had it all in my filing drawer mind. Traffarro knew this because I had relayed all the information to him. The mob probably knew it too because Brufalo and his boys were at too many parties not to hear the conversations. The question was, did Costa and the Justice Department know? When Justice found out that I could tie all the pieces together, they would be on me like white on rice and that would mean that Costa couldn't let me live.

Merzone strolled into my office at 9:30 the next morning to inform me that the meeting with Massarro was set for 11:00 at the coffee shop on Bleeker Street. We could go down in Merzone's car and have lunch afterward. Since things were seldom as they appeared, and I was a little nervous on the trip there, I knew that all the guessing I had done was just that, guessing. It didn't help matters any that Merzone talked constantly. He told me about a bid-rigging situation that Massarro and Big Nappi were involved in on a huge State highway program. Did Merzone have a death wish? He must have because if Massarro found out Sammy was telling anyone about his business dealings, he was as good as dead.

When we walked into the coffee shop Massarro was sitting at a table at the front of the shop. This struck me as very unusual. Although I had never met Massarro before, I was pretty sure I knew the type. I was damned sure that Traffarro would never sit in the front of anyplace. Not only was Massarro sitting at the front table, he was sitting at the table next to the front window. Since the entire front of the shop was glass, it made Massarro and his men look like pastries on display. The FBI couldn't have asked him to sit in a better location. As Sammy and I approached the table, everyone got up except Massarro. He was a shriveled old man who appeared to be well into his seventies and whose health couldn't be all that good. His clothes hung loosely on his bony frame and either he had lost an awful lot of weight or he shopped at the Salvation Army. With Big Nappi sitting next to him, it just made Massarro look even smaller. The other two men were in their fifties or sixties and were of standard Italian issue.

"Please sit down, Mr. Quinn," Massarro began. "I understand that you've been very helpful in getting Sammy situated. You did him and us a big favor and I wanted to express my gratitude."

"You're very welcome I'm sure, but it was good business for us, Mr. Massarro," I replied. "Sammy brought a significant amount of revenue to our office and we're fortunate to have him." I figured that this was a good standard, harmless reply. I didn't have a clue why I was sitting there with a well-known mobster on display for all to see, but I was damned sure not going to say anything that I might later regret hearing on a recording. The FBI had the best surveillance equipment that taxpayer's money could buy. Hell, they could hear a flea fart at a hundred yards.

"We have several securities operations that are very profitable for us, Mr. Quinn," Massarro said. "We are always searching for enterprising individuals such as yourself and their companies to support our efforts. I think you might find it very interesting and profitable. Maybe we could get together sometime and discuss the possibilities?"

The Massarro family wasn't what you'd expect in a mob family. They didn't pull armored car jobs or rob trucks loaded with computers and although they would kill someone every now and then, they really did think it was bad for business. These guys were a modern version of the Mafia. They didn't rob because it was safer to fence stolen goods. They did sell a few drugs every now and then, but it was better and cleaner to launder money for drug gangs. It wasn't smart business to steal securities because they were hard to get rid of. What made more sense to them was to use one of their shell companies and run a 'Pump and Dump' operation. They'd form or buy a small brokerage operation and get a bunch of guys on the phone to start peddling a worthless company's shares at a feverish pace. All the activity would run up the price of the stock and they would dump their remaining shares at a huge profit. The public of course got killed. The NASD would get a mountain of complaints which meant they were forced to take action against the brokerage company who would just disappear and open somewhere else under another name. This produced a ton of money with no violence and minimal risk since trying to catch a company that constantly moves and changes its name isn't easy. They had their fingers in the unions for decades before I got involved. You couldn't get to many goods shipped, buildings built, or roads constructed without the mob getting some piece of the action. It was all a hell of a lot safer. You get convicted of murder and you can kiss your life good-bye. Under this plan, if you were dumb enough and the government was smart enough—both of which were rare events—you got nailed for a white collar crime and did a short stretch in a federal country club rather than a Super Max facility.

"We are always looking for good business, Mr. Massarro," I replied. "Why don't you have someone give myself or Sammy a call and we can set a date to meet." I kept thinking about the tape recorder I could almost hear running. I didn't want to turn Massarro down flat for fear that it might raise suspicions but on the other hand I didn't want to appear to enthusiastic to the FBI.

Massarro turned away from me to speak to Brufalo. The shift in gears surprised me. It seemed that one-minute I was part of the discussion and the next it was as if I didn't exist. *What the hell is going on,* I thought?

"Nappi, I understand we might have a problem with a friend on our highway job," Massarro continued, totally ignoring me. Massarro owned a state highway commissioner. It seemed the commissioner had a lust for fast women and slow horses. It doesn't take long for that kind of habit to put you into a very deep hole and Massarro was very good at finding the right people and encouraging them to dig deeper. The only way out of this mess was for the commissioner to do what he was told or he'd wind up as an 'upstanding citizen of the community.' It was one of the cuter phrases used by this crew. It meant they would dump his body into the form for a bridge column just before the concrete was poured. It was always cheaper for Massarro to let someone's vices get them in so deep they had to help him rather than pay bribes. What Massarro needed was help to secure some state contracts for certain construction companies, who in turn would pay kickbacks to Massarro over the life of the contract.

"Don't worry about it," replied Brufalo. "I'll stick my finger in his fuckin' eye. He won't be any trouble."

"Excuse me, Mr. Massarro," I interrupted. Brufalo shot him a look that made my mind race to choose the right words. "I'm sure you have business to discuss that you would want to keep private. I think it would be better if I just waited outside for Sammy. It was nice meeting you."

I rose and extended my hand to Massarro who shook it, but never said a word. I acknowledged the others and told Sammy that I'd wait outside. I couldn't imagine what the hell that was all about. Was I being sized up? Was that a genuine business discussion and would I really receive a call later on? Were they trying to link me to organized crime by having such a public meeting? I knew I could stand there and think about this all day and never come up with the right answer. The one thing I knew for sure was that if I didn't maintain my composure, I'd be in some very deep shit.

Chapter Nine

Someone New

I met Traffarro at our regular Saturday lunch. We had a brief discussion about the Massarro meeting but neither of us could figure out what it meant. While we were eating, two women walked into Salvatore's and sat at the bar. I had met one of them before. Sandy Smith dated Nicky briefly, but she was a lot more than Nicky could handle. Sandy was the kind of woman that wouldn't throw you a life preserver if you were drowning and she was standing hip deep in them. I figured it was that independence that drove Nicky to pursue her. It made him crazy that she wouldn't melt under his charm. Sandy knew Nicky would be at Salvatore's on Saturday because he was always at Salvatore's on Saturday, along with myself, Traffarro and the other regulars in the crew. It was like religion. She probably came in just to break Nicky's balls. I could care less because I couldn't take my eyes off of the other woman. She took my breath away. She had a full head of soft blonde hair, big blue eyes and soft pink lips, a beautiful face and a figure that made my heart skip. She was Jane Russell, Marilyn Monroe, and Jean Harlow all rolled into one.

"Nicky, who the hell is that?" I asked, pulling anxiously on Nicky's arm.

"You know her. That's Sandy." Nicky responded as if he could care less, but I knew otherwise. I had seen Nicky bite the knuckle of his index finger in total frustration over this woman too many times.

"Not her you idiot, the other one."

"Oh, hhheeerrr," he said with a big smile, taking sweet pleasure at watching my rapt attention. "That, my friend is Rane Harold. She's not my type."

"*No shit*!" I said in fierce defense of the vision I was looking at. "She's not built like a swizzle stick. Who *is* she?"

"I told you, that's Rane Harold. She goes out with Pete Mastro. He's some lawyer who does some work for the boys out in Cleveland. The guy's a genuine asshole. He acts like he's connected all over the country. You want me to introduce you?" Nicky said, recognizing an opportunity to torture me some more.

"Thanks, but no thanks," I replied. "I'm perfectly capable of handling that myself."

Sandy Smith was having a similar conversation with Rane Harold. Sandy knew who all the players were in the city and she enjoyed playing games with the men who moved and shook it. It was the one thing that really got her blood up and the more powerful the person, the more fun it was to mess with their head. She thought playing *in* the lion's cage was a lot more exciting than standing in the crowd and just watching. Sandy and Rane were just having a girl's day out. They planned to go to a couple of bars, have some drinks, meet some of Sandy's friends, and maybe go to dinner. They had known each other from high school. Rane moved away shortly after graduation and since she had gotten back to the city, she and Sandy hadn't been able to catch up on old times, new boyfriends or their new lives.

Rane Harold grew up poor. Her mother was an alcoholic and her father had left her and her three sisters and brother when she was seven years old. She had worked since she was nine and knew what a hard life was all about, living in a cold water flat in Florida. Life was tough and the people around her were tougher. She had built a cold steel exterior to protect herself and few people ever got through to find the loving person inside. When her first husband managed to break through, she was rewarded with being beaten up regularly. The marriage ended after she got fed up and threw his miserable ass down a flight of stairs. But, she liked men, even if she thought they never knew what color her eyes were because they didn't bother to look above her chest. She was a 'take no crap and take me as I am' woman.

"I don't know why you drag me into places like this," Rane said as she sat down at the bar. "It's just the same low life mob crowd that Pete hangs around. I'm really getting sick of this type."

"I know what you mean, but believe me this is a better class low life crowd," Sandy countered, lighting a cigarette. "Besides, there's somebody I wanted you to meet."

"Oh, no!" Rane protested, raising her hand as if she were stopping traffic "I'm just getting rid of Pete and I don't need another one of his kind in my life."

"Yeah, and what are you going to do, sit at home and knit? I'm not saying you have to do anything. Beside, nothing says you can't window shop. For example, see the big guy on the far end of the long table?" Sandy said as she pressed on. "He's definitely *not* like these other guys. He runs a big brokerage operation here in the city and I've met him. He's really a nice guy."

"Yeah, I see him and ya' know what? He's *way* too good looking." Rane said. "Believe me, I know the type. They're *soooo* impressed with who they are and how good looking they are. I really don't have time for this bullshit, Sandy. Let's go."

"For God's sake, have some patience. Look...here comes Nicky," said Sandy as she tried to keep Rane in her seat.

"Heyee! I haven't seen you in a long time. You look as beautiful as ever," Nicky crooned, swaggering over to the bar. "Where you been? I always thought we had some good times together."

"We did. I've just been busy lately," Sandy said as she leaned forward for the kiss that she knew would be coming. She could have cared less. She stored men like cordwood...to be used when needed. Things had been a little slow in her life for the past couple of weeks and it was one of the reasons she called Rane. She knew the two of them would stir up a fire wherever they went. Nicky was always good for some good times and great gifts

"Nicky. This is Rane Harold. We've known each other since high school. I just thought I'd bring her in for a drink, and I wanted her to have a look at your friend Quinn," Sandy said as she flashed Nicky a sly smile.

"Christ, Sandy!" Rane said, rolling her eyes in frustration. "Give it a rest!"

"Hi, Rane," Nicky said in as sweet a voice as he could muster. "Please don't be embarrassed. She drives me crazy, too. That's why I love her," he continued as he leaned over to give Sandy a kiss on the cheek.

Rane leaned back on the barstool and shot Nicky a 'drop dead' look.

Nicky could see an opportunity for mutual gain here. He could get back with Sandy and I could stop drooling and meet Rane. While he was devising his plan, Nicky couldn't help but wonder if I could handle this Ice Queen. He figured I might lose a hand or an eye if I made a wrong move on this woman.

"Next Friday night, there's going to be a small party at the Shoreline, just some of the guys from the Union and their friends. Why don't you and I go with Rane and Quinn?" Nicky said to Sandy. He figured Sandy would have to say yes if she was really up to her old scheming self. "You and I could get caught up and they could get to meet each other over dinner. Nice-nice, cheech-a-cheech, quata-quat." That was a phrase that Nicky often used and I never understood what the hell he was saying.

Before Sandy could open her mouth, Rane offered her opinion of the arrangement. "Whoa! Hold it a minute. I haven't done a blind date since high school and I'm a little past old for that crap. If your friend wants to go to dinner with me, he can ask me himself...unless he's not man enough."

Nicky wanted to leap across the bar and choke the bitch but he managed to keep his composure and thanked God that it was me that would have to deal with her. "First, he doesn't know anything about this. Second, I wouldn't have suggested this if he hadn't expressed an interest in meeting you when you walked in. Why don't I go over and explain what's happening and we can see 'if he's man enough.'"

"Why don't you do that," Rane said dismissing Nicky as one would a small child.

Walking back to the table, Nicky was slowly shaking his head. If it wasn't for the fact that he wanted to go to bed with Sandy so much, he would tell me that Rane was committed to Pete Mastro and that she had no interest. But the 'brain' in his pants was doing all the thinking at this point and *it* knew what it wanted. When he got back to the table, he figured he'd tell me some of the truth and let me make up my mind.

"Quinn, you were absolutely right. She's some kind of woman," Nicky started with a bit of diplomatic sarcasm. If he told me what he really thought of the Ice Queen, he'd never get his chance with Sandy. "I told her about the dinner next week and that I thought you and I could take her and Sandy. We could have a nice dinner and you two could get to know each other. But, she said she felt a little uncomfortable with me making the arrangements like this. She was concerned that maybe you might not want to take her. So, she wants you to ask her yourself just to be sure you really want to go with her. Maybe she's a little shy and uncomfortable. You know how women get." Nicky was impressed with the line of crap he just fed me. The best entertainment of that night would be watching poor me getting torn to shreds.

Rane Harold watched me as I got up from my chair and headed in her direction. When I reached the bar, I couldn't help noticing Rane's full breasts being slightly exposed in her partially unbuttoned blouse. I instinctively knew I had better keep my eyes on her face or I'd be just like every other guy who met her.

"Hi, Sandy," I said, trying to be as casual as possible. "It's good to see you again." I wanted to be careful in my choice of words. "Ms. Harold, I'm Parker Quinn. I would like to apologize for my over-zealous friend. He sometimes gets overly enthusiastic in his efforts. However, this time he couldn't have been more accurate. I feel fortunate to have met you today and I would very much like to take you to dinner next week. If you're going to be available, I could pick you up around seven next Friday? I hope you'll accept the invitation."

She looked up and appeared to be lost for an instant. Her natural defensive instincts overcame her body's enthusiasm. "I think that might be nice Mr. Quinn, but I'd rather take my own car if you don't mind." She was thinking that as gorgeous as this man was and as nice as things sounded, she was still pretty sure it was just another guy who would turn out to be a jerk and she didn't want someone new to know where she lived. Besides, if the evening turned out to be a bust, she could leave anytime and drive home. There had been too many disappointing men in her life and she had no interest in dealing with another one.

"Sure, that'll be fine. Why don't we meet at the Shoreline at 7:30? I'll meet you on the front deck and we can walk in together. Don't get me wrong. It's a nice place but I don't think a lady should walk in alone."

Rane thought that was a nice touch. It was better than the usual 'I'll meet you at the bar.' She was sick of walking through crowded restaurants with men looking down the front of her dress. If this guy were half the man he appeared to be, she doubted that would be a problem. Besides, she could handle herself.

Rane kept looking at me as I walked back to the table. Sandy's voice brought Rane back from deep thought. "*Holy Christ, Rane!* Whoa, the heat between you two. I swear to God, I could feel it."

"Give it a rest, girl," Rane said as she played at being composed and only mildly interested. "We'll see if he's for real. I still say he's way too good-looking and just a little too smooth."

The next week proved to be fairly uneventful, considering everything that was going on. I had mixed feelings about my date with Rane. On the one hand, I couldn't wait until Friday, but on the other, I didn't relish going through a long evening with someone who turned out to be less than hoped for. I had been dating different women for some time now and it was getting a bit old. They were all nice and they certainly provided sexual gratification, but not one of them had what I was looking for. I had finally found the extended family I was looking for and I was starting to think about finding someone I could share my life with and that meant someone with a strong character. I wanted a woman that loved me for who I was not what I was or what I had.

Friday finally arrived and I got to the Shoreline at 7:15. I didn't mind being early. It was a beautiful warm evening and there was no way I wanted to arrive after Rane. I have this set of rules; such as, never make a woman wait. I couldn't remember where I picked them up, but they were ingrained in me and violating them made me extremely uncomfortable. It was about 7:30 when I saw Nicky's Corvette pull up to the front of the restaurant and I was surprised because Nicky was always late. When the valet opened the passenger's door, one of God's greatest pair of legs unfolded themselves into the parking lot. I couldn't help notice that if her skirt were any shorter; I'd certainly know whether she was a natural blond. As Nicky approached the restaurant, he put his arm around

Sandy who was definitely dressed to appeal to Nicky's most basic instincts.

"Heyee! Quinny, you're looking very sharp tonight," Nicky said as they came up the stairs to the small front deck. I had taken great care in picking out what I wore for the occasion. I had on a pair of black pleated pants and a navy blue crew neck shirt and a taupe silk jacket. It was my Miami Vice look and it was nice to hear somebody confirm my choice, especially Nicky, being that he was the clothing industry's best friend.

I insisted that Nicky and Sandy wait inside. I didn't want anything to distract me from Rane's arrival and about five minutes later, a black Jaguar pulled up. When the valet opened the door and the driver got out, butterflies started to flutter in my stomach. Rane Harold was even more beautiful than I remembered. She strode elegantly and confidently toward me. She wore a simple black dress that stopped at mid-thigh. It was folded closed across the front and plunged down between her breasts revealing just enough of her soft skin to announce the greater rewards inside. Rane had the legs of a lingerie model and I was surprised I hadn't noticed them before.

"I'm sorry I'm late, Mr. Quinn. It's really not the way I am, but I had a hard time finding the place. I'm somewhat geographically challenged" She said as she extended her hand. She too had spent the week in anticipation of the evening, but she thought she had this handsome man figured out. Rane Harold was no novice to relationships and she was growing tired of the parade of empty liaisons that had past through her life. She figured that this guy Quinn was probably just another hollow pretty boy but Sandy and Nicky were going to be there and they were always good for an evening's entertainment. As I walked down the stairs to greet her she felt a chill even in the warm night air.

"I can truly appreciate that. This is a bit hard to find the first time you come here," I responded in sympathy. "I would have been far more disappointed if you hadn't found it at all. You look absolutely beautiful. By the way, please, can we get past the Mr. Quinn? Everybody just calls me Quinn and only my mother ever called me Parker."

"Well, I'm not everybody," she said. "I'm sure your mother was a fine woman and personally I like her choice. So if you have no objection, I'll use Parker. Besides, that way you won't have to wonder who it is if I ever call you." She raised her hand to make a point. "Now *my* mother on the other hand, called me every name imaginable and I certainly wouldn't recommend any of them. Why don't we just keep it simple with Parker and Rane?"

"I like the sound of that very much."

At first, I was taken back by Rane's fiery independence. Most people just went along with the standard 'Quinn' and never thought much about it, but she seemed to take such things more seriously and as I thought about it, I liked the idea. I especially liked the 'Parker and Rane' part. It had a certain ring to it that made me feel strangely comfortable.

I extended my arm for her to take and as we walked inside, I told her that Nicky and Sandy would be waiting at the bar. Entering the restaurant, I recognized many of the people at the bar. It seemed strange that as we walked the length of the room to find Nicky and Sandy, people just turned their heads and stared at us. I felt as though I had grown a third eye or something. When we arrived, Sandy pulled Rane close to her and whispered in her ear.

"Christ, you two look *fabulous* together. The place actually quieted down when you both walked in," said Sandy with a certain amount of satisfaction at being part of the center of attention caused by this stunning couple.

After we sat down for dinner, Rane and I fell into a conversation that totally consumed us. It was as if we had been friends our whole lives. She was surprised to find that I was a man of character and understanding. She saw a man who was totally devoid of pretense and who had genuine humility. I knew this was more than lust at first sight. She had a wonderful insight. This was a strong independent woman who had built up a shell around her as a defense against a hard life, but who was warm and caring in her heart. Dinner came and went without much notice and we continued to be absorbed in our conversation.

"Tell me something about your family. Do you have any brothers and sisters?" I asked, hoping she would be like everyone else and enjoyed talking about whom they were and what they had done more than listening to what other people had to say.

"I have a brother and three sisters. We're spread out all over the country. My mother was inclined to move around a lot and I guess as we made friends in various places and we tended to go back there and settle in. My sister Barbara and I are very close. We needed to be just to survive childhood." This was about as far as Rane felt comfortable going. She really wasn't like everyone else and she certainly didn't enjoy bringing up the past. She also didn't want to sound like she was offering up some sob story about her difficult childhood, because that definitely was not her style. *I think it's about time I divert this little inquiry in a different direction,* she thought

"I can't imagine a man like you has been single your whole life," she said in a gentle probe into his background. They had been talking long enough that she was genuinely interested in finding out more about him.

"Well," I started with a little hesitation. I didn't want to parade my past mistakes in front of her, but I felt a need to be honest. "I was married. I think we got married for all the wrong reasons, but stayed together for all the right ones. We were both very young and as the years passed we just grew in different directions. After a while, we had very little in common. I have a son and a daughter that I love very much and it was extremely difficult twisting their lives out of shape when the divorce finally came. It's not something that I take a lot of pride in, but in hindsight I think it was probably best for both of us. My daughter's in college and I think she's reconciled the situation. She's a very special person and we talk on the phone quite often. My son on the other hand is trying to find his place in the world. I think the divorce affected him more than anyone else and we don't seem to be able to talk the same language. I'm hoping that as time passes and he gets more of life under his belt that he'll possibly understand that things happen. How about you? I can't imagine that someone didn't manage to tie you down."

She was taken by his sensitivity. So many men had an arrogant attitude toward their divorce. It always seemed they found more faults in their ex-wives than with themselves. She was a firm believer that it took two to get married and the exact same number to end one. Quinn appeared to be a man who knew his role in one of life's most common mishaps.

"I guess it's somewhat the same with me," she said after a long look into my eyes. "Married young, had a baby young, and divorced young. I didn't have the luxury of trying to decide whether I wanted to stay or not. He was a hitter and I don't think any woman should stay in that situation. My son goes to high school here in the city. He's a great kid and we get along very well." She paused and took a sip of her cocktail. "Have anyone special in your life right now," she asked, deciding to get right to the point.

I was pretty sure I knew the point of this question. I enjoyed talking to Rane and it was something I didn't want to give up. She was bright, funny and beautiful and that was a combination I hadn't seen in many years. Rane appeared to be a person that said what she thought and didn't have the time or interest in playing games. I wanted the choice of words to be just right so that a response would be called for. If she wanted information of this type, I figured I was entitled to the same.

"Well, I don't know," I said as my mind scrambled to come up with an end to the sentence. "I'll have to ask you."

Nice move, she thought. She searched for a positive response that was without commitment.

"Well, you never know. It's a possibility," she said with a warm smile.

The dialog was like a friendly game of tennis. There was the serve, the return, and a good amount of volleying back and forth. It had been such a consuming conversation that the world around us disappeared. Then a voice came from the distance and brought us both back to the present.

"I know you two could care less if we just fell in the lake, but it's getting late and I've got to get Sandy home sometime tonight," Nicky said in mock annoyance. Things with Sandy were always on and off. They both had strong wills and sooner or later there would be an assumed challenge and the game would end. Tonight, however, the game was very much on.

"Oh, damn Nicky, I'm sorry. I guess we haven't been the greatest dinner companions, but apparently we had a lot to talk about," I said apologetically.

"Actually, I couldn't be happier," Sandy said. "Nicky and I got a charge out of watching you two consume each other. Soooo...Miss Rane, I guess he's not such bad guy after all?" The "see I told you so" was evident but tactfully not said.

"No, he'll do in a pinch," Rane said jokingly, reaching across the table and giving my hand a pat. After she did that, she was surprised that there was a fleeting moment of real connection.

"Look, why don't you guys stay here and have a good time," Nicky said. He was definitely eager to get back to Sandy's house for some recreation. "I don't know if I'd stay too much longer. There's a storm coming. I can hear the wind starting to pick up outside." They all turned to look out the big windows overlooking the lake. The trees were behaving as if giants had grabbed each one and were trying to choke the life out of them and the lake had developed quite a chop. Maybe Nicky was right. Maybe it is time to go.

The thought didn't last very long because Rane and I stayed at the table for twenty more minutes and although neither one of us wanted the night to end, the wind was really howling outside and a serious early summer thunderstorm was approaching. Rane was sorry she had brought her car because she knew what the perfect ending to this evening was. As we walked past the bar, I noticed five or six of Massarro's men having some drinks. I frowned slightly as I wondered, *what they hell are they doing here?* Although it wasn't unusual to see a few of them at the Shoreline from time to time, it struck me as odd that this many would be here at the same time. I decided it was a touch of paranoia. It had been a wonderful evening, but the sight of these goons brought my whole situation crashing back. *I've gotta learn to relax,* I thought

When I opened the front door the wind grabbed it with such force that I was nearly thrown across the deck. Before I could say anything Rane went passed me and headed for her car with a short stepped run that made her hips move in a very sensual way. I wondered why she hadn't waited for the valet until I saw their small valet checking station had blown over and they were nowhere to be seen. I ran after her and caught her just as she was opening the car door.

"I really think you should wait until this blows over," I shouted over the roaring wind. "I wouldn't want to lose you after we just met."

She was seated in the driver's seat and the force of the wind through the partially opened door was frantically blowing her hair. She looked around for a moment at the leaves and branches as they raced passed the car. Huge drops of rain started to pelt the car with such force it sounded like hail. She quickly looked up at me and yelled, "Oh for God's sake, get in before you drown!"

I ran around to the passenger's side as she reached over to open it for me. When I was safely inside we both just sat there and looked at the fury that now consumed the car. The lightning was flashing so quickly that the parking lot appeared to be lit by a giant flickering light bulb. Thunder rolled and crashed, shaking the sides of the Jaguar. While watching nature's mighty display, we happened to turn towards each other and became lost in each other's eyes. In an instant, the chaos around us went silent. We leaned toward each other and gently kissed

"That was very nice," she said. "I think we might be here for a few minutes and this can't be very comfortable for you." With a few graceful moves, she turned and plopped into my lap with her beautiful legs laid across the center console. I cradled her head in his right arm and as she reached her arms around my neck, we melted into a long embrace.

It was forty minutes before the storm subsided. Sex was definitely on my mind, but I thought it wouldn't be the right move to try anything on this first date. If we were right for each other, we would have plenty of time for that. We sat quietly just holding each other and talking.

"I think it's safe for me to drive home now. This has been a wonderful evening and I don't want it to end."

"Neither do I. Why don't I call you tomorrow and see when we can get together again?"

"I'd like that." She reached into the glove compartment and pulled out a business card.
It read, 'Rane Harold - Vice President - Commercial Lending'. "Call me on my cellphone. I'm usually out seeing clients."

One last long kiss and before I realized it, I was walking back into the Shoreline. When I got to the door, Massarro's men were gathered around it peering through the glass.

"Why didn't you guys go home?" I asked not comprehending the sight before me.

"How the fuck could we go home?" said Bobby Primo. "You was out in the car with that lady. We wasn't gonna go out there and disturb you."

I couldn't believe what I was hearing. These guys would just as soon kill you as look at you, but they waited patiently for Rane and me to cease our activities.

"I ain't seen nuttin' like it," Primo continued. "It was like a fuckin' hurricane out there and yous' two was goin' at it like nuttin' was happenin'. We thought we was never gonna be able to get outta here." I just shook my head and headed for the bar. I just wanted to sit and reflect on the evening and the woman I had met.

Eleven o'clock the next morning, I got a call from Nicky. "Heyee, Quinny. You are fuckin' unbelievable! You two were so hot last night that people were stopping by the table to look. And that stuff in the parking lot—fuckin' forget about it!"

"How the hell did you know about the parking lot? You two left an hour before we did."

"What do ya' mean how do I know?" Nicky said. "The whole fucking city knows. You two are like legends. The wind's blowin' sixty miles an hour, trees are gettin' knocked over, limbs are breakin' off and blowin' through the air like fuckin' paper, and you two are in her car makin' out like nothin's happening. Quinn you never stop surprising me."

"I'm glad we were able to provide the city with so much entertainment," I said with some embarrassment. "What's up?"

"I'm meeting Sandy at Terrabella's at 4:30. Why don't you call Rane and see if she can meet us there. We can have a few drinks and well, we'll see what happens."

There was nothing that I wanted more than to see Rane Harold again. She stirred my blood like no other woman ever had. It wasn't just that she was a beautiful woman with an incredible body. There was something inside her that I couldn't quite put my finger on. She made me feel more complete. It was as if two pieces of a puzzle that had been on opposite sides of a table and were finally joined for a perfect fit. I sensed her being with me even when she wasn't.

When I arrived at the restaurant, Gina Terrabella jokingly admonished me about the dangers of being in a parking lot during thunderstorms. I just smiled and shook my head. It occurred to me that I must really be a part of the Eastside Italian crowd if news of my exploits traveled that fast. After every one arrived, we spent an hour and a half having drinks and talking about the famous 'parking lot incident' and everything else going on in the city. When things appeared to be winding down Rane leaned over to me.

"What would you like to do now?" she said.

I almost couldn't believe I said what I did. I knew exactly what I wanted to do now, but I didn't think the restaurant was the best place for those kinds of activities. I didn't want to appear to be moving too fast but on the other hand I didn't want to come across as timid. This didn't seem to be a woman that would suffer a timid man. *Oh, what the hell*, I finally concluded. *If you never swing the bat, you'll never hit the ball*

"I'd like to take you back to my place and spend the night with you." The words hung in the air like fragile crystals waiting for her to shatter them.

"I'd love to," she said in a soft voice. "Why don't I follow you in my car and don't worry, it's not there for a fast escape." *Thank God*, she thought. *If you know what you want, just say it.*

105

My home appeared very modest from the street. I was single and couldn't see the need for some big house when I knew I would only use a few rooms. The house didn't stand out from the other forty-year-old homes on the street, but inside was another matter. A construction supervisor had owned it. He was a bachelor and thought himself a ladies' man. There was no doubt in anyone's mind about his intentions when they saw the interior. He had gutted the place and turned it into a single man's paradise. The living room ceiling had been removed so that the walls ran straight to the roof giving you the feeling that you were in a new A-frame out in the country. The ceiling over the living room was covered in tongue and grooved knotty pine along with the walls. A huge fieldstone fireplace dominated one end of the room and when it was burning, the walls glowed with a honey colored warmth. The entire second floor was dedicated to the master bedroom, complete with skylights, and a bar area that overlooked the living room. Everyone was amazed by the contrast between the modest exterior and the lavish interior of the house. It really was like walking into another world.

I made us each a cocktail and at Rane's request showed her the rest of the house. After the tour we found ourselves back in the living room.

"I think I'll start a fire," I said as he motioned toward the fireplace.

"Parker, it's seventy-five degrees outside," Rane said in mild disbelief at the suggestion.

"That's okay," I said "I'll just turn on the air conditioning."

"You're crazy!" she said with a soft laugh. "But, I love it."

Within a few minutes the fire was casting its warm glow through the room. I placed my drink on the mantle and cradled her face in my hands as I leaned toward her and gave her a soft kiss. She placed her drink next to mine and undid the top button on her blouse. I hadn't felt like this in years and it was wonderful.

Chapter Ten
Things Start to Pick Up Speed

While Rane and I were falling in love, the Justice Department was drawing closer to the conclusion of their investigation. Kevin Norris rose through the ranks of the Justice Department to become the Chief Federal Prosecutor in the city. He moved up quickly and had a reputation for being ruthless. His passion for attacking unions and their leaders was legendary and his almost fanatical desire to put Renato Costa in prison and tear apart the union had some people in the Government wondering if he had lost perspective. Norris needed to bring in extra agents from the FBI, Treasury, and the Department of Labor in an effort to gather massive amounts of evidence against Costa and the people around him. There was no way he was going to let Costa slip through his fingers. He wanted evidence piled to the ceiling when he brought the case to court. Norris swore that Costa would 'rot in prison for the rest of his miserable life.'

Kevin Norris had grown up the only son of a solid well-heeled Boston family and his fate was sealed at birth. His mother was Lucille Barrington Norris. Costa's Union had destroyed her family's textile business, Barrington Mills. The disgrace of her father's lost fortune brought him to suicide and she vowed revenge. It was a passion that consumed her. She had pursued and captured Charles Norris as her husband because she needed to regain some of the lost wealth and power her family once had. He came from a prominent Boston family and was a partner at the law firm his grandfather founded decades ago. The firm wielded considerable influence not only in Boston, but also in Washington. Lucille Norris had a plan, and after the birth of two daughters, that plan started to take on life with the birth of her son Kevin.

When young dogs are beaten and abused, they will turn out one of two ways. Either they will be cowering shadows or vicious fighting monsters. The right balance of verbal and psychological torture when combined with moments of apparent love and caring can produce a lethal character. Be assured that Kevin Norris was just such a person.

Norris was a large man standing well over six feet tall with light brown hair and dark green eyes that hinted at an intensity which bordered on the insane. Norris went off to law school at the University of Pennsylvania, and was expected to become a corporate lawyer like his father. However, the young Mr. Norris had been groomed with a desire to prosecute people and an especially deep hatred of unions and their leaders. There was no place more likely to have the money and unlimited resources needed to pursue this passion than in the United States Government. At his mother's insistence, his father reluctantly used the law firm's considerable influence in Washington to secure a position for Kevin with the Justice Department. No one worked harder at their job that he did. The long hours left little time for anything else and now in his late thirties, he was very much alone.

His offices took up half a floor at the Federal Building. Entry to his area was through electronically controlled doors that required a proper code or announcing ones purpose into the keypad microphone. The entire place was buried in a sea of paper.

It was Friday morning and Bill Douglas was waiting for Norris when he arrived. He had been one of the FBI agents assigned to Norris's new task force. This was nothing new for Douglas because he had been following Costa's activities for over twelve years and it wasn't the first time he tried to put Costa away. He didn't particularly like Norris, but he had to give him credit for his determination. Norris's predecessor was a strictly "by the book" type. On the other hand, Norris made more illegal wiretaps in the past year than Douglas had seen in his whole career in the Bureau. Norris wanted every piece of information he could get and because of his obsession, he didn't care how he got it. He planned to sort out all the pieces and use only those he could prove were obtained by legal means.

"What have you got, Bill?" Norris said as he walked into his office. "Anything on that new player, Quinn?"

"Well, I'm still pretty sure he's up to his neck in this thing," Douglas responded. "We had some guys follow Massarro to a meeting in the city this week and who should come strolling in with Sammy Merzone, but Parker Quinn. The strange thing was they sat at the front tables practically in the window. They had to know we were watching. It was like they were on display. We used a directional microphone to pick up the conversation."

"What did they talk about?"

"Massarro seemed to be offering Quinn some kind of job dealing with some stock operation they had," Douglas said. "Quinn didn't give him an answer and told Massarro to have someone call him later."

"Well, it sounds like this Quinn is looking to move up. I want his miserable ass along with everyone else. We got a tap on his phone?"

"Not officially," Douglas replied. He didn't really like going around the law, but Norris was relentless in his demand for information. Douglas sat through enough of Norris's temper tantrums about his 'apparent inability to produce fresh information' to know when to resort to 'unofficial' means.

"I gotta tell you Kevin, I can't quite figure this Quinn out," Douglas continued. "He's gone to meetings with Costa, socialized with Costa and Merzone, and had a meeting with Massarro and his boys. Then he's going to meetings and socializing with Traffarro and his crew. He hangs around with Tagliano all the time. This guy sits right in the middle of this whole thing and when I think I've finally figured out which side he's on, BAM! He's over on the other side."

"I really don't give a shit what side he's on," Norris fired back as he slammed his hand on the desk and finally cast a chilly look at Douglas. "I want this son of a bitch's ass."

"Look, I agree with you. We don't have shit on Traffarro. If he's got his hand in the pot, I sure as hell can't find it. I know he would love to see Costa out because he's next in line. Christ, if it weren't against their bullshit code, he'd probably be helping us. I'm wondering if Quinn isn't bouncing back and forth because he's feeding information to Traffarro and if he is, he might know enough to connect the dots for us on that mountain of information we have in the other room."

"I said it before but apparently I need to say it again. I really don't give a shit! After I'm done nailing Costa and his lot, we can start on Traffarro. If there's one thing I've learned, it's that they're all the same. When one leaves, the next one just comes in and starts screwing up the system all over again. They're like fucking cockroaches. You kill one and there's always more coming out from under a rock. These unions are ruining this country and it's our job to put them all out of business. Sooner or later this Quinn will step on his dick and by God you better be there when it happens."

I had a luncheon meeting with Traffarro and Nicky and when I arrived I noticed a new face as I walked toward their table. It was a tall slender man with a pock marked face and eyes that seemed to be dead. When we exchanged greetings the man never said a word. I didn't know why but I felt very uneasy in his presence.

"Quinn, this is Tino Drazzetti," Traffarro said, while I sat down. "I know I've asked you to do a lot for us over the past year or so, but I've got to ask one more. If there's no way you can help I'll understand, but I've gotta ask."

"Anthony, you know I'll help if I can," I said. I wasn't at all comfortable with the way this conversation was going, particularly whenever I looked at this new guy.

"Connie tells me that things are going very well at your office and that the girls in the back are really busy," Traffarro continued. "Tino's wife Nina got laid off over a month ago and he's come to me for some help. Tino has been a reliable friend to me in the past and I'd like to return the favor if I could."

"Excuse me, Mr. Quinn," Tino interjected. "I know that this might be tough for you, but I would take it as a personal favor if you could help out my wife."

I didn't need anyone and I didn't want anyone. I was sick of being used as the dumping ground for displaced wives and girlfriends. Enough was enough. I looked over at Nicky who was giving me a subtle nod of the head to indicate that this was something that I should do.

"I'm pretty sure we can find a place for her," I said nearly choking on the words. "Have her call my office in the morning and we'll see when she can get started." As the words were coming out, I was wondering if the slow burn I was feeling was visible to the men around me.

"Mr. Quinn, I owe you a personal debt. Thank you very much." He rose from the table and left the restaurant.

"Nicky, tell him," Traffarro said with a wave of his hand as if the information could be pushed through the air.

Curiosity quickly replaced my anger. What the hell was this all about? Nicky leaned across the table so he could speak softly enough for me to hear him without the rest of the customers being able to eaves drop.

"Quinn that was Constantino Drazzetti. He was one of the biggest enforcers for an old mob family here in the city. Their action dried up when the Feds decided to clean up the place. He's been freelancing by contract ever since. He's whacked people all over the fucking country. If something should...well...let's say go wrong, and somebody wants to put a hit out on you or me or Anthony, they're probably going to call this guy. If not, it's a safe bet he'll hear about it anyway. Let me put it this way, this is a very good guy to have owe you, and you heard him say it...he owes you."

Oh, I thought. *Now I know why I had that 'be careful what you say' feeling when I sat down across from Drazzetti.*

The Massarro family could have taken in Tino but they already had Big Nappi and his protégé Little Nappi. Big Nappi is controllable and could be counted on to deliver a message in the stated fashion. Tino Drazzetti on the other hand, was created by some malevolent thing with all the compassion and finesse of a cornered rattlesnake. Suffice it to say that Big Nappi isn't likely to cut your throat if you cut in front of him in the popcorn line at the movies. The same can't be said about Tino.

Things had to be heating up and Traffarro appeared to be buying insurance in the form of one of the most dangerous killers in the country. For the first time, I felt as if I might actually have a weapon on my side and an independent source to watch my back. I had been in the Italian community long enough to know the code of honor that many of these people had. Tino Drazzetti may have been a contract killer, but he was at least fifty years old and that meant he was 'old school'. The new people coming up in the mob were second generation Americans who laughed at the old ways of the 'Moustache Pete's' from the old country. They could care less about traditions. It was a game of fast money and imagined self-importance and they had become the most important contributor to the decline of the mob's strength. I believed that Drazzetti would honor his self-stated obligation. If this whole thing was going to blow up soon, I was glad Traffarro was planning ahead.

The next month was deadly quiet. *Nothing* happened. I went to the usual Saturday lunches with the boys at Salvatore's, but nothing was really discussed. Sammy hadn't been in the office that much and when he was, he was unusually quiet. The money from Sammy's business was pouring in and my override was paying me handsomely. Rane had started spending her weekends at my house and we were falling more deeply in love. We had taken day trips up to the lake and would end the day with dinner at the Shoreline Restaurant. I noticed one night that the crowd had changed at the Shoreline. I hadn't seen one of Massarro's guys there in a month and the one thing you could count on was a few of them sitting at the bar. Costa hadn't been around either. I was having too much fun with Rane to analyze this strange change in the pattern of movement in the world. I just gave a mental shrug and proceeded to focus on my relationship with Rane.

As the end of the month drew near, Traffarro arranged a birthday party for Connie at Terrabella's. Connie decided she wanted to have the party in a more 'civilized place' than Junior's restaurant. She had become close to some of the women working in Quinn's office, so in addition to the usual crowd, some of the women and their husbands would be attending. It would be the first time that Rane and I would attend an 'official' social function together. Despite my assurances that Rane would be accepted like a long lost sister, Rane was a little anxious about meeting the families of my friends. She was very much in love with me and she knew how important these relationships were to me. Rane was comfortable in any social setting because for the most part, she hadn't really cared what anyone thought, but this was different. This time, she was with someone she didn't want to lose over conflicts with friends.

The last thing Rane had to worry about was being accepted. She was with me. I had done so much for so many people that she would have had to be the Wicked Witch of the West for these people not to take her in. Connie knew how I felt about Rane and she made it her mission to make her feel welcome. It took only five minutes of Rane being with Connie before Rane's steel curtain was gone and she had the women laughing at her stories about me.

I was having a good time laughing at the stories being told and now that I had been around long enough, I was able to contribute some of my own. At one point, I happened to notice Tino Drazzetti sitting at a table alone. Nina had fit right into the office environment and was very flattered to be invited to the party. She and Tino didn't attend too many social gatherings and she looked forward to this night. I was the odd man out too many times to see someone sitting by himself and not feel for them. I didn't know what I would say to Tino, but I was pretty sure I shouldn't start out by saying, "Hi, killed anyone lately?"

"Hey, Tino. I'm glad you and Nina could come tonight. She's fit in at the office very quickly and I know everyone likes her a lot," I said as an opening attempt at a conversation.

"Yeah, she likes it there," Tino replied. His tone was that of a man who was very tired. "I told you I appreciated what you've done and I meant it. I owe you."

"Look, Tino. You really don't owe me anything," I said. I was never comfortable having people feel like they owed me anything. Hell, I wasn't even comfortable when I gave someone a gift and they would say thank you. I helped so many people throughout my career I couldn't count them. Yet I would rather peel my skin off than ask any one of them for a favor.

"That's not the way I see it," Tino responded in an almost hostile tone.

"Well, I'll tell you what," I said in an effort to extricate myself from this situation. "You know what's going on around here. If you wouldn't mind lettin' me know when somebody might want to put a bullet in the back of my head, I would consider us even."

Tino never even acknowledged the remark. He just said, "You're not afraid to be sitting here with me?"

"Why, you planning on killing me?"

"No." Tino said calmly and then waited a moment before he said. "I don't have too many friends. Maybe it's just my line of work?"

I thought that probably would have been *my* first guess and I thought it would be better if I didn't pursue that line of discussion.

"Look, Tino. You and I don't really know each other, but if you're looking for somebody to apply for that 'friend' job, you let me know," I said as I rose to my feet. I wasn't looking forward to spending any amount of time with this man, but I sure as hell didn't want to piss him off either and I figured having people know that someone like a Tino Drazzetti was a friend might give certain people second thoughts about stuffing my mangled carcass into a fifty-five gallon drum.

As I started to turn and walk away, Tino said, "There's gonna be a get together down at this guy's house in two weeks. He's got a big place on a lake just a little down south of here. It's kind of an annual thing. There's gonna be all the lobster, steaks and all the booze you could ever want. There'll be a ton of broads, too. Why don't you come down with me and I'll introduce you around? You'll have a great time. We party all night."

"Well, damn Tino. That's really nice of you. Let me make sure I can get free and I'll call you," I replied with a mix of surprise and dread. It was time to go back to the others and when I got back, Anthony pulled him aside.

"That was a nice conversation you had with Tino," Traffarro said with a touch of sarcasm. "What did he say?"

"Nothing really," I responded. "He was saying how he owed me for helping Nina. I told him it wasn't necessary but if he wanted to help, he could keep me from getting my ass shot off. He wanted me to go with him to some annual cookout."

"That's nice, but you're not going," Traffarro said emphatically. "That cookout will have more guys from the mob in one place than any other during the year. The only thing there'll be more of is Feds with cameras and I don't want the government to associate you with them. It'll ruin everything."

"Don't worry," I quickly added. "I didn't really think it was a good idea and now I know it's not."

I felt like I was being pulled in six different directions at once, but I trusted Traffarro's judgment. It was bad enough that I already met with Massarro. If the Feds were wondering where I fit in all of this, going to this cookout thing would remove all doubt.

Connie and Lorie Tagliano had collapsed at a table together. They had been talking, eating and drinking for several hours and it was time for a break.

"Did I tell you what happened to Nicky the other night?" Lorie began. "He was out late with Anthony, *as usual*, and he was so tired he had to pull off the side of the road and had to sleep in his car. He didn't get home until seven the next morning. I told him he had to slow down. I don't know why they have to have meetings until all hours of the morning all the time.

Connie just looked at her in complete amazement. "Lorie, grow up. He's not out with Anthony." She knew Nicky was using the Union and Anthony as an excuse to be fooling around on his wife and Connie had reached the end of her rope. How could this woman be so stupid? She and Lorie were like sisters and sooner or later she was going to find out. Connie hadn't said anything because Anthony had told her to stay out of it, but working for me this past year had changed her and she felt like getting this off of her chest.

"What else could it be?" Lorie asked

"For God's sake woman, *wake up!*" Connie said in a hushed voice so that she wouldn't be over heard. "Nicky's been screwing around on you for years. Anthony and the Union don't have a damned thing to do with it."

Lorie just looked at Connie with a touch of resentment. "I don't believe you." How could she? Nicky had two beautiful children and a wife who worshipped the ground he walked on. How could it be possible for a man to give all that up? No. *This can't be happening*, she thought.

"Fine!" Connie said in total disgust. "I've got to go to the ladies room."

The party went on until nearly midnight before people started to leave. Rane and I said our good-byes to the remaining guests and headed back to my place. About half way there Rane turned to me and asked, "Was that Nina's husband I saw you with in the corner?"

"Yeah, why?"

I hadn't really told Rane a great deal about what was going on. I didn't think we had been together long enough to tell her that I stood at the center of a triangle formed by the Mob, the Union, and the Feds.

"He didn't seem to spend much time socializing. It was like he spent the whole night alone except for you. What does he do?" she asked.

"Aaaaahh...he's an Independent Contractor," I said hoping it would end there.

"Houses or big buildings?" she asked.

"Neither, Honey." This was as good a time as any to let Rane know what was going on. I didn't want to lose her, but I knew that to keep these types of secrets would be worse than telling her the truth. If she was going to move out of my life because of this, then it was better to get it out and over with.

"He's a contract killer," I continued.

"*What*? You're kidding, right?" It wasn't that Rane had never met anybody who was a hit man. She went to enough dinners with Pete Mastro that were attended by people in the Cleveland mob not to suspect that some of them must have killed somebody sometime. It had just become too real too fast and she was caught by surprise.

I told her everything about Costa and Sammy, about Traffarro and cleaning up the Union, about the Feds and their very active investigation and about Massarro. When we got to the house, I got out but Rane just sat there. As I looked at her, I had a sinking feeling in my heart that our relationship was slipping away. I consoled myself with the thought that if this were truly meant to be, then we would be able to get past this. When Rane finally got out of the car, we sat at the kitchen table for over an hour. I answered every question she had as best and as honestly as I could. When she was satisfied that she knew everything, she just sat quietly again for a few minutes.

"Parker, I think I'm deeply in love with you," she said as she put her hand lovingly up to my face. "You're a wonderful man and I think what you're trying to do is noble, but be careful. I know these types of people and they're dangerous. So help me God, Parker Quinn," she said with the volume of her voice rising sharply. "If you get yourself killed, you're gonna really piss me off."

"Rane, I love you, too," I began. "I've spent my whole life looking for you and I don't intend to get my ass shot off now that I've found you."

She got up from her chair and reached her arms out to me. When I stood up she threw her arms around me and kissed me passionately. After a moment she turned and grabbed my arm.

"Come on ya big ape, let's go to bed," she said with a little laugh. "Parker, you never cease to amaze me."

"I try," I said with a smile as I turned out the kitchen light. "I try."

Chapter Eleven
Trying to Catch a Fish

Norris had spent eighteen months on the case and he knew he had all the pieces he needed. Unfortunately, the whole thing still lay before him like a giant puzzle. The big picture was becoming clearer, but he wasn't entirely comfortable with exactly how all the little pieces fit. It was time to move to the next phase. He would convene a Grand Jury. This would allow him to subpoena witnesses and give him the power to get the additional documents he was sure would give him the last bit of detail he demanded for a successful prosecution. There would be no escape for Costa this time. This would be the high point of his career and he wanted all the 'I's dotted and all the 'T's crossed.

Bill Douglas had spent the better part of his career chasing after Costa and this time he thought they had it right. It would be good to change his focus to something else when this was all over. He was sick of this case and was looking forward to a change of pace. He knew Costa and his crew better than most of his own friends. He'd be happy if he never heard the word Union again. Traffarro, Nicky and I really didn't interest him. He wanted Costa, Merzone and the others. Massarro might even fall before this was over, but that would just be a bonus. If Norris wanted to continue to pursue the Union after he put Costa away, let him. Douglas had had his fill of Norris and his insane obsession with union busting.

Norris was desperate to put the final nail in Costa's coffin. If he could get one of the players to turn on Merzone and Costa and testify against them, he'd have everything in place. He would grant them immunity from prosecution in exchange for their testimony. It didn't matter to Norris if one of the small fish got away if it would seal the fate of the rest. He decided to start with someone that was closely involved with the kickback schemes and that made Vincent Maldanado a prime target.

"Ms. Avery," Norris called to his assistant on the intercom. "Is Bill Douglas in the building?"

"No, Mr. Norris. I'm sorry but I think he's in his car downtown."

"Patch me through to his radio."

"Yes, sir. Right away"

In a few minutes, Norris had Douglas on the radio. "Bill, I want you to see if you can get Vincent Maldanado some place alone. Sweat him hard and see if you can get him to testify in exchange for immunity. Maybe you can get him to wear a wire and get either Costa or Merzone to discuss the kickback on that Capital Development deal. Don't push him too much on the wire, but I want the little bastard to testify. If we can get one of these punks to roll over, we'll have this thing nailed shut."

"We gonna do this on a warrant?" replied Douglas.

"No. Just do it in an unofficial capacity. If you can turn him, I'll issue a subpoena and have him sit before the Grand Jury to make sure he stays with the deal."

Douglas sat in his car for two hours waiting with Treasury Agent, Felix Garcia, for Maldanado to show up. Maldanado owned a duplex on the Eastside and showed the rental income from one side as his visible means of support. This made Maldanado one of the thriftiest people in America considering his ability to purchase a new Cadillac, expensive clothes, and a Rolex watch. Norris had accumulated a significant paper trail on Maldanado's finances and if he couldn't make a bribery charge stick, he could easily get him on income tax evasion.

"Here he comes now," Garcia said to Douglas as Maldanado pulled into a parking space behind their car.

As Maldanado got out of his car, Douglas got out of the car and approached Maldanado.

"Vinny," he said in a cheery voice. "I'm Special Agent William Douglas with the FBI and this is my partner Agent Felix Garcia with the Treasury Department. We'd like to talk to you for a few minutes."

"Go fuck yourselves," Maldanado replied, bumping into Douglas as he passed him.

"Now that wasn't very sociable of you, Vinny," said Douglas, grabbing Maldanado's shoulder and spinning him around. "We're gonna talk whether you like it or not. We can either do it now in the privacy of your house or we can come to one of your favorite little shit holes and pull your ass out in front of all your friends so everybody can see. Now, which would you prefer?" Douglas said as he jabbed his index finger into Maldanado's chest.

"What the fuck you want?" replied Maldanado.

"Why don't we go inside and talk about it before everybody in the city sees us," Garcia answered, grabbing Maldanado's arm, and dragging him along.

Once they were inside, Douglas and Garcia looked around Maldanado's sumptuous living room. They just looked at each other and smiled. There had to be twenty grand worth of furnishings in the living room alone.

"Nice place you got here, Vinny," said Garcia. "You gotta tell me how you can afford so many beautiful things on the shitty little rental income you report."

"I buy on sale," Maldanado sneered.

"Look, you stupid son of a bitch," Garcia said as he shoved Maldanado. "I don't like you, but I've been ordered to give you a choice. You can do five years for income tax evasion and another five to seven for bribery or you can help us and get a pass. We've got enough to put you away for a long time buddy boy, but today's your lucky day."

"I don't know what the fuck you're talking about," Maldanado shouted. "You fuckers don't have shit on me."

"We know all about your deals with Capital Development and the money you kicked back to Costa," Garcia yelled as he pushed Maldanado down onto his leather recliner. "We're gonna bust your ass for those payoffs and every other little deal you did with Sammy Merzone."

"Good fuckin' luck asshole," shouted Maldanado as he tried to get up from the recliner. "I reported those deals and paid taxes on them. So fuck off!"

Garcia just leered at him as he put his hand on Maldanado's chest and pushed him back into the chair, nearly knocking the chair over backwards. Douglas reached over and grabbed Garcia's arm.

"Come on Felix, take it easy. I'm sure Vinny here will be more than willing to help us if we just calm down and explain things a little more clearly." Garcia turned and walked across the room leaving Douglas with Maldanado

"Vinny. You really need to do a better job of hiding the trail of the money," Douglas continued in a calm soothing voice. "We know how much you were paid for the commission on the building loan, and we appreciate that you paid taxes on the money, but the deposits and withdrawals just don't add up. There's about a hundred and thirty-five grand missing, and we know where it went. We saw you giving it to Sammy Merzone, and we know that moron gave it to Costa. We've got the paper trail and we've got you on video. Now, if you help us on this and testify, we can offer you immunity on this beef. Why don't you help yourself out here? You're too young to spend that much time in prison with some guy shoving his dick up your ass three times a day." They didn't have any video or paper trail but running a bluff like this was standard operating procedure for the FBI. The only suspect that absolutely knows they don't have anything is the one who didn't do anything. In this case, they knew Maldanado was up to his neck in this and if they pushed hard enough they could turn him.

"Get the fuck out of my house," Maldanado yelled as he attempted to get out of the chair again. "If you pricks got anything on me, use it. Go ahead and arrest me. Otherwise get out!"

"Vinny, Vinny, Vinny," Douglas sighed; sticking his index finger into Maldanado's chest and forcing him back into the recliner. "Look asshole, I'm tellin' you...you're gonna do hard time. We're only trying to help. When we walk out that door, there's not gonna be another offer. Why don't you take a minute to think about this? It's really in your best interest."

"Like I said, I didn't do shit, and you ain't got shit so fuck off," Maldanado said, nearly crying over the humiliation of being pushed around.

Douglas and Garcia looked at each other. Neither of them thought that Maldanado would ever say anything. He'd been in this culture too long and what was worse; he wasn't all that bright. They slowly turned and walked out the door. When they got back to the car they called Norris and told him the news.

"These guys have seen this before," Douglas explained to Norris. "We've tried to bust Costa before and he beat the charges. This guy figures it's just more of the same and they don't want to be left on the outside if Costa walks again. He also doesn't want to be found face down in a swamp either."

"Costa's never going to walk," Norris shouted into the phone as if somebody had insulted his intelligence. "I want you to lean on this guy until he breaks."

"I understand," Douglas replied, letting his head fall back against the headrest in frustration. He turned his head to Garcia and with a look of irritated amusement said, "He wants us to follow Maldanado to see if we can shake him up a little. Maybe he'll give it up if he thinks we won't let go. I doubt it, but what the hell. It's either that or go listen to Norris rant and rave for an hour."

Fifteen minutes after Douglas and Garcia left his house; Maldanado was on the phone to Sammy Merzone. He asked Merzone to meet him at the Shoreline that evening. Maldanado was nervous and afraid he'd be left swinging in the wind if the Feds tried to pursue the case. When he met Merzone at the Shoreline, he told him about his meeting that afternoon and Merzone was visibly shaken by the news. He heard that the Grand Jury was meeting and calling witnesses, but this was the first time anyone so close to him had been contacted. He and Vinny went back many years and did a lot of deals together. Sammy knew that if they broke Vinny, he was done. It was starting to get very real and the growing chance that his world could come crashing down was becoming a nagging ache.

Merzone had been talking to Maldanado for about thirty minutes when Big Nappi Brufalo walked into the restaurant. Merzone, in his nervous state, thought it might be a good idea to tell Brufalo what was happening. He told Maldanado to wait at the table while he asked Brufalo for advice. Maldanado choked on his drink when Merzone told him what he was going to do.

"Sammy, are you fuckin' crazy? Nappi's gonna kill me." Maldanado said as he started to feel like the main course during the feeding of a Great White Shark. But, Merzone assured Maldanado that he had nothing to worry about and walked over to Brufalo. They had a drink together while Merzone explained the latest developments.

"Tell that fuckin' Vinny to come over here," Brufalo said to Merzone. Sammy promptly went to Maldanado and before he brought him over to Brufalo, he reassured Maldanado that everything was all right. Maldanado had turned a pale gray and his face was getting numb. It was as if he had been drinking too much. All he kept thinking was that stupid fucking Sammy was going to get him killed.

"Look, Vinny," Brufalo began, grabbing Maldanado by the throat. "I don't gotta tell you to keep your fuckin' mouth shut, do I? Because you know if I even think you was talking to the Feds, I'd fuckin' kill you." Brufalo released Maldanado when he realized that the wheezing he kept hearing was Maldanado's desperate attempt to take in some air. He smiled at Maldanado as he slapped him firmly in the face." I like you and you been around a long time. I trust you to do the right thing, 'cause if I didn't, you'd been down swimmin' in this fuckin' lake right now," he said as the volume of his voice picked up to a low roar. "You understand?"

"Nappi, honest. You know me. I wouldn't say nothin' to nobody," Maldanado replied nervously.

"Now why don't you two fuckin' mooks relax," Brufalo said in a calming voice. "Go fuck some broads or somethin'," he said, waving his hand to dismiss them.

The next day Brufalo went to Rocco Massarro and told him what had happened the night before. "You did the right thing," Massarro said. "I don't want Maldanado saying anything and I don't want him dead either. It'll make it look like we're afraid of this investigation. We've got enough distance from this thing that Norris shouldn't bother us. Besides, it's easier for Norris to pick the low hanging fruit like that degenerate Costa and his babbling idiot Merzone. All we have to do is get this thing out of the way and it'll take some of the heat off the Union *and* us. In a couple of years we'll be able to go back to business as usual with the Union. Look, get in touch with some of your guys in law enforcement. Tell them to keep their ears open. If this thing starts to turn against us, we'll have to deal with it ourselves, but for now...leave 'em alone.

"Boss, why is Norris tryin' to get Maldanado to talk? I thought he had all he needed to put those assholes away."

"I'm not sure. Norris likes to have all his packages wrapped up with a nice little bow," Massarro said, moving his hands as if he was tying a bow. "I don't want him to keep hounding Maldanado. He's like a fucking dog with a bone. It's just possible that Maldanado knows too much about our operation from that talking parrot Sammy. I don't want to whack Maldanado and give any ideas to the Feds, but...let me think about it some more."

Massarro sat for a few minutes carefully figuring out the best way to placate Norris and not give him any new trails back to the Organization. The Feds had been after him for fifty years and he knew them better than they knew themselves. If he could keep giving them easy scores, they'd stay out of his way. Besides, he wanted Costa and his crowd out of the way. They were getting far too reckless.

"Here's what I want you to do," Massarro finally said with a smile on his face, stroking his chin with his hand. "Contact Anthony Traffarro and see if he can get that guy Quinn to talk to the Feds. Quinn's been in the middle of this for a while and my guess is he knows as much as anyone about Costa and Sammy. He's also smart. I could see that by the way he acted at the meeting we had. He's a cautious man. If we can get Quinn to tell the Feds everything he knows, then maybe we could actually give Norris the 'bow' he wants for his package. He's also far enough removed from us that I don't think the Feds will even ask about us and if they do, Quinn's smart enough not to say anything. Besides, he doesn't really know anything anyway. Now, go on and make this happen."

Chapter Twelve

... And Now the Last Favor!

Traffarro was having a nice quiet lunch at Salvatore's with Nicky when an attractive young woman walked into the restaurant. She patiently looked around the restaurant and spotted Traffarro sitting in the far corner. As she came near Traffarro's table, he looked up.

"Mr. Traffarro?" she said, when she reached the table.

"Yes," Traffarro replied with some surprise. He knew everyone who came into Junior's restaurant and he was damned sure he hadn't seen this beauty before.

"I wonder if I could speak to you alone?" she asked.

Traffarro glanced at Nicky "Nicky, would you do me a favor and get me another drink while I speak to this young lady? Please...sit down, uh Miss?" Traffarro said as he motioned with his hand toward the empty chair.

"My name isn't important," she said, sitting down. "I have a request from your friend down south, Mr. Traffarro. The Federal Prosecutor, Kevin Norris, is putting a lot of pressure on people your friend would like left alone. It seems Mr. Norris would like someone close to the situation to testify at the Grand Jury and to make sure this thing goes the way your friend wants, he would like to have someone he can count on to provide Norris with that testimony. Your friend would like to avoid any unnecessary publicity."

"I hope he's not suggesting that someone should be me," Traffarro said with a touch of hostility.

"No, Mr. Traffarro. Your friend has suggested, Mr. Quinn."

"*Quinn?*" Traffarro said. *What fucking maniac thought this one up*, he thought.

"That's right. He believes that Mr. Quinn knows a great deal about this situation and that Mr. Quinn can be relied upon to be discrete about your friend's business. This is a get-well card," she said as she passed the card to Traffarro. "If Mr. Quinn agrees to help, you are to mail it to the address on the envelope...unsigned of course. You have five days to respond. If he doesn't hear from you by then, he'll assume you were unable or unwilling to convince Mr. Quinn."

"How do I know you represent who you say you do," Traffarro asked, waving the card slowly back and forth in his hand.

"The gentleman who sent me said you would recognize this," she said as she placed a bullet on the table. She got up without saying another word and left.

Traffarro picked up the bullet and recognized the .44 Special Reloads with their scored tip as the preferred tool of Big Nappi Brufalo. He released the bullet from between his thumb and forefinger and let it fall into the palm of his other hand. He was looking across the restaurant at the woman leaving when Nicky came back to the table.

"What the fuck was that all about?" Nicky asked.

"Trouble!" said Traffarro, still looking at the restaurant's front door and bouncing the bullet in his hand.

Rane and I had made Wednesday nights somewhat of a ritual. We went to Terrabella's for a quiet dinner and afterward Rane would spend the night. It really was a 'hump day' celebration. Rane had come to grips with my 'crusade' with the Union and everything had been fairly quiet. We had just finished our coffee, when Gina Terrabella came over to the table and told me that I had a call at the bar. When I went to the phone I found Traffarro waiting on the other end. He asked me to meet him the next morning at 7:00 A.M.

at the coffee shop. I slowly placed the receiver back into the cradle as I thought about the call. It wasn't like Traffarro to call me while I was 'involved' with a woman. When I got back to the table, Rane asked me what it was all about.

"To be honest, I'm not really sure. Anthony wants to meet me tomorrow at the Coffee shop. Don't worry. It's probably nothing."

The next morning, I walked into the coffee shop looking somewhat less than refreshed. Traffarro was at his usual table in the back.

"Christ Quinn, didn't you sleep last night?" Traffarro asked with a laugh.

"I must really be lettin' myself slide," I said as I pulled out a chair and sat down with a big sigh. "One thing is for sure, that women's either going to kill me or get me into shape...but, *what* a way to die."

Traffarro leaned back and laughed. "She's a great girl. You're a luck man," he said. "Quinn, I'm not going to bullshit you," Traffarro continued, leaning forward and resting his arms on the table while he looked from side to side to be sure no one was close enough to hear. "We've got a problem and your name has come up as a solution."

Solving problems occupied the better part of my average business day and I was good at it. Unfortunately, the problems usually associated with Traffarro and the Union were the kind that tended to get very messy. Traffarro went on to explain about Norris's attempt to get Vinny Maldanado to roll over on his friends. He explained what Massarro wanted to get done and that there was no way he trusted Maldanado to keep his head if the pressure got turned up. Massarro didn't want Norris poking around anymore for fear he might get in the way of his business. He wanted to give Norris a nice little package that would take care of his problem with Costa and Merzone.

I was a close friend but Traffarro knew this wasn't going to be a walk in the park. He also knew that Massarro certainly wasn't going to be the problem. It was all his idea and as long as Massarro didn't change his mind, I'd have nothing to worry about from him. Norris shouldn't be a problem either. Christ, I could give him the whole case on a silver platter. Traffarro's fear was that the problem would be Costa. Costa couldn't go to Massarro for help, but that didn't mean he was without resources and when things got really hot, I'd be a sitting duck.

"You want me to go to the Feds and tell them everything I know?" I asked in total disbelief. This was a turn in the course of events that I hadn't foreseen. Keeping an eye on Sammy Merzone was one thing, but now I was being asked to jump headlong into the center of this shit storm.

"I don't know what you've heard about Massarro and his operation, but whatever it is forget it," Traffarro responded. "As far as going to the Feds, don't bother they'll come to you. I'll get you hooked up with Mario Rizzelli. He's done a lot of work for me. He's a friend and a damn good lawyer. If you have any questions about testifying, he's the one you should ask. Mario will do this pro bono, so don't worry about the cost. He owes me big."

"You have got to be shitting me! No fucking way!

"Quinn, I really need you to do this. This is the only way we can ever hope to have any control over what happens."

I just sat there staring at the ceiling. *Are these people out of their fucking minds*, I thought. *Sure...get this one a job or get that one a job but this?...**Shit**!* I was taking deep breaths and Traffarro was quietly sitting and waiting for what he was sure would be a reluctant but positive outcome. Finally, I brought my head down and gathered my thoughts.

"I'll be honest with you Anthony, a few things bother me," I said. "No...fuck that! ...a lot of things bother me but these are the ones that really matter. First, I'm glad this is Massarro's idea and all, but is he going to back me if Costa decides to get somebody else to shut me up? I'm not so much worried about me, but Rane and I are a public thing. Anthony, you and I both know this could get every ugly and there's no way I want to put her in any danger. Shit! It's going to be hard enough when I tell her what's going down. She's gonna flip out. I'm not going to go near this crap unless I know she's safe. I want Massarro to guarantee that nothing happens to her. Second, I really don't like going to the police, the Feds, or anyone else and ratting someone out. Costa and Sammy may be pieces of shit, but if I testify I'm no better than they are. Third, I haven't done anything. What the hell do I need a lawyer for?

"I'll get word to Massarro." Traffarro replied. "I can guarantee you that he would never hurt Rane. If Costa tries to contract you out, odds are that Massarro will hear about it. As far as being a 'rat', all your friends will know what you're doing and they'll support you a hundred percent. Everybody else can kiss my ass. Besides, Massarro is fed up with the old man and Sammy. As far as I can tell, it's either going to be this or something a hell of a lot nastier. Lastly, you're right. You haven't done anything, but I don't trust the Feds and I want somebody I do trust watching your back from the legal end. Look Quinn, I'm not telling you this is going to be easy, but if you can get this done, we can clean up this Union and do some good for the members. Not to mention, there'll be a lot of people who'll owe you big."

"Wonderful!" I said as I leaned back in the chair again. "I can see my tombstone now. Here lays Parker Quinn. He tried to do the honorable thing and oh yeah...by the way...everyone owes him big time."

It was a week later when I got a call from Bill Douglas. Douglas received a phone call from the local police, advising him that if he wanted to know what was going on in the Union, he should talk to

Parker Quinn. He was very polite and asked if I could meet him at the Sheraton Hotel downtown. I was filled with mixed emotions. On the one hand, there was a certain amount of excitement generated as I wondered who would screw me first, the Feds or Massarro. My bet was on the Feds. Finally, to wrap these thoughts up in a neat little bundle was Costa and Merzone. What would *they* do?

When I finally found the right room at the Sheraton, there was Douglas and Garcia waiting for me. Garcia didn't say very much and I guess Douglas was as pleasant as he was capable of being.

"Come in, Mr. Quinn," Douglas said as he opened the door. "I'm Bill Douglas with the FBI and this is Agent Felix Garcia with the Treasury Department. Please come in and sit down."

As I entered the room I nodded toward Garcia, but his coal black eyes just stared through a scowl as he sat down. I went over to the table by the window and pulled out the chair across from Garcia who sat there motionless. I smiled and sat down crossing my legs and folding my arms across my chest. I was desperately trying to appear relaxed.

"What can I do for you fine gentlemen today?"

"You're looking at seven to ten years in federal prison for bribery and conspiracy", said Garcia as he pointed his finger at me.

"Believe me, we can help you with that", Douglas said as he sat down on the edge of the bed. "Just tell us what you know about Renato Costa, Sammy Merzone, the Massarro crime family, and their involvement with the Union."

Frankly, I was expecting a little better reception than this. I knew someone had called them and tipped them to what I could give them. I was thinking I should have been welcomed with open arms, but I decided I might as well get right to the point.

"Well, let's see," I said, breathing in deeply in preparation for a deliberately long sentence. "I don't know exactly what you gentlemen want to know about, but I've witnessed Merzone passing envelopes filled with money to Costa, buying Costa hundreds of lunches and dinners, expensive gifts bought for other people by Merzone at Costa's instruction, kickbacks to Costa from loans made by the Union with fees run through people such as Vinny Maldanado and probably a lot of other things that they've done that are illegal, but that I just can't think of right now."

Douglas and Garcia didn't say a word. They just looked at each other. It isn't often that a case gets neatly wrapped up in the form of a cooperating witness, especially one they didn't have to threaten first.

"I don't want to sound ungrateful, Mr. Quinn." Douglas finally said as he got up from the bed and paced around the room. "But, why are you willing to tell us all of this? What's in it for you?"

"First of all you can take your seven to ten fucking years and shove it," I said looking at Garcia.

"Yeah, please forgive Felix, Mr. Quinn. He's not used to people actually cooperating with us," Douglas said. "But I'll ask you again. What's in this for you?"

"There's a certain satisfaction in cleaning up a corrupt Union," I replied with sincerity. "Beyond that I don't see how I could gain anything. I might be able to pick up some of the Union's business, but there's no guarantee and the firm that I represent stands to lose a considerable amount of business from the Union if I testify. Oh, and let's not forget that I get an override on all Merzone's business and that would definitely be gone."

"So let me get this straight, Quinn. You're willing to testify before a Grand Jury about what you know and then testify in court about the same things?" Garcia asked in a tone of disbelief.

"Yeah, I'd do that."

The two agents sat and talked to me for over an hour. They were like two kids in a toy store with dad's credit card. They couldn't believable I knew so much. As far as they knew, I had been involved for a little more than a year with Merzone and the Union funds. How the hell did I learn this much so quickly? Obviously, they hadn't spent much time with Sammy. Douglas and Garcia were convinced that their search for *the* key witness was over but Douglas wanted to test me on one final point.

"What do you know about a man named Rocco Massarro?" he said.

"I met him once," I replied. I wasn't about to lie about Massarro. Let's face it, they had to know about the meeting at the coffee shop. The fact was I really didn't know that much about Massarro and denying the meeting was pointless. "Sammy invited me to sit down with him and some of his people. He offered to do business with me——I think. To be honest, it was a strange meeting. To this day, I'm not exactly sure what the hell I was doing there. Beyond that, I don't know anything other than he's supposed to run the mob in the southern part of the State."

Douglas looked at Garcia and smiled. He asked Garcia if there was anything else he wanted to ask me. When they were both satisfied they knew who they were dealing with, they told me I could leave and that I would probably have a meeting with the Federal Prosecutor in a few days to review my potential testimony. Neither of them could wait to call Norris with the news. Finally!! They caught a break. Now their lives would be a little easier since they hoped they wouldn't have Norris breathing down their necks twenty-four hours a day.

I was somewhat relived and a little amused that the two agents seemed amazed at what I knew. It was a relief in a sense to have gotten the things under way. There wasn't that nervous anticipation, wondering what I would say and what they would ask. Now I knew. Now it was over as far as the initial phase. Douglas didn't seem like a bad sort to me, but I didn't trust Garcia at all. Garcia looked like a man who enjoyed watching people suffer. The difference between

Big Nappi Brufalo and Garcia was that at least with Brufalo everything was up front. With Brufalo it was "Hi, I'm Big Nappi Brufalo. I'm here to kill you." But with Garcia it was "Hi, I'm with the Federal Government. I'm here to help you." Either way you were screwed.

Douglas and Garcia waited until they got back to Norris's office to tell Norris the good news. They couldn't want to see the expression on his face.

"Well Kevin, Felix and I got you your witness," Douglas said as they walked into Norris's office.

"I knew that if you stayed on Maldanado, he'd roll on those bastards," Norris said in his best 'I told you so' voice.

"It wasn't Maldanado. It's Quinn."

"Quinn?" Norris asked in total disbelief. "What the hell would Quinn know about this?"

"Quinn is like a walking encyclopedia of information about Costa, Merzone, Maldanado, and other shit we didn't even know about," Douglas said, collapsing in one of the chairs in front of Norris's desk. "He told us that the bribes that Merzone pays aren't half what it costs him in lunches, dinners, and gifts for Costa and his lady friends. He also said that the Shoreline is a cash cow for Costa. Costa's even got the money managers on a fucking schedule buying four to five thousand in dinners five or six times a year. They do all this at Costa's Shoreline Restaurant which then pads the bills. Not only that, but Costa washes his bribe money through there too! Merzone feeds hot New Issues to Costa to keep the old man happy. For Christ's sake, on just that scheme, Costa's made over three hundred thousand this year alone. Believe me...Maldanado isn't worth shit compared to what Quinn knows."

"How the hell did this Quinn get to know all this?" Norris asked. This was far more than he had ever hoped for and unless there was a nasty wrinkle in all this good news, he knew he had the whole lot of them on a bus to prison.

"Quinn's kind of a special sort," Douglas said opening the folder containing his notes from the day's meeting. "We talked for a little over an hour and I could tell I'd really like this guy if the situation were different. He's one of those people you take to right away. Quinn's like a priest. You meet him and you tell him your life story before you even know it. He said that Merzone told him most of what he knows and the rest he picked up from other people. The money managers would *love* to tell their story. They've got nothing to lose. They buy dinners all the time and it's perfectly legal, but they're getting hosed on *this* deal. They'd love to get these bastards off their backs. Christ, if we put these guys away, they'd save a fortune. All we have to do is subpoena the business records from the Shoreline and match up the food purchases against the sales and we've got more evidence to nail Costa. The number of new issues alone is de facto bribery."

"Where's the catch?" Norris asked wanting to get the bad news out before he even considered celebrating.

"That's the best part," Douglas went on. "Quinn's as clean as the driven snow. He's got no record Costa's defense team could use against him. The guy's only had one speeding ticket in the past three years for God's sake and we don't have to make any kind of a deal with him, so no one can say we bought his testimony. He even stands to lose a huge piece of revenue if he loses Merzone. Yeah, it's possible he could pick up some of the business when Merzone's out of the picture, but he says there are no deals out there and I believe him. It's like this guy was sent from heaven."

"What about Massarro. What about his meeting? Does he know anything about Massarro's operation?"

"We asked him if he knew Massarro," Garcia said. "We specifically didn't mention that we knew about his meeting with him. We wanted to see what he would say."

"....And?" Norris asked impatiently.

"*And*...he said he met with Massarro once at the coffee shop," Garcia replied. "He said Massarro seemed to offer him some kind of work, but he wasn't sure what Massarro meant and he never pursued it. He knows who Massarro is, but nothing about his business. Bill checked with the Bureau and they have no record of any other meetings between Massarro and Quinn. The guy seems to be on the level."

"I want to see Quinn the day after tomorrow, "Norris said. "What's the potential threat against this man? Does he need protection? Are we going to have to call Witsec?"

"I asked him if he needed help along those lines," Douglas said. "He said he felt safe enough. I think somebody's behind this guy and they're pushing him in our direction. The lead came from the local P.D. and we know some of those guys are on the take from the mob. My bet is that Costa's gotten to be a liability for somebody and that somebody wants Quinn to testify. Obviously, Quinn knows who the players are and there's no way this guy is going to volunteer this information out of the goodness of his heart. He knows he'd be dead inside a week. If you ask me, I think the mob wants Costa out as much as we do."

"But, you said that Quinn wasn't connected to Massarro."

"No, I don't think he is," Douglas responded with some exasperation. "I think somebody else talked to Quinn and asked for his help. I think that once Quinn agreed, they went through the local cops to feed us the lead. I think this is exactly what it appears to be. Quinn's got the information that we need and he's willing to cooperate. The only reason I brought up the subject was in response to your protection question. This is a clean deal Kevin, let's not get overly paranoid and screw this up." Douglas was getting frustrated with Norris's obsession with the minutest details. He should be jumping for joy rather than trying to find eight sides to a three-sided argument.

I was in my office at 4:30 when I received a call from Mario Rizzelli. He told me that he had been asked by a friend to supply whatever help I needed. I noticed that Rizzelli was careful not to use any names on the phone. Even the attorney believed the phones were tapped. He asked if I wanted to accompany him to any meetings with the prosecutor. It made me wonder how safe I really was with the Feds. Why would it be necessary for Rizzelli to come along on any meeting if I had nothing to hide? Rizzelli strongly recommended that he go along with me to the Grand Jury when I get called to appear. He explained that no attorneys were allowed in the Grand Jury hearing room, but if something didn't sit right with me, I would have the right to stop the proceedings and come outside to consult with counsel. As Rizzelli was explaining the 'ins and outs' of the meetings and the Grand Jury, I realized that if I had an attorney present, it might look like I had something to hide. I figured I'd be better off going it alone.

No sooner did I hang up the phone with Rizzelli then Douglas called. He wanted to know if "it was convenient" for me to meet with Norris on Thursday morning at 10:00. I wasn't surprised to hear Douglas say that Norris was anxious to meet me. After I hung up the phone, I realized that I hadn't told Rane anything about this. I was pretty sure I knew how she would receive the news. Although I was sure she wouldn't be thrilled with me sticking my neck out like this, I knew her well enough to realize that she would be behind me all the way. I wanted her to be aware of the things that happened around her just in case someone might use her as leverage against me. It would be a delicate thing to keep her from becoming totally paranoid rather than just careful. We had our regular Wednesday dinner the next night and I thought that would be the best time to talk. The dinner was wonderful as usual but it was obvious I was distracted by something.

"Okay, Parker. Out with it," she said. "What going on? You're a lousy liar and even worse at hiding things. I know something is on your mind and it's bothering you and that bothers me"

I went through the whole story from the meeting with Traffarro to the hotel room scene with Douglas and Garcia. Rane's reaction was about the same as mine when I sat down with Traffarro. She just sat there for a few minutes. I thought I would use the same tactic as Traffarro and just keep quiet.

"Please tell me you're joking"

"Nope"

"Really?"

"Yup"

"To be honest I'm not very happy about all of this but I trust you and I know you'll do what's right." she said after she finally resigned herself to the situation.

Chapter Thirteen
The Game Starts

The short drive to the Federal Building and Kevin Norris's office didn't give me much time to think, but the one thing that kept crossing my mind was that Norris might start a line of questioning that I wouldn't want to answer. I'd be flying very close to the flame and I just hoped I wouldn't get my wings burned. It was 9:55 when I rang the buzzer next to the door to Norris's offices. It was a minute or so before Norris's secretary's voice come out of the speaker. Once she buzzed me through, I had to wait fifteen minutes for Norris. I was not very good at waiting. I hated going to the doctor's office and having to wait in the reception area, followed by the mandatory wait in those little examination rooms, followed by five minutes with the doctor and another fifteen minutes waiting for whatever the doctor decided to prescribe. It makes you wonder, if the doctor only took five minutes to see a patient, why does it take an hour for a visit.

"I'm sorry to keep you waiting," Norris's secretary said. "Mr. Norris will see you now. Please follow me."

After she finished her little speech, I followed her down a short hall. I couldn't help thinking that this was exactly like being at the doctors. I even had that nervous feeling I got before the doctor finally told me that I really wasn't dying of some horrible disease and it was just a bad cold. One thing I did notice was the doctor kept his office a lot neater than Norris. The place was a *wreck*. There were files and paper everywhere. *How the hell does he find anything in this place*, I thought.

"Please come in and sit down, Mr. Quinn," Norris said, walking from behind his desk.

Douglas and Garcia were already seated to one side of Norris's desk. I hadn't really given much thought about what Norris would look like, but if I had, I wouldn't have picked this guy. I made Norris to be in his mid-thirties and well over six feet tall. He was a beefy guy. I didn't think this man spent too much time shopping. The suit he had on fit him like skin. I thought I recognized Norris's suit as the one I remembered being buried with my grandfather. He had those wire rimmed glasses the preppy types always thought were so cool. I realized I must have been staring at Norris for a long time when I heard Norris's voice seemingly come from some distant place.

"Mr. Quinn, are you alright?" Norris asked as he looked at me with a most puzzled expression.

"Oh! I'm sorry. I was just admiring your suit, Mr. Norris. Versace?" I replied trying to cover his lapse. I noticed Douglas and Garcia glance at each other when I mentioned Versace. It was obvious that the comment had struck them as funny because Garcia had pursed his lips and Douglas had to bring his hand to his mouth to catch a phony cough.

"Well thank you, Mr. Quinn, but no. It's something I picked up at a local store," Norris replied with all seriousness. "I'd like to get started if there are no more questions or observations about my attire, Mr. Quinn."

"Nope"

"Mr. Quinn, you told agents Douglas and Garcia that you saw Sammy Merzone give an envelope full of money to Mr. Costa," Norris began as he leafed through Douglas's notes. "How did that come about?"

"I don't really remember what the meeting was about, but we hadn't been in his office very long when Sammy reached into his pocket a laid an envelope on Costa's desk."

"How do you know there was money in the envelope?"

"It wasn't sealed and when he laid the envelope down, the open side was facing me. I could see a stack of bills in the envelope, but Costa slammed his hand down on the envelope before I could tell what denomination they were. He looked at Sammy like he wanted to kill him. I think he was pissed because Sammy had passed the money in front of me."

"Did Merzone ever reveal to you how much he was paying Costa?" Norris asked.

"He told me he paid out over thirty thousand to him in one month," I replied. "I took it from his comments that it was a particularly heavy month. He never said how much was in that or any other envelope. He did say that whatever he paid Costa in hard cash was nothing in comparison to what he had to shell out in lunches, dinners and gifts. He also told me it was costing him over two hundred thousand a year."

Norris looked at Douglas and Garcia. He couldn't believe what he was hearing. He knew that Merzone was shelling out to Costa, but this was a lot more than he realized. "Why did Merzone tell you all of this?" Norris still couldn't believe that anyone involved in payoffs would broadcast it to a relative stranger.

"Frankly, I don't know. I couldn't possibly tell you what motivates another person. What I can tell you is that I wasn't the only one. I met quite a few people over the past year that expressed amazement that Sammy told them about how expensive Costa was."

"Tell me about the Capital Development payoff?"

"Vinny Maldanado was named as an agent or broker or some such thing for the placement of a twelve million dollar loan from the Union to Capital. He received two hundred and forty thousand as a fee. He set aside something for taxes, kept twenty-five for himself and issued a check to the Bleeker Investment Company. The Bleeker Investment Company only has one person in it and that's Sammy Merzone."

"Who the hell told you all of this?" Norris asked in a voice that echoed his disbelief.

"Maldanado and Sammy," I responded in a matter of fact tone. "They were bragging about it. They were asking me how it might be possible for Sammy to get a tax deduction on money paid to Maldanado."

Norris let his head fall forward and he just slowly shook it back and forth. The gall of these people was indescribable. It might be possible for one or two transactions to slip through the Governments cracks, but these guys were doing things week in and week out. Why anyone would brag about his or her illegal activities was something that Norris would never understand.

"What about the lunches and dinners, did Merzone ever tell you how much he was paying out for these?"

"Not really." I replied. "He did say he bought lunch for Costa and any other guests every day except Sunday. It didn't matter if Sammy was present or not. If he wasn't there, Costa would have the restaurant hold the bill until the next time Sammy came in. I did see several lunch checks that Sammy signed for and they ran a hundred and fifty to two hundred. By the way, if you really want to know all you have to do is request a copy of Sammy's monthly tab from the restaurants that they went to. He always signed the check and received a bill monthly. I would think it must make your job a lot easier when the crooks keep *such* good records. The dinners were another thing. He bought dinner three or four nights a week and they were a hell of a lot more expensive than the lunches. Sammy said it cost him almost ten grand a month for lunch and dinner."

"Speaking of dinners, what's this you told these two gentlemen about the money managers and the money they paid out for lavish dinners?" Norris said as he pointed his finger toward Douglas and Garcia.

"I was at quite a few dinners put on by the money managers. There were usually about thirty to forty people at these gatherings including trustees of the funds, friends of Sammy, business agents for the Union, and God knows who else. I became friends with a few of the managers and one of them told me the cost to him was usually between four and five thousand dollars per event. I've eaten at the Shoreline. The foods good, but no way could you spend a hundred a fifty dollars a person for dinner. Somebody was padding the bills."

The question and answer session went on for over an hour. Norris was convinced that I was the genuine article. This was the break that he had hoped for and with my testimony, there was no doubt that Costa and his crowd would go away for a long time.

"Mr. Quinn," Norris said as he started to wrap up the session. "I want you to appear before the Federal Grand Jury in two weeks. I would bring you in sooner but there are already other people who are scheduled to appear. Are you comfortable with appearing? The questions that I'll ask you will be nearly identical to those we talked about today. Do *you* have any questions?"

"No," I replied, standing up from my chair. "I can't think of any at this time."

When I left Norris's office, I felt like a weight had been taken off my shoulders. I knew this was a long way from being over, but at least I had this meeting behind me. I was reasonably convinced that Norris wouldn't try to screw me. Norris wouldn't want to risk compromising his star witness by playing games. At least, that's what I hoped.

The Justice Department and the FBI are about as secure as a sinking ship. Only they have more leaks. I couldn't have been out of Norris's office for more than one day before everybody who needed to know what was going on heard about my meeting.

Sammy Merzone arrived at the office at 9:30 A.M. as usual, and as he passed his brother's office, Ralph called him.

"Sammy, we've gotta talk," Ralph said as Sammy passed by the door. "Get the fuck in here and close the door."

"Hey, how you doin'?" Sammy said as he walked in and sat down.

"How am I doing?" Ralph said in a sarcastic tone. "Not too fucking well and neither are you. Did you know that Quinn got called into talk to that prick Norris yesterday and that he was in Norris's office for over an hour?" What did you tell him about Reno and us?"

"Nothing! I don't know. I mean...he's around a lot," Sammy replied defensively. "How hell would I know what he heard?"

"Sammy, you fucking talk to everybody. I've told you a hundred times to keep your fuckin' mouth shut," Ralph said as he started to raise his voice. Ralph would have given anything to be in Sammy's shoes. Ralph made a lot of money working with Sammy, but it was nothing in comparison to what Sammy brought in. He wanted to be the center of the action. In his mind, Sammy wasn't half as smart as he was and Ralph believed he'd be able to make twice the money as his blabbermouth brother.

"So what! So...yeah...okay, maybe I said a few things to Quinn over the past year. So what! Quinn's not going to say anything. He's a good guy and besides I got him photographed with Massarro in the coffee shop. The Feds aren't going to believe a word he says. He's up to his ass in our business. If we go to jail, he goes to jail."

"Have you *completely* lost your fucking mind?" Ralph yelled. "A thousand people have been photographed with Massarro and they didn't all wind up in jail. Even if the Feds had something on him, don't tell me you never heard of immunity from prosecution? Sammy, for God's sake...don't you get it? This guy can bring everything we've got to an end. Not to mention the fact that I don't want to go to some fucking federal country club."

"You're crazy. First, I've got one of the best lawyers in the country working on this. The fucking guy's already cost me two hundred grand. You don't think he's going to let some chicken shit prosecutor throw us in jail? Besides, Reno's beaten these guys off for years. I'm telling you, there's no way this thing even goes to court."

"*I'm* crazy?" Ralph shouted. "*I'm* crazy? *I'm* not the one who's been running around telling everybody about payoffs to Reno. *You're* the crazy one! I'm going over and tell Reno exactly the position you've put us in. Let's see what he thinks we should do. I'm not going to the can just because you can't keep your fucking mouth shut."

"No!" Sammy yelled. "You go to Reno and tell him about your stupid ideas and he's gonna to throw us both out. Keep your mouth shut!"

Ralph left work early that day and went straight to Costa's office. He didn't give a shit what Sammy said. There was no way he wanted to spend any time in jail regardless of what his idiot brother thought. He might even be able to convince the old man that Sammy was a loose cannon and it might be possible that Costa would replace Sammy with someone more sensible like him. When Ralph got to Costa's office, he laid out the entire scenario for Costa, complete with all the information that he imagined his brother could have told Quinn. Costa kept pounding his desk at every new point Ralph brought out.

"How the fuck could your fucking brother be that stupid," Costa screamed. "I treated him like my own son, for Christ's sake. I knew that idiot was saying things to some people and I told him to shut his fucking mouth. But no! He's got to go and talk to somebody like Quinn." Costa stopped for a few minutes to collect his thoughts. If it was going to be necessary to take drastic measures, he didn't want to scare Ralph and Sammy into hiding. "I don't want you to worry, Ralph. You're a good boy. You've done the right thing telling me this and I'll make sure you're taken care of. If that fuckin' Quinn is talking to the Feds and if he knows what you say he knows, then everything I've built could disappear and I'm not going to let that happen."

"What do you want me to do, Reno?"

"I want you to be a good boy and keep your ears open," Costa answered. "If you think of anything we could use against Quinn, you let me know. And for Christ's sake, don't tell your fucking brother you talked to me!"

I hadn't talked to Traffarro since I met with Douglas and Garcia. Nicky had told me that Traffarro figured the Feds would be watching me to see whom I met with so they could figure out who the players were. We had been going to lunch at Salvatore's on a regular basis for months and the Feds were familiar with the routine. It might cause just as much suspicion if I stopped going on Saturdays as it would if they had any extra meetings. Nicky told me Traffarro wanted us to be at Salvatore's thirty minutes early so we could talk about my meetings.

When I arrived at Salvatore's, Junior was behind the bar.

"Junior, why do you keep working like this? You'll spoil your reputation."

"Don't start with me, Quinn. I'm not in the mood," Junior shot back. "I seen your Caddy in the parking lot here for the last three days, *but*...I didn't see you. What's up?

"I lent my car to Carmine," I said. "I came in here one day after work and Carmine was tending bar. He said his car was in the shop and he was having trouble getting around. He knew I had two cars so he wanted to know if he could borrow the Caddy."

"Yeah, I know," Junior said as he slammed his hands down on the bar. "Fuckin' Carmine is a low life piece of shit. He doesn't *own* a fucking car 'cause his ex-wife took it when she found him fuckin' around on her. Carmine's been stayin' at my place for three weeks now, the lazy bastard. I told him to bring your car over to your place this afternoon or I'd have Tino play baseball with his fucking head." Junior leaned over the bar and put his hand on my shoulder. "Quinn, you're a nice guy and I appreciate the fact that you're helpin' Anthony, but your fuckin heart is *too big*! These other 'mooks' around here will try to take advantage of you. If anyone asks you for a favor, I want you to let me know. I take care of these idiots and I know who needs what. Don't go worrying about idiots like Carmine. I'll take care of him."

"Whoa, Junior, I'm sorry. I was just trying to help," I said as a sincere apology. I felt that I had somehow stepped on Junior's territory and I really liked Junior and wouldn't hurt him for the world.

"Aaahhh! It's all right," Junior replied. "I just don't want some of these pricks taking advantage of my friends like you." Junior stepped back and pointed his finger at Quinn. "You gonna sit there with that stupid fuckin' look on your face or you gonna order a drink? I got bills to pay, ya know. I can't have people hangin' around here and not buyin something."

"I'll have a beer," I said as he slammed a five-dollar bill on the bar pretending to be offended by the remark.

"Fuck you!" Junior sneered. "Your money's no good here."

I just shook my head as Junior poured me a beer and as he placed it down he gave me a friendly slap on the cheek. "Your fuckin' lucky I like you, Quinn," Junior joked as he turned and walked away.

Traffarro and Nicky walked through the back entrance to the restaurant. When Traffarro saw Junior behind the bar he leaned across it and gave his cousin a kiss on the cheek.

"Christ, Junior," Traffarro said. "All this fuckin' work is gonna kill you."

"Fuck you, Anthony," Junior said. "First it's Quinn and now you. I gotta get a better class of customer in this joint. Maybe some new curtains would help," he said, looking around the restaurant.

Everybody laughed. They knew Junior wouldn't give up his current clientele for anything. He loved them and they loved him. Junior was an institution in the city. People would go on vacation and send him postcards before they would send any to their own family.

Traffarro, Nicky and I gathered at our usual table in the corner. Traffarro wanted to know everything that was said at my meetings with the Feds and Norris. When I ran down the list of all the points that I covered with Norris, Traffarro was surprised. There were a number of things he had forgotten. He was happy with the way things had gone. He was especially happy that I hadn't been pressed about Massaro. Traffarro could get a report back to Massaro and let him know that for now, the Feds were not looking to go after him.

"Well, everything is going along better than I had hoped for," Traffarro said. "All we have to do is go about our regular business for a while and everything should be fine. Is everything okay with you and Rane about all this?"

"Yeah, she's a little worried about what might happen to me, but nothing out of the ordinary." I certainly hoped that was true. I loved Rane and I didn't want her involved in this mess any more than possible.

"Good," said Traffarro, pointing across the restaurant. "Look. Some of the guys are coming in now. Let's go have some lunch."

Chapter Fourteen
Marriage and Murder

Nearly two weeks went by without incident. It was Wednesday evening and Rane and I were once again having dinner at Terrabella's. I was going to appear before the Grand Jury on Friday and I had something very important that I wanted to discuss with Rane.

"Rane, you and I have been seeing each other for some months now. I think you know me about as well as you ever will. I'd like to think we could spend more time together," I said as he reached into my pocket.

"I'd like that," Rane said not really knowing where I was going with the conversation.

I reached over and held Rane's hand and for a moment just looked at her. Rane sat there with one eyebrow raised and a total 'what-the-hell-is-this-about' look.

"Rane will you marry me?" I asked softly. I put my hand in my pocket and proceeded to show her an engagement ring. Nicky had arranged for me to meet with a friend of his that specialized in fine jewelry at substantially discounted prices. I suspected the ring was part of a shipment that never quite made it to the intended buyer but I had seen a lot of merchandise sold from the back of cars. It was almost the normal way to buy things on the Eastside.

Rane just sat there and looked at what she thought was the most beautiful thing she had ever seen.

"Look Rane, my life is like the Chinese curse," I said holding the open box in my hand. "It's always interesting, but I love you and I can't promise that things will ever be normal or easy in my life.

But if you'll have me, I'd love to spend the rest of that crazy life with you."

"I don't know what to say," she stammered. The more precise truth was that she didn't know what to say at that particular moment. I knew she had thought about being married to me and it seemed like a good idea, but she didn't think that I was ready for that kind of a commitment. Living together was all that she had hoped for and it would have been fine with her. Neither of us wanted to have any more children, therefore marriage wasn't a requirement. Marriage was a strong public declaration of unity to her and when she found the right man, it was something that she wanted. She said I was unlike any man she had ever met and she loved me deeply. "I love you, too," she said looking up at me. "So I guess...yes."

She reached over and threw her arms around me. "I can't believe you did this," she said. "I mean...don't get me wrong...I'm *glad* you did this but...When did you want to get married?"

"I thought we'd wait for a few months. There's so much going on right now I didn't want anything to interfere with our wedding. Besides, after you think about it, you might want to change your mind."

"Shut up, Parker," she said jokingly. "If anybody changes their mind it'll probably be you. Of course, if you do I'll have to kill you."

"Yeah...well, get in line," I said with only a little humor.

We had a wonderful dinner and afterward, Gina brought out a bottle of Dom Pérignon. I couldn't remember when I had felt this good. She was talking about wedding plans and all the things that she wanted to do. I felt a wonderful peace come over me as I listened to her enthusiastically talk about our future together. I thought back to that evening walk by the ocean in Hawaii and how great it would be to share that moment with her. If I had spent forever planning this night it couldn't have gone any better. The restaurant was nearly empty by the time we left.

I hadn't driven two blocks before I heard sirens and saw three police cars scream past the car. Pulling up to a stoplight, I smiled as I glanced over at Rane and saw her admiring the ring on her finger. A car pulled up next to us and purely out of habit, I looked over to see who it was. I was kind of surprised to see the passenger's window start to roll down. Maybe it was someone I knew and they wanted to say hello. I stared for a few seconds before I realized that I was looking at a man in a ski mask with a very large gun pointed in my direction.

"Rane!" I shouted. "Get down!"

As I dove toward the passenger's seat, I instinctively reached for Rane and tried to pull her down toward the floor. I heard the gun fire four or five times and the glass flew at me with such force that it imbedded in the side of my face and neck. The sound of the shots was deafening. I lay motionless on top of Rane for what seemed like an eternity.

"Rane," I cried, looking over at her. "Are you all right?"

She was slumped over with her head resting on the dashboard. I moved quickly over to see if she was hurt and as I did, he saw that blood had started to run down her neck from beneath her beautiful blond hair.

"Oh, God...Rane! No! This can't be happening."

I pulled her back so that her head was resting on the seat's head restraint. I grabbed her wrist to see if I could find a pulse. The blast of a car horn startled me and I realized that the car was still running and had drifted out into the intersection. I grabbed the stirring wheel and turned the car down Main Street. St. Peter's Hospital was only three blocks away, but it seemed like miles as I sped through the light traffic.

The car careened around the corner to the emergency entrance and I rushed to the passenger's door. Rane nearly fell into my arms as I opened the door. I bent over, carefully putting her head on my shoulder as I lifted her into my arms and ran into the emergency room.

"Nurse!" I shouted to the woman behind the counter. "This woman's been shot. Get a doctor, now!" I stood there with Rane cradled in my arms. I had never lost anything so precious to me and the thought was tearing me apart.

The nurse rushed from behind the counter and ordered me to follow her. We hurried down the hall and through the double doors to the emergency room. The nurse called out for a doctor as we approached a vacant emergency bed.

"Please sir, put her down on the bed and stand back."

The doctor came into the curtained area and bent over Rane. "How did this happen?" the doctor said as he moved Rane's blood soaked hair back to reveal the gaping wound. The whole left side of her face and neck were covered in blood. "How long ago did it happen?" He was almost shouting as he tried to get me out of my obvious stupor.

"Five minutes at the most," I said as I suddenly recovered my senses and anxiously looked at the woman I loved. "We were stopped at a traffic light and a car pulled up next to us. The passenger rolled down the window and opened fire on us. If I hadn't looked over at them, we'd both be dead"

"Sir," the nurse said as she pulled on my arm. "Please come over to this bed and lay down. You're bleeding heavily." I hadn't felt a thing and was totally oblivious of the blood that soaked my shirt.

"No." I shouted. "I want to stay with Rane." I didn't want to take my eyes off her for fear that I might lose her if I did. I wanted to find a way to take the strength from my body and put it in hers. A feeling of complete helplessness overwhelmed me.

"If we don't stop the bleeding from your neck, you'll both be dead," she said as she pushed me toward the bed next to Rane. "Now get over here and lie down! I'll pull back the curtain and you'll be right next to her. Now move!"

Several more nurses and another doctor rushed into the room. The doctors worked feverishly on Rane. Her blouse was covered in blood and they stripped it off to see if there were any other wounds. A nurse held a compress on her head to control the bleeding while another took her blood pressure. The doctor checked her wound again and then replaced the heavy compress on Rane's head and they started to rush her out of the room.

"Where are they taking her?" I anxiously inquired. The sight of the gurney rolling quickly out of the room amplified the fear of losing my beloved Rane.

"Please sir, calm down," the doctor working on my neck said. "We need to get an MRI to see if there's any brain damage. Now, relax," he said as he surveyed the damage. "I've got a lot of glass to pick out of the left side of your head and neck so *please*——stay still."

The doctor put his hand on my head and moved closer to survey the damage. I lay quietly on the bed as the doctor worked with a pair of tweezers to pick out all the small pieces of glass. I kept playing the evening over and over in my mind. How could things have gone from one extreme to the other so quickly? I kept seeing Rane slumped in her seat with the blood running down her face. Who did this? Did that fucking Massarro double cross me? Maybe it was Costa or Sammy. The more I thought about them and what they had done to Rane, the angrier I got. I wanted to kill whoever hurt her.

The doctor's voice brought me back to the emergency room. "I've gotten the glass out," the doctor said, reaching for the surgical tray at his side. "I'm going to have to put in a few stitches before I bandage you up. I want you to stay here over night as a precautionary measure," he said as he pulled the first stitch through my skin. "You've lost a lot of blood and it's better to play it safe."

"What about Rane?"

"We haven't heard anything yet," the doctor replied. "They'll take her straight to a room after the MRI. I'll arrange for you to see her as soon as she gets settled. The nurse will take you over to admitting and get all the information on you and your friend and then you can go to her room."

While Rane and I and been ending our engagement dinner that night, Traffarro was at one of the local bars having a club soda with two of the business agents from the Union. It had been a quiet week and it was a good time to catch up on some Union business and tell some old war stories.

"Did you hear the latest on Reno?" asked Danny Fitz. "It seems that somebody told the old man that the fat black bitch he hangs around with is seein' some other guy, which personally I find quite amazing. After all, who could possibly want anyone else when they could have that shriveled up dick on the old man," Fitz said with a sarcastic laugh. "Anyhow, he says he doesn't believe it, but it must have been eating at him 'cause he called up Sammy at two in the morning and tells Sammy to have one of his guys follow her. Sammy calls Carlo Bonaface and tells him to watch her. About two nights later, Carlo follows her and some guy back to her place. He sneaks up to the window and there they are fuckin' like rabbits. So Bonaface leaves and calls Sammy. Sammy tells the old man, but he refuses to believe it. He tells Sammy he wants pictures. Now get this. He doesn't want just any pictures. He wants a picture of the guy *actually* stickin' it in her! Otherwise he says they could be doin' anything, he says. Can you believe that old fuck? Actually stickin' it in her!"

All of a sudden Fitz turned and yelled, "Jesus Christ!"

A man had come up behind Traffarro and had pointed a sawed off shotgun at the back of Traffarro's head. Fitz lunged at the man and grabbed the barrel of the gun pushing it toward the ceiling as it went off. The blast blew a two-foot hole in the ceiling. They wrestled with the gun for a few seconds before the second barrel discharged only inches from Fitz's ear. Pulling the gun free, the man ran from the bar and into a waiting car.

"Bobby, throw me that piece you got behind the bar," Traffarro yelled to the bartender. By the time Traffarro reached the street, the car was roaring away and Traffarro fired five shots into the fleeing vehicle shattering the rear window. He stood there in the street and watched the car careen around the corner.

When Traffarro went back inside, he found Fitz lying on the floor holding his right ear.

"Christ, Fitz. Are you all right?"

"My fucking ear!" Fitz yelled. "I think the motherfucker blew out my fuckin' eardrum."

"Bobby, call the cops! Somebody get a fuckin' chair for Fitz."

Within a few minutes three police cars came around the corner with their sirens screaming out the emergency. Six cops charged into the bar and found Traffarro sitting next to his friend. It took an hour for the police to gather everybody's statement. They advised Fitz to go to the hospital and get his ear check by a doctor.

"Come on, Danny," Traffarro said to Fitz as he pulled him up from his chair. "I'll take you to the hospital. We'll go over to St. Pete's." Fitz staggered out of the bar leaning on Traffarro's shoulder.

By the time Traffarro got to the emergency room, I had just left to go fill out some hospital paperwork. Traffarro recognized the doctor as an old friend from the neighborhood.

"Hey, doc," Traffarro said as he greeted the approaching doctor. "I think Danny here got his eardrum blown out."

"Bring him over here Anthony and let me look at it," the doctor said as he led the two men to the bed. "What happened?"

"Some asshole tried to take my head off with a shotgun," Traffarro explained. "Danny here saved my life, but the gun went off right by his ear"

"That'll do it. It's a big night for attempted murders."

"What do you mean?" Traffarro asked, watching the doctor dab a small trickle of blood from his friend's ear.

"We just had a man and a woman come in here. Somebody tried to kill them at a traffic light."

"Anybody I know?" Traffarro asked.

"I don't know. Their names were Quinn and a woman named....."

"Harold?" said Traffarro cutting the doctor off.

"Yeah, you know them?"

"Yeah." Traffarro said in a low voice. "I know them." He just looked off into that empty place that we sometimes view when things don't quite make sense. *Who the fuck had the balls to try this,* Traffarro thought. He couldn't believe that Massarro had gone back on his agreement.

I was in a wheelchair next to Rane's bed. I just sat there holding her hand and rubbing it softly. I was so angry I could hardly contain myself. All I could think of at this point was revenge.

"Mr. Quinn?" a man said as he entered the room. "I'm Doctor Morris. We've done a full screen of tests on your friend and I'm pleased to tell you that she's going to be just fine. The bullet grazed her skull and caused a mild concussion but I don't foresee any complications. So far, there doesn't appear to be any swelling of the brain or any fluid build-up in the area. She has a bad bruise on her forehead that I imagine she got by hitting the dashboard when you tried to get her out of the way. We'll keep her here for a few days just to be sure. I would expect she should wake up any time now. You can stay here as long as you like. I'm sure she'll be happy to see a friendly face when she wakes up. She's a lucky woman, Mr. Quinn. If her head had been turned just a fraction the wrong way or if the gunman's angle were a few degrees different, we would have a far greater tragedy on our hands. The police have been notified and I would expect they would be here shortly. Please call the nurse when she regains consciousness. I want to check her reactions."

"I will. Thank you, doctor. Oh, and doctor...could we keep the dashboard thing between you and me. I don't think she really remembers it and I know she appreciates the fact that I tried to protect her and all but...well, the truth is I know her and she's gonna break my balls for years with that one."

The doctor just smiled and shook his head. "No problem. Believe me, I understand,"

Twenty minutes passed before I heard Rane exhale a low moan. I got up from the wheelchair and stood over her. Her eyes were barely open.

"Rane," I said. "How ya doin' baby?"

"Parker?" she said in a faint soft voice. "Did some son of a bitch just shoot me?"

"Yeah, baby. Luckily they hit you in your head and the bullet bounced off." This was not a joking matter, but I was so glad to see her open her eyes I couldn't help myself.

She reached her hand up to her head and felt the bandages. Rane slowly rolled her head to one side and looked lazily around the room.

"Where am I?" She asked, becoming more aware of her surroundings.

"You're in St Peter's Hospital, babe," I said as I slowly rubbed her hand. "The doctor said you're going to be fine."

Traffarro was walking briskly down the hall and was stopped by a nurse coming out of a patient's room.

"Sir! Sir! It's way past visiting hours. You can't be up here."

"Yeah, I know," Traffarro said as he totally ignored her and continued on his way.

"Sir, please. I must insist!"

"Yeah, sure...whatever," he said as he kept on walking. The nurse took a few more steps before she realized that the situation wasn't really worth her time. He seemed like a man on a mission and if there was any trouble she could always call security.

Rane rolled her head to the other side as if she wanted to see if her neck still worked. As she turned her head toward the door, she noticed a man standing there.

"Hi, Anthony," she said in a low whispery voice as Traffarro entered the room. "Some asshole tried to kill us, Anthony."

"Yeah, I know baby," said Traffarro as he approached the bed and softly picked up her hand and gave it a kiss. "There seems to be a lot of that going around tonight."

"Who did this Anthony?" Rane said softly.

"I don't know yet, sweetie. But I promise you, we'll find out. I'll have their balls wrapped up in a nice little box for you, Rane," Traffarro said with a controlled intensity in his voice. The sight of her in the bed only made him more furious. It could be Connie laying there.

"What do you mean, there's a lot of this going around tonight?" I asked.

"Somebody put a sawed of shotgun to the back of my head in Gregorio's Bar tonight," Traffarro explained. If Danny Fitz hadn't grabbed the guy, I'd be on a slab in the fucking morgue right now."

"Jesus Christ! Who's did this?"

"Shit, Quinn! You look like you got a pillow stuck to your head," Traffarro said as he finally got a good look at Quinn. "You okay?"

"Yeah, it's just some cuts from the glass. The shots came through the car window and blasted it all over the place. Anthony, what the fuck's going on?"

"Like I said, I don't know. But I don't want you two to worry about it tonight. There'll be fifty fuckin' cops in here in a few minutes. Nobody's gonna try anything again tonight," Traffarro said and slowly bent over Rane and gave her a kiss on the forehead. "Baby, I just want you to relax and get better real soon. Connie'll come up tomorrow and visit you I promise. In the meantime, I gotta find out who's behind this. *Fucking pricks!* Ooops, sorry about the language Rane," Traffarro said as he brought his hand to his mouth.

"That's okay Anthony. I want to know who the fucking pricks are, too."

It was four in the morning and Norris was at home in a deep sleep when his phone rang. He had been getting some of the best sleep in months as a result of his conversation with me. Everything was set. I would testify before the Grand Jury in two days and that would assure the indictment of Costa and his crew. This was the strongest case he ever prosecuted and he couldn't wait to see the look on Costa's face when the marshals led him off to prison.

In a half wakened state, Norris reached over for the phone on the nightstand. "What!" he said with a sleepy voice.

"Somebody tried to kill Anthony Traffarro tonight," the voice said.

"So?" Norris barked, still trying to find a better level of consciousness.

"So, they also tried to kill Quinn and his girlfriend, too."

"What! Is Quinn all right?"

"Yeah, he's staying in the hospital overnight, but he's fine. Just some cuts from flying glass. They tried to kill him and his girlfriend at a traffic light about three hours ago."

"Get one of your guys over there to watch Quinn and the woman."

"Why don't we have some of the local LEO's do that? We don't have the manpower to keep guys watching him day and night," Douglas replied.

"For Christ sake, just do what I tell you. You know as well as I do that some of the cops are on the take. I don't want anything to happen to him and I sure as hell don't want anybody trying to get to him through her. *Son of a bitch!* Call me at the office in the morning." Norris started to put the phone back down, when he suddenly put it back to his ear. "...and for Christ's sake keep Quinn alive! You got that? *God damn it!"*

Ten o'clock the next morning, Big Nappi Brufalo lumbered into Massarro's home to find him having breakfast on the back porch.

"Boss," Brufalo began. "I got a call from Tino Drazzetti about an hour ago."

"Yeah, how is he?" Massarro responded before bringing a cup of coffee to his lips.

"Not too fuckin' good, Boss. Somebody tried to whack Anthony Traffarro last night."

"What!" Massarro shouted as he threw his napkin on the table.

"That ain't the fuckin' half of it," Brufalo continued. "They tried to take out Quinn and his girl a half hour later. Tino's fuckin' *pissed*. He thinks you put out the hit. For some reason he likes this guy Quinn. I think Quinn did him a favor or somethin'," he said, pulling out a chair next to Massarro. "Anyway, I told him it wasn't us and we didn't know who fuckin' did it. I told him Quinn was doin' you a favor and that he would be the last person you'd want to see whacked."

"Fuckin' cocksucker stupid sons o' bitches!" shouted Massarro. "I want you to make some calls. I want to know who the fuck authorized this. If it wasn't one of our people, I want you to find out who it was...and don't come back here until you find out. *Motherfuckers!*"

The police questioned me for what seemed like hours. Bill Douglas showed up and contributed to the whole process. He told me an agent would be assigned to Rane and me twenty-four hours a day and at this point, I certainly didn't object. I wanted to be sure someone was watching Rane whenever I wasn't. I decided to spend the night in the wheelchair next to Rane's bed. I slept with my head on her bed and held her hand through the night. I couldn't believe I let this happen to her.

"Mr. Quinn. Mr. Quinn," the nurse said as she gently shook his shoulder. "I need you to go back to your room. The doctor wants to check your wounds. If everything is okay, I'm sure he'll release you."

I nodded my consent and she wheeled me into my room. The doctor had the nurse change the dressing as the wounds had oozed more blood during the night. About two hours later, I was being wheeled to the exit with an FBI agent close behind.

"Mr. Quinn," the agent said. "I'll be glad to drive you home. In fact, I think I'll have to insist."

"I appreciate it," I said, pulling myself out of the wheelchair. "But, I really want to drive myself. Why don't I wait in my car and you can follow me."

I walked slowly to the car. I wanted to go home and change my bloody clothes before I returned to the hospital to be with Rane. I opened the door and slid onto the soft leather seat never noticing the man seated in the passenger's seat.

"Shit!" I yelled as I realized that I wasn't alone. "Tino! You scared the shit out of me! God damn it!" I sat with my back against the car door. I started to realize that maybe I was about to be killed. "What do you want, Tino?"

"Relax, Quinn," Tino said in his raspy voice. "If I wanted to kill you, you'd already be dead. I'm not like these fucking amateurs. I came to tell you that it wasn't Massarro. If I know him, he'll have Brufalo make some inquiries. He wants you alive as much as the Feds. I already spoke to Anthony, and I told him we'll find these guys and whoever put them up to this. Massarro's gonna to put out the word. Nobody's gonna touch you or Rane."

"Thanks, Tino. My eyes happened to catch the sight of a tan Ford pulling out of a parking space at the far end of the lot. "Shit! You better get out of the car quick. I've got the fucking FBI following me for protection. I don't want them shootin' your ass."

"Don't worry pal," Tino said as he smiled and patted my shoulder. "We'll find out who did this."

Tino wasn't gone but a few seconds before the tan Ford sedan pulled up behind my car. *Great*, I thought as I let out a long sigh. If this is their idea of protection, I'm a lot better off with Tino and the mob. I felt a small sense of relief and irony. It was strange to think that I was feeling so much better because I knew Massarro wasn't trying to kill him. I was thinking that if it wasn't Massarro then it had to be Costa. The more I thought about that little piece of shit and what he had done to Rane, the more I couldn't wait to testify.

I drove to the house with the agent close behind. I could feel the anger settle into my gut and I knew it would be there for a long time. The events of the past twenty-four hours had changed me. I had become a part of Traffarro's world and the world of mob violence. I made some powerful new friends and...new enemies.

I drove to the rear of the house and the agent parked next to me but didn't get out of his car. I went over and tapped on his window and invited him into the house. Somehow it didn't seem polite to leave someone sitting in his car just waiting for me to come back out. Besides, they could shoot me just as easily in the front of the house as out here in the back.

"Would you like a cup of coffee?" I said to the agent as we went into the kitchen. "I've got one of those one cup machines. It only takes about a minute to brew a cup. The cups are in the cabinet over the coffee maker and the coffee and the milk are in the fridge. Make yourself at home. I'm going upstairs to take a shower and change my clothes."

"As long as I'm inside, why don't I just walk through the house to make sure no one left you a surprise?"

While the agent walked through the house, I pulled out the coffee and the milk and started to make him a cup of coffee. I felt stupid just standing there and waiting. I suppose walking through the house was a good idea and at least it gave the guy something to do. It was only a few minutes before he returned.

"This is a great place you've got here, Mr. Quinn," the agent said, turning back and looking at the living room. "You'd never know it by looking at it from the outside."

The phone on the wall rang as I was leaving the kitchen. The sudden sound caused me to jump away from the phone. My sudden movement caught the agent by surprise and he threw open his jacket and had his hand on his gun before he realized what happened.

"Sorry about that," I said apologetically. "It's the first time somebody's tried to kill me. I think it's made me a little edgy." I went to the phone and snatched the receiver off the wall in a little fit of anger. It was Bill Douglas

"Hello," I barked. "Yeah, Bill I'm fine. Yeah, he's right here, do you want to speak to him? No. I understand. I'm glad Norris postponed the Grand Jury date. Next week would be fine. No, really I'm not worried. I've got you and half the city watching out for Rane and me. It's nice to know you've got friends you can count on, especially when some asshole's trying to kill you. Look Bill, I don't know why you'd ever think that I would have second thoughts about testifying. If I ever wanted Costa and that fucking bunch of miscreants of his in jail before, I sure as hell what them there now. It's bad enough they tried to kill Traffarro and me, but those bastards nearly killed Rane. They're fucking lucky I don't have a gun or I'd already be on a killing spree. No Bill, I'm not about to do anything stupid. Massarro? What about him? Why would Massarro want to risk killing me? (A) I don't know anything about him and (B) I'm not testifying against him. Yeah. Yeah. Okay. No, I'm going to take the next week off. I want to spend the time with Rane. God willing, she'll be coming home in a few days and I want to be here with her for at least a couple of days to make sure she's all right. Yeah, okay. Yeah, right. Bye."

"Douglas is like a mother hen," I said as I hung up the phone. "The TV's in the living room. I'm going upstairs and finally take a shower and I think I'll lie down for a few minutes. I feel like I just ran a marathon. Make yourself comfortable. If you're hungry, there's cold cuts in the fridge and the bread's out there somewhere." The sentence trailed off as I was suddenly tired of being nice.

I arrived back at the hospital three hours later. I couldn't believe my eyes when I walked into Rane's room. It looked like a flower shop. There were bouquets everywhere. Junior, Connie, and Nicky were all standing around Rane's bed. I walked over to Rane's bed and gave her a kiss and said hello to everyone there.

"Hi, sweetie. How ya doin'?"

"I'm doin' good. I've got the worst headache of my life but other than that I'm fine." In the few hours I had been gone, Rane's color was back and her voice was a strong. "Can you believe all these flowers? Wasn't it nice for Connie, Nicky, and Junior to stop by?"

"I couldn't let my favorite girl lie in the hospital and not stop by," Junior said. "Christ Quinn, they really did a number on your face. Everything's gonna' be all right with you."

"Yeah, Junior," I replied. "Now, I guess you'll be the best looking guy in the city again."

"Bullshit!" Junior snapped back. "What makes you think I wasn't?"

"You doin' okay, Quinn?" Connie asked.

"Yeah, Connie. I'm fine. What's Anthony up to? I'm sorry I didn't get over to see you. This whole thing must have really upset you. I mean somebody trying to kill Anthony and all."

"Well, I was pretty upset as you can imagine, but Anthony said he had it under control," Connie replied, not truly believing her own words. "He's out making some calls to see what he can find out. He got some of the Union guys to stay over at the house while I was home. He's worried that somebody might come after me. I've seen this happen before, but it's the first time for my family. I think it pissed me off more than really scared me."

"So, Quinn," Junior said. "Rane tells me you two are gettin' married. I tried to talk some sense into her and have her marry me, but for some reason she wants you. No accountin' for some people's taste."

"Yeah," I said with a long sigh. "Nice start to our new lives, uh?"

"Quinn," Nicky chimed in. "This'll be over in a few days. You do what you gotta' do and we'll do what we gotta' do. Don't worry, you guys'll be fine."

Chapter Fifteen
Who Did It?

Rocco Massarro made some inquiries with some of the other families. No one said they knew who put out the contracts on Traffarro and Quinn, and each offered their assistance in finding out who did. Big Nappi Brufalo had sent his men out to shake down the local low lifes to see if anything turned up. The following Monday he received a call from a bar owner in a small town near the state line. He told Brufalo that some 'wanna be' hood was showing a big roll of bills and talking about shooting up a car in the city. The owner said the guy was a regular and would probably be in again that night. Brufalo thanked him and said that somebody would stop by and take care of him. All he had to do was point the guy out when he came in.

"Angelo!" Brufalo yelled into the phone. "I want you and Tony to go out to that joint on route forty-six. What's it called? Yeah, The Last Stop. Ask for a bartender named Jimmy. Give him five hundred. He's gonna' point out one of the fuckin' asshole that tried to pop Quinn. Bring the guy over to the warehouse and call me when you've got him there. Don't fuckin' touch him 'til I get there." Brufalo was shouting at the phone with such force that Angelo could have heard him without the phone. "You understand?"

It was ten o'clock when Brufalo's phone rang. After he hung up, he went to his closet and picked up a small gym bag. It contained fifty feet of rope, a ball peen hammer, a blowtorch, a pair of pruning sheers, and an assortment of boning knives. He threw the bag on the floor of his Lincoln and drove over to the warehouse. When he arrived Angelo and Tony had a thirty something year old man seated in a chair in the middle of the large room.

Brufalo walked up to the man and dropped his bag in his lap. The sound of all the metal tools in the bag made such a loud clanking sound that the man jerked back in absolute terror. "You know," he said. "You are one *stupid* son of a bitch. You tried to whack a friend of Rocco Massarro's. What were you fuckin' thinking?" he said as he put he hands on his hips and cocked his head with a perplexed look on his face. "Now, you got a' choice. You can tell me who fuckin' hired you and maybe I give you a break, or I'm gonna start cuttin' you up in little fuckin' pieces until you tell me. Either way, I fuckin' guarantee you're gonna' tell me everything I want to know." He shot his hand out and grabbed the man's head under the chin. The huge hand squeezed the man's face until it was doing an imitation of a goldfish. "So, what the fuck's it gonna be?"

"I swear to you, I don't know what you're talking about. I swear," the man cried.

"Angelo, Nicky, take off his fuckin' clothes."

"Wait! Wait! Okay, I'll tell you. I work with Johnny Lupo out of Cleveland," the man said as he held up his hand to stop Big Nappi. "I got a call from Pete Mastro who gave me a number for some guy who had a job he wanted done. I called him and he tells me he'll pay twenty five grand to take care of a problem for him. Me and my brother were suppose to whack some guy name Quinn and another guy named Traffarro. Johnny don't mind if we do a job out of town if it don't mess with his business."

"Yeah, well listen smart ass. You just fuckin' messed with Mr. Massarro's business!"

"How the fuck was I supposed to know?"

"You stupid prick...ya shoulda gone to Johnny and got the okay."

"Yeah...well...maybe you're right. I promise I will next time," in an apologetic tone.

"Next time...next time!" Brufalo hollered. "What the fuck make you think you're gonna be alive for a next time you stupid shit?"

"Come on guys, give me a break." The man was looking up at Big Nappi and his boys with his arms stretched out pleading. The men just stood there and looked at each other.

"Listen stupid. You're gonna tell me everything you know and God help you if you leave out anything."

"Yeah...Okay...Just...just don't kill me...Please?"

After about fifteen minutes of conversation with the occasional slap across the face, Brufalo was sure he got all he was going to get out of the guy. He walked a short distance away to call Massarro.

"I'm sorry to bother you at this hour Boss, but I knew you'd want to hear the news,"

"That's okay, Nappi," Massarro replied. "Tell me what you found out. I assume you found the people who did this?"

"We found one of the guys, Boss. It was some guy named Dino Maretti."

"Tino Drazzetti?"

"No boss. Dino Maretti," Brufalo replied. "Shit boss, if it was Tino, they'd all be dead and they still wouldn't have found all the pieces. It was this guy Maretti and his brother out of Cleveland who took the contract. Angelo and Tony brought him to the warehouse and we persuaded him to tell us who was with him and who hired them. Theses idiots sometimes work for Johnny Lupo."

"Lupo! He told me he didn't know anything about this."

"He might not have," Brufalo said. "Maretti and his brother aren't made guys. I don't even think they're regulars in any crew of Johnny's. They're just low life wanna be's. They probably took the contract as a normal piece of business. I think they shoulda known who Traffarro was...but Quinn...eh, not so much. He shoulda asked before he tried to whack him, but Anthony's not close to the family and maybe they thought it was okay."

"You know who called these idiots?"

"Pete Mastro."

"Mastro?" Massarro said in disbelief. "This doesn't sound like something that Pete would ever get involved in. Are you sure?"

"Boss, I dropped my bag in this asshole's lap and shoved his fuckin' face in it and told him what I was gonna do. Christ boss, he started to cry and pissed his pants. No way is this fuckin' mook's lyin'. All this prick said was that Pete called and gave him a number to call and that the other guy would pay him?"

"He collect yet?"

"Oh yeah, half up front, but he said he just went to his mailbox in the morning and a package was there with the money in it. He don't know who put it there. Boss, what do you want me to do with this asshole?"

"Let him go. I'll call Johnny Lupo and explain what happened and let him deal with it. He'll owe me for this and you never know when collecting on that will come in handy. I'm going to get in touch with Pete. This must have been someone very special for Pete to do something as stupid as this," Massarro said as he hung up the phone.

"Angelo! Give our friend here a good-bye kiss and let's get out of here."

Angelo looked down at Maretti and smiled. He swung his right arm back and punched Maretti as hard as he could on the left side of his face. The force of the blow knocked Maretti across the floor and rendered him unconscious. When Maretti finally woke up fifteen minutes later, he was alone...and very happy to be alive.

Rane came home from the hospital on Sunday. I brought her to the house and refused to allow her to do anything except sit and let me wait on her. What I hadn't realized was that Rane wasn't accustomed to just sitting around.

"Parker, I've got to go and take a shower," Rane said as she walked into the living room with her hands fluffing her hair. "The hospital really screwed up my hair. I look like a Chia Pet gone bad. In about fifteen minutes, would you make me a nice cup of tea? I would really appreciate it. The stuff they serve in the hospital is like dishwater. Yyaacckk," she said in disgust as she reflected back on the hospital's food.

Twenty minutes later, Rane came down stairs looking her usual radiant self, except for a small disruption in her hair were the doctors had to shave her before stitching up the scalp wound. "Oh, thanks honey." Rane reached for the cup of tea that I had made. "I almost feel like a human being again. It'll be good to get back to work next week. I feel like I've been gone a year." She blew gently across the tea before she took a sip.

"Look, Rane," I said slowly as I searched for the right words while I paced the floor. "I'm really sorry for what happened."

"It's not your fault," she replied, placing the cup down on the table. "It's not like you put an ad in the paper saying 'Please Shoot Me'."

"No, that's true," I replied as a thousand phrases swirled through my head. "Rane, there's no easy way to say this except you can't go back to work next week."

"Bullshit!" Rane said emphatically. "Why not? I'm not going to let some two-bit asshole gangster run my life."

"Well, it's not exactly like that. First of all, the two-bit asshole gangster I think you're referring to didn't do it. In fact, he's got men out as we speak looking for the people who did. They know who negotiated the contract and they're trying to locate him to find out who put up the money. The word is out on the street that we're not to be touched. That doesn't necessarily mean the person behind this is going to stop trying to kill me. It's just going to be harder for them to hire someone for the job and until I testify or the person is caught or killed, neither you nor I are safe. That's why, if you look out the window, you'll see a patrol car parked across the street. The mob's doing what they can to protect us on the streets and the police are watching the house. The Federal Prosecutor has already contacted the bank and they've agreed to let you take as much time off as necessary to clean up this business. Oh, I almost forgot, you get full pay and it doesn't go against your sick time or vacation."

"I don't care. I've got clients and I don't need someone else at the bank trying to take them from me."

"The one thing I can guarantee is that no one at the bank will take your clients."

"Oh, really," Rane said in a cynical tone. "And how my I ask, can *you* guarantee that?"

"Because, my beautiful intended, the Union uses your bank as its primary bank. They run millions through it each year. They fuck around with you and the Union will pull the accounts."

"Oh," Rane said. She sat back down on the couch and thought about the situation. There was no doubt that she still wasn't happy with the position she was in, but there didn't seem to be much she could do. "Parker, how are you holding up through all this? Everybody's been so kind to me and asking how I'm doing, but I'm worried about you."

"Well," I said, shifting nervously in my chair. I'm not the best when it comes to expressing my feelings. "I think I'm more surprised than anything else. Not that I'm totally surprised that somebody's trying to kill me. I do know that I'm worried about you. When I saw you lying there in the hospital, I was very afraid I might lose you and that, my love, would kill me."

"I feel the same way," she said as she leaned forward. "I feel like I'm in a movie. I get nervous when the killer is stalking the victim through the house, but I know it's not real. When I think about it, I'm more nervous waiting for the movie killer to jump out of the shadows than I am now. As bad as all this has been, I think it's made me realize just how right you and I are together."

I sat there and looked at Rane. *God, she's beautiful*, I thought. She was looking longingly at me when I raised my eyebrows and slowly rolled my eyes. "You up for a little—you know?"

A smile slowly crept across her face. "You are *such* a dog. Let's go," she said, jumping from the couch.

Chapter Sixteen
Johnny Lupo Sends His Apologies

Rane had the police take her back to her apartment to pick up whatever she needed for an extended stay. That turned out to be the highlight of our stay so far. After three days of being house bound, Rane and I were feeling a little stir crazy. It wasn't so much that we had so many places we wanted to go as it was that we felt like prisoners. I was getting particularly antsy. I did whatever business I could on the phone, but seeing the same four walls day and night was getting under my skin.

"Honey, it's hump night," I declared. "I don't give a shit what anyone says, we're going out tonight. Let's go to Salvatore's and have a nice dinner so we can feel like human beings again. I've got two more days before I testify and we need to get out. Hopefully, we'll see somebody down there we know and we can have a few laughs."

"You've got my vote," Rane replied enthusiastically as she jumped to her feet. "Let me go make myself presentable and we'll leave."

As I drove out of the driveway, the light on the patrol car started to flash. I pulled up alongside and explained where we were going. The officers in the patrol car protested vehemently, but to no avail. I had my mind made up and short of putting us in jail, we were going out.

When we arrived at Salvatore's, the parking lot was nearly full. I pulled around to the back and parked near some large bushes at the edge of the lot. Just being out and moving around made us both feel as if we were going to a New Year's Eve party. I looked around the parking lot before we started towards the restaurant. It was dark, but I was comfortable that no one was in the lot. I noticed the patrol car faithfully parked across the street.

We came in through the back door and immediately saw some familiar faces. It felt good to be back in circulation even if it was only for one night. I started to feel there was no monetary benefit that I could derive from my association with the Union that could compensate for what Rane and I had gone through. This wasn't something either of us would ever forget.

"Hey, Quinn," Carmine said from behind the bar. "It's good to see you two out and about again. Anthony and Connie are around the corner."

"Thanks, Carmine. Is Junior in tonight?"

"No. He's comin' in later."

We walked into the dining room and found Anthony and Connie seated at Anthony's usual table. It was nice to see a friendly face after being stuck in the house.

"Hey, look who's here," Anthony said with enthusiasm, getting up from his chair. "How you two doin'? I thought you were under arrest or some bullshit like that. I didn't expect to see either of you until after you testified."

"We couldn't take it any longer," Rane said. She bent over and gave Connie a hug. "Another couple of days being cooped up like we were and we'd have been at each other's throats. We had to get out and see how normal people live."

"Well, I don't know how normal *we* are, but it's good to see you," Traffarro said, standing up and giving Rane a kiss on the cheek. "How you feeling Rane? Come on and sit down."

"I'm fine. Did you hear anything more about who tried to kill us?"

"No, not really. It's not like these guys call on a regular basis and report in, but don't worry though. They'll get the bastards. You could say it falls into their normal line of work."

Traffarro and his wife had already started to eat, but insisted that we join them. Everyone had a good time talking about the events of the past week. It was strange that such a traumatic event could actually contain some moments that we all thought were funny. After the coffee was brought out, Carmine came up and tapped Quinn on his shoulder.

"Quinn, could I borrow your car for ten minutes," Carmine said. "I swear I'll have it back before you know it. I need to run over to the pharmacy and pick up a prescription for my wife. She and I are back together and she asked me to pick the prescription up this afternoon, but I forgot and now she's got the car."

"Carmine, so help me, if Junior finds out I lent you my car, he's going to kill both of us,"

"He won't," Carmine said. "He's not gonna be back for another hour and I swear I'll be right back."

I reached into my pocket and pulled out the keys. Traffarro shot an icy stare at Carmine as he took my keys.

"You're too fuckin' soft, Quinn," Anthony said, watching Carmine hurry out the back door. "Junior's right. You keep helpin' these idiots and they'll never leave you alone."

"Yeah, I know," I replied with embarrassing resignation.

The waiter came by and asked if they'd like another cup of coffee. Before I could respond, I jumped out of my seat and grabbed Rane dragging her to the floor. It was almost as if I had anticipated the massive explosion that rocked the building. Tables in the dining room were lying on their side and customers lying on the floor or hiding under the remaining upright tables. I looked across the dining room and saw the back door of the restaurant lying in the middle of the dining room with smoke rising from it. It wasn't until a few moments later, that I realized that I *had* felt the concussion of the blast and *had* heard the bottles and glasses in the bar come crashing down from their shelves. It just seemed so unreal. One minute we were having a nice conversation and the next we were in a war zone. What the hell happened?

People started to get up and look around to see if anyone was hurt. We were all in a daze. The two police officers that followed me to the restaurant bolted through the front door with looks of total disbelief at the sight that greeted them. The force of the blast was so great they weren't sure if it came from inside or outside the building.

"Is everyone all right?" one of the cops shouted moving hurriedly from one person to the next. Everyone looked around to see once again if anyone had been hurt. Responses came from all over the dining room. Although a few of the women were crying, no one appeared to have been hurt.

"Parker, what the hell was that?" Rane said as I helped her off the floor.

I turned to Traffarro and we just stared at each other for a few seconds.

"Carmine!" I said. "He just went out to my car."

One of the officers came over to our table while the other checked the other customers.

"You folks all right?" he asked with a voice that sounded as if he dreaded the answer he might hear. "Mr. Quinn, Miss Harold, are you two okay?"

"We're fine," I said quickly, waving my hand to motion the cop away. "Go out back and see what's happened."

When he returned, the look on his face told the story before he could say a word. "Christ! Your car is a burning pile of shit and the two cars next to you are gone, too. The God damned back of the building is on fire. My partner radioed the fire department. I want you two to stay right here until I call the FBI."

As he turned and walked away he shouted "Son of a bitch!" Traffarro turned to me and told me that he was going to take Connie home. He didn't want to be around when the Feds got there. If there was one thing that Traffarro hated to do, it was talking to the Feds. It was their nasty habit of making you feel guilty even when you were the victim.

This was one call this cop didn't want to make. "Central...patch me through to Bill Douglas at the FBI." It was a few minutes later that Douglas was on the radio.

"What!" Douglas screamed. "What the fuck were you thinking...I don't give a shit what he wanted...Hell no. You keep them both right where they are. I'll be there in a few minutes."

I grabbed Rane by the arm and brought her over to the bar. I went behind the bar and searched for two unbroken glasses and a bottle of bourbon. Rane picked up one of the barstools from the floor and sat down as I poured us each a heavy drink.

"I told you, your life would be interesting if you married me," I said. "You still want to go through with it."

Rane took a long drink from the glass and said, "You're not getting off that easy mister. Besides, things are starting to look up. At least, I didn't get shot in the head this time."

"I'm serious, Rane," I said, putting my hand on top of hers. "I love you very much, but my life is like this. Weird shit seems to happen. I just want to be sure you know what you're getting into."

Rane just looked at me. She picked up her drink and finished it. "Parker, shut up and pour me another one."

I poured us another drink and then went to the back door to see the carnage the explosion had caused. The fire department was pouring water on the burning wreckage and the back of the restaurant. I had to jump back as one of the hoses came close to the door and the spray hit me in the face. My car wasn't even recognizable. You could tell it had been a car at one point in time by the few remaining parts that hadn't been total distorted by the blast, but forget about what kind it might have been. The cars on either side hadn't fared much better. The sight before me was so incredible that I couldn't believe I was in any way connected to it. It happens in movies or you read about it in the newspaper. 'Car Bomb Kills Four in Lebanon'. This crap happens to other people not me. As I was standing there in my own little world, I felt a hand on my shoulder. It was Junior. We both stood silently for a minute looking at the destruction in the back of the restaurant.

"I'm sorry for Carmine," Junior said in a sad voice. "But for once I'm glad you didn't listen to me. You sorry son of a bitch, that could have been you."

"Yeah, I know. I'm getting real tired of this shit, Junior."

"Quinn!" a voice shouted behind them. We both turned to see Bill Douglas charging through the restaurant.

"Oh, crap," we both said in unison. Junior started to leave me and head for the kitchen. "First you blow the fuckin' place up and now these assholes. I'm gonna have to start charging you double if you wanna keep comin' in here, Quinn. I love you, but you're a real pain in the ass."

"What the hell were you thinking, Quinn?" Douglas said as he made his way toward me. "Did you think we had those cops there watching you because they needed something to do?"

I really wasn't in the mood to listen to Douglas chewing me out about leaving the house.

"Hello, Bill," I said calmly, forcing a smile on my face. "Whatever you've got to say, I don't want to hear it."

"Frankly, I don't give a shit because you're going to hear it anyway," Douglas said as he poked his index finger into my chest. "You almost got yourself and your lady friend killed ... *again!* Do you think this is some kind of a game? Somebody is trying very hard to keep you from testifying and I want you to hear me loud and clear. They probably aren't done. You keep running around the city like this and sooner or later they're gonna be successful."

"I hear you. I hear you." I hated to be chastised like a five-year-old and if Douglas didn't stop poking his finger into my chest, I was going to beat him senseless.

"I spoke to Norris. You and Miss Harold are going to a hotel were you will stay in the room with a guard at the door until you go before the Grand Jury. Don't even think about stepping outside that room or so help me God I'll shoot you myself."

"Fine," I said. "But, first we go back to my place and get some things. I'm *not* spending two days in a hotel with Rane without her having comfortable clothes and her stuff...You know...her woman's necessities."

"No." Douglas said in a very strong tone. "We go to the hotel and I'll send someone back for whatever you people need."

"Yeah, right," I said with a sarcastic laugh. "That's just what she wants, one of your guys rootin' through her personal stuff. I'm not asking you, Bill. I'm telling you. Just do it my way. *Please.*

"You know, Quinn? You're a real pain in the ass," Douglas said, pointing his finger at Quinn.

"Yeah, I've been hearing that a lot lately," I said flatly as I turned toward Rane and walked away. "Come on honey. We've got to go back to my place so we can pick up a few things. We're going to be the guests of the Government at a nice hotel. Room service! Pay-per view! Champagne! Oh, my!" I said in his best imitation of the Wizard of Oz.

Douglas drove us back to the house. Although no one wanted to admit it, the past week had taken its toll. When we got to the house we all went inside and went upstairs to gather our essentials. Douglas just stood there with his arms folded across his chest like a scoutmaster watching his troop. When the suitcase was packed, we headed down stairs.

"Let me go and check the mail," I said as he opened the front door.

"Are you out of your fucking mind. I'm not letting you walk out to the curb to get the mail, Quinn," Douglas said as he grabbed me by the shoulder. "You amaze me. Why don't you paint a big target on your back and walk up and down Main Street?"

"There's a box is right outside the door," I replied, extending his left arm and pointing to the door with his hand.

"Good. You stay here and I'll get it," Douglas said as he walked passed me to the front door. "Here. You also had a package inside the storm door for Miss Harold." Douglas just handed the mail and the package to me and walked toward the kitchen, hoping we were leaving soon.

"Rane?" I asked. "Did you order anything through the mail?"

"Yeah." Rane said. "I had a prescription filled. I had them send it here since I've been here more that at my place. Let me see it." I handed her the small box. "I don't know why they sent it in a box," she said. "They usually put it in one of those padded envelopes."

Before I could say anything, Rane had the box opened. "Oh, shit!" she cried, handing the box to me.

I looked at the contents of the box and said, "Fuck me!" It must be male instinct, but I couldn't help bringing his hand down to my crotch. Unfortunately, there wasn't much comfort even after my hand gave me physical confirmation that all the vital parts were still in place.

"What the hell's going on now," Douglas said as he came back from the kitchen.

I held the box out so Douglas could see the contents. Inside were two sets of male genitals tied together with a pink bow. They all stood there and just looked.

"What the Christ does this mean?" Douglas said.

"I think it means these two sorry pricks weren't the ones who tried to blow us up." I said. I knew exactly what this meant and so did Rane. I sure as hell couldn't give all the details to Douglas without making it look like I was cozy with the mob.

"Who the hell sent this to you?" Douglas demanded.

"How the hell should I know?" I said putting on my most surprised voice. Traffarro said he'd like to give Rane the shooters balls in a box and here they were. "I'm guessing somebody wants to make it very clear the attack on Rane and I wasn't a mob hit. This does look like something the mob would do, doesn't it Bill?" I continued to put on a show of complete naiveté.

"Yeah, I guess. Give me that. We'll need it for evidence," Douglas said, reaching his hand out to me. "You keep dangerous company, Quinn."

I reached down and picked up their suitcase, hoping to end Douglas's questions. However, it didn't stop my mind from formulating a few of my own questions. It was fairly obvious that the men who tried to kill me were dead. Who the hell had so many people available they could lose two and still have more to bomb my car? The horrific message in the box was sent to make a clear point. They wanted us to know that it wasn't the mob that was responsible for the murder attempts. There was no way they'd be sending us something like this if they were the ones trying to kill us. Could Costa reach out to that many people to keep this up? If the bomb wasn't in the car when we left for Salvatore's, then how did they know where we would be?

Rane and I made ourselves comfortable in our new home at the hotel. It had been a long evening and we were both tired, but sleep didn't come quickly. Our present location served as a constant reminder of the danger that we were in. After Rane unpacked our clothes, we found ourselves lying on the bed staring at the ceiling.

"When does this end, Parker?"

"Honestly, I don't know," I replied as my mind reached for the answer. "Obviously, when and if they find who's behind this. Possibly, after I testify on Friday. If Norris's case is very strong, it might be that everyone just plea bargains and it all ends. If on the other hand it goes to trial, I'll have to testify at the trial. I'm not sure though whether my Grand Jury testimony could be used at trial if I was dead. If it could, then I guess the Grand Jury would be the end. Bottomline, I haven't a clue."

"Remind me never to ask you a question that I don't want to hear the honest answer to," Rane said as she rolled over and laid her arm across my body. A moment later she moved her hand down to my crotch and gave a gentle squeeze.

"Yyyeeeessss," I said very slowly.

"Never mind," Rane said in a sleepy voice. "I was just checking."

Chapter Seventeen
Problem Solved

The next day seemed to be seventy-two hours long. There are only so many movies you can watch without ultimately becoming screaming bored, particularly when you have other things on your mind. It was like waiting in an airport for a delayed flight. It just drags. We had to fill the time with our limited entertainment choices to fight off the boredom. I was permitted to make out-going calls to check on my clients and the status of the office. I made one call to Nicky to see what was happening around the city. Nicky gave me some information that helped ease my mind a little.

"Quinn, I've been talking to Tino," Nicky said. "He thinks he can find out who's behind all of this. Tino said there aren't too many places somebody can get the type of explosives that blew up your car and Carmine. He's checking out the sources and should know in a day of two who this motherfucker is."

"Well, tell him to hurry up. By any alley cat's method of counting, I've only got seven lives left."

On the morning of the Grand Jury testimony, I was a little nervous. I wasn't worried that they would ask me a question that I *couldn't* answer, but I was worried that they might ask questions that I didn't *want* to answer. Rane's little gift box had achieved one of its desired goals and that was to make sure that I focused on the task at hand. The mob's point was clear.

Douglas arrived at 8:30 with three other agents for the five-minute ride to the Federal Building. My 'appointment' with the Grand Jury was set for 9:00 and the only people more obsessed with being on time than me was the FBI. They had a plan to get me to the Federal Building without getting me killed.

"We want you to wear this bullet proof vest over your suit," Douglas said as he handed me the vest. "There will be one agent on each side of you and one both front and back. We'll move as a pod to and from the car. Once you're in the building you'll be safe. We've cleared everyone off the floor so there wouldn't be any surprises. Do you understand what I've said?"

"Absolutely," I said, handing the vest back to Douglas. "You want me to wear a sign that in essence says 'Shoot This Fuckin'Guy' and 'Oh yeah, By The Way, Shoot Him in the Head'. Thanks, but no thanks. Here's how we'll play this. Bill you and I are about the same build. *You* wear the vest and as you walk, keep your face pointed toward the ground. Hopefully, that will be enough to hide your identity. I'll walk behind you with your sunglasses on. Some people seem to think I look like the FBI so why not use it to our advantage. If your plan works, than you shouldn't get shot. If it doesn't...well, then at least *I* won't."

"Thanks, Quinn," Douglas replied with a sarcastic tone. "I hate the plan but it does make some sense."

Rane sat on the edge of the bed listening to the discussion. She had to turn away and put her hand over her mouth to keep from laughing. It was clear to her that I was coming into my own in this new environment I had become even stronger in my handling of the situation and more comfortable in this perilous ordeal. She said she didn't think that I had ice water in my veins but she was sure that my blood ran pretty cool.

What could Douglas say? He put on the vest and they went out of the room in formation. It ultimately didn't make any difference because nothing happened. Shuffling my feet along as we moved in formation into the Federal Building, I felt like I was part of old time football's famous Flying Wedge. We hustled straight to the elevators and up to the sixth floor and the jury room. The halls were empty and I had to wait fifteen minutes, sitting on a solitary chair flanked by two of the Bureau's finest. Inside, Norris was preparing the Grand Jury for his prize witness.

The Grand Jury room was about as far removed from what a typical courtroom looked like as possible. The room was fairly large. Rizzelli had given me all the details about Grand Juries. The jury was composed of eighteen men and women seated in groups behind four tables along the far wall as you entered the room. Maybe the fact that you had to face thirty-six eyes as you entered the room was an effort by the Prosecutor to intimidate the witness. The Prosecutor and the assistant Prosecutor were seated at a long table at the left end of the room and the witness had the honor of sitting next to a small table just inside the doorway. Sitting behind another small table at the right end of the room was the court recorder. There were no seats for anyone else because no one else was permitted to be in the room. There is no judge to rule on the defense attorney's objections because the witness is not permitted to have an attorney present in the room. He can have an attorney outside the jury room, but basically the witness is on his own. That's exactly the way the prosecutor wants it. It's *his* show. The jury starts out with the belief that the Federal Prosecutor is a righteous man who wouldn't be trying to put these people in jail if they weren't guilty. The Prosecutor gets to chat with the Grand Jury members throughout the entire process, as if he were in one gigantic summation. He's the dealer in this game and all the cards are marked. If a Prosecutor can't get an indictment under these conditions, then he's either an idiot or the target of the investigation is actually innocent.

Norris was nearly salivating over the anticipation of having the Grand Jury hear my testimony. He had laid all the groundwork with pounds of documentary evidence and now they would get an opportunity to hear the story from someone near the center of the storm.

"Ladies and gentleman, you're about to hear sworn testimony from a man who was at the epicenter of these crimes. He is the branch manager of the office were Sammy Merzone conducted his business for over fourteen months. It was during this period that Sammy Merzone and several others told him about the schemes they used to funnel enormous amounts of money to Renato Costa. His testimony is so damning that two attempts have been made on his life. He is not a target of this investigation and we have no reason to believe that he took an active part in any crime."

Norris then motioned to the Court Recorder to bring me in. When I walked through the door every eye in the room was on me and I felt truly alone. Score one for Norris. I stood in front of my chair and was sworn in by the Recorder. I sat down at Norris's instruction and waited for him to begin.

"Mr. Quinn," Norris began. "Would you please state your full name and address and occupation for the record?" Then it really began.

"Mr. Quinn, how long did you know Sammy Merzone?"

"Mr. Quinn, what if anything did Mr. Merzone tell you about his relationship with Mr. Costa?"

"Mr. Quinn, did you ever see Mr. Merzone give any money to Mr. Costa?

"Mr. Quinn, explain what a New Issue is to the Jury.

"Mr. Quinn, how did you become aware of large numbers of these profitable transactions being directed by Mr. Merzone to Mr. Costa.

"Mr. Quinn, tell the Jury about the lunches and dinners that Mr. Merzone bought for Mr. Costa and his friends."

The Mr. Quinn, Mr. Quinn, Mr. Quinn, went on and on for nearly four hours. Norris had more questions than I thought I had ever heard asked in my entire life. I had to give this bastard credit, he was thorough. I was amazed at the amount of information Norris had. It made me uncomfortable to know the extent to which the Government was willing to go to gather evidence on a suspect. The power of unlimited resources was being demonstrated before my eyes and it made me nervous. God forbid I would ever be in Costa's situation.

It was nearly one o'clock before Norris stopped for lunch. He was on a roll and he didn't want to quit, but he could see the jurors starting to squirm in their seats. They were told that lunch would be brought in and they would have forty-five minutes before Norris started again. I was permitted to eat in the hall from the same menu the jurors had. I wouldn't be alone. The two agents assigned to guard me stood there and watched me eat. I felt like jumping from my chair and beating the two of them to death. It's like having somebody watching you while you're trying to go to the bathroom.

"Don't you two have a magazine or something you can read? I feel like a fucking science experiment here. You're actually starting to affect my digestion."

There was no response. I thought this must be some kind of FBI revenge thing for making Douglas wear the bulletproof vest. I kept trying to think of some inane thing that I could ask these two assholes to do. Although some ridiculous things came to mind, I figured I was better off leaving things alone.

The afternoon session started as if Norris had taken a forty-five minute break in the middle of a sentence. He never missed a beat. While Norris was in the middle of a question, I drifted off with the thought of being paid a whole fifty dollars for my appearance in court. This was to offset my lost wages. I wondered when they came up with that figure.

"Mr. Quinn, did you hear what I said," Norris said as I snapped back to reality.

"I'm sorry, Mr. Norris. Could you repeat the question," I replied as I gathered myself together and tried to pay attention to Norris's droning delivery.

Ninety minutes later, Norris was through and it was the members of the jury's turn to ask questions. This surprised me. I had seen a lot of trials on TV and never once did the Prosecutor turn to the jury and ask them if they would like to ask any questions. I was starting to get irritated. I had been at this forever and now the jury gets to play lawyer? *What kind of bullshit was this*, I thought.

Two of the jurors asked some very good questions about the nature of my business and I was glad to give them as much information as they wanted. The next juror I figured must have been a professional wise ass. He started to ask me some questions of a more personal nature and after the third question; I just sat there and stared at him. I was visualizing jumping up on the table in front of this asshole and kicking him in the face. Thankfully, Norris interrupted my fantasy by instructing the juror that the question was out of bounds. Norris then asked the jury if they had any more questions of the witness and when he received no response, Norris released me.

"Mr. Quinn, the two agents outside will bring you home. Thank you for your testimony."

Thank God it's over, I thought. All I wanted to do was to go home and have a nice dinner with Rane. Being on your toes for an entire day, listening to every word and their meaning and intention is exhausting, particularly when the words are coming from a Federal Prosecutor like Kevin Norris. Move incorrectly in one direction and the Government tries to put you away. A wrong move in the other direction and somebody is lopping off some of your most cherished body parts. I felt good in spite of being tired. I had run the gauntlet and survived. Now maybe things could get back to normal. Whatever the hell that was.

Tino had been busy while I was waiting to testify. He checked with a number of suppliers and found that they all led him to one person, Myron Handelman. Handelman was a small time hustler who ran a pawnshop in the sleaziest part of the city. He was the man to go to for hard to find items that are normally associated with terrorists and the mob. Tino knew Handelman and he didn't like him. The 'No honor amongst thieves' phrase was probably created to warn people about Myron Handelman.

Tino opened the door to Handelman's store and walked down a cluttered aisle to the rear. Handelman came out from the back, but judiciously stayed behind the bars of the clerk's area. He was a puffy little man in his fifties. Handelman was one of those people that make your skin crawl and what to count your fingers when you shook his hand, just to be sure he hadn't stolen one.

"Myron," Tino said with false enthusiasm.

"Hello, Tino. What can I do for you?"

"I'm looking for information, Myron."

"I suggest you try the library, Tino. They have all kinds of information."

Tino just stood there for a moment and stared at Handelman and slowly ground his teeth together. "Some asshole tried to blow up a friend of mine behind Salvatore's Restaurant a few nights ago. I've asked around and everybody says that the rig that was used was a design that you specialize in, Myron. All I want to know is *who* you sold it to. Tell me and I'll walk out of here and leave you alone. I don't have a beef with you, Myron. This is your business and I don't have a problem with that."

"I don't know where you're getting your information from, Tino, but they're wrong," Handelman said, leafing nervously through the ledger pages. "Even if I sold this merchandise to whoever you're looking for, you know I can't tell you. It's not ethical."

"Myron," Tino said calmly as he reached his hand under the left side of his leather jacket and pulled out a silenced 9MM Beretta. "I'm gonna put a bullet in one of your fuckin' wings and then I'm gonna come around there and start carving on you like a fuckin' Thanksgiving turkey if you don't start telling me what I want to know. *Now tell me who bought the fucking merchandise!*" Tino shouted the last line with such sudden force that Handelman nearly fell over.

"Honestly, I don't know. Some guy came in here and paid me ten grand for the bomb. Ten grand, Tino! That was enough money that I didn't ask who he was." Handelman cried. He knew Tino and his reputation and had no doubt he meant every word he said.

"What the fuck did he look like, Myron. Tall. Short. Fat. Thin What!!

"I don't know. Average guy. Forty, maybe. Kinda well dressed. That's all I know, Tino. I swear."

"Myron, if I find out your lying...well, you know what that means."

"Yeah...I know"

I got back to the house late in the afternoon. The agents told me that Rane had been dropped off an hour earlier. I walked into the living room and gave her a kiss.

"How'd it go?" Rane asked, closing the book on her lap.

"Actually, it went pretty well. They asked me a thousand questions and much to my surprise I had an answer to all of them without giving them anything to indict *me* on." I went to the front window and looked out at the street. "I see we lost our protection. I hope that means they think we're safe now."

"Well, I'm going back to work Monday whether they like it or not," Rane said emphatically.

"I agree. So am I," I said as I collapsed in the recliner. "I've stayed away from my business long enough. I'll have to wear a sign around my neck so people will know who I am."

Two days passed before Rocco Massarro was able to speak to Pete Mastro. Massarro knew there was no way he could call Mastro on the phone because no one knew whose phones were tapped. What he needed to do was get to Mastro by surprise. It would have an impact on Mastro and there was less chance that the wrong people would be listening. He found his opportunity when Mastro was having lunch.

"Hello, Pete," Massarro said has he sat down. Big Nappi was standing right behind Massarro's chair.

Mastro, who had his head down reading the newspaper, jumped slightly. "Shit, Rocco! You scared the crap out of me."

"Peter, Peter, Peter. I always thought you were a smart man," Massarro said calmly.

Mastro knew immediately this was no social call. Men like Rocco Massarro don't just go out to find people to talk to. He decided to get right to the point. "How can I help you, Rocco?"

"You should stay with what you know Pete. You got a call from someone who asked you to do them a favor. They wanted to find a hitter and you gave Dino Maretti their phone number. That was a big mistake. Now...I called Johnny Lupo and told him what happened and that his people were making my life a living hell. I'm sure you know Pete, that I don't like problems. I told Johnny that since they worked for him, it was up to him to decide how to handle this.   Pete...Johnny was not very happy and as a gesture of good faith and peace between our families, he got rid of those two assholes and sent a present to Parker Quinn's girlfriend. Now Pete...I'm only going to ask you this one time and if you don't tell me the absolute truth, my dear friend behind me is going to escort you out side and do some very bad things to you. Do I make myself clear?"

"Perfectly," Mastro said with a long sigh.

"Who called you? Was it Renato Costa?

"No."

"Who then, you stupid son of a bitch!" Massarro said as he slammed his hand down on the table causing all the silverware to jump and clatter around. Everything in the restaurant came to a momentary halt.

"It was Ralph Merzone. Honestly, Rocco, I thought he was doing it for you."

"That's bullshit and you know it! You should have made some calls. No...the reason you did this isn't only because Ralph called you. You were going out with that woman that's with Quinn now, weren't you?" Massarro put his hand up as Mastro was about to speak. "Shut up, Pete. That's right. You thought you could get even with her for dumping you by getting rid of her boyfriend. This must have looked like a gift to you. I'm going to give you some good news, Pete. My friend and I are going to leave you alone. Oh, no...I'm going to leave you to Johnny," Massarro said as he got up.

When they got outside and back in the car, Brufalo turned toward Massarro in the back seat and said, "You want me to take care of Merzone, boss?"

"No. We're too close to this and I don't want anything to come back on us," Massarro said as he brought his fingers to his chin and looked thoughtfully out the car window. "We're making progress now that Quinn is on board and testifying. We can get rid of that pig Costa and his idiot friend Sammy Merzone. No, we need to get someone on the outside to take care of this." Massarro paused for a moment before he spoke. "You said you thought Tino Drazzetti was a friend of Quinn?"

"Yeah, boss. That was the feeling I got when Tino asked about the thing with Traffarro and Quinn."

"Good. I want you to get to Tino and tell him who was really behind all this. Don't tell him we want anything done. You're just giving him the information as a courtesy. That way, we won't be involved and it won't cost us anything. If I know that lunatic, he'll take care of Merzone for us."

It was 10:00 Saturday night when Ralph Merzone left the Blue Lounge bar. Try as he might, he couldn't find any peace of mind in a bottle. He had spent all day trying to think of what he should do. I had testified and he couldn't find a reason to try to kill me now other than revenge. Merzone figured he had gotten away with two attempts on me since no one had asked him a single question about any of it. The hit on Traffarro had been screwed up, but no one had traced anything back to him. He was thankful he was so careful in hiding his identity. It didn't make any difference how much he wanted to kill us now because he didn't want to risk being caught. He got into his car and tried to clear the fog the alcohol had caused to settle in his head. As he put the key into the ignition he sensed that he was not alone. Looking into the rear view mirror he saw the figure in the back seat. The form leaned forward and revealed it's self.

"Tino!" the startled Merzone said. "How the hell did you get in my car?"

"Car alarms aren't all they're cracked up to be, Ralph."

"What do you want?" Merzone asked nervously. He knew who Tino was and combined with what he had done started to make him tremble.

"I want to know why you tried to kill some friends of mine, you stupid piece of shit," Tino whispered softly into Merzone's ear.

"What are you talking about?" Merzone said, starting to turn his head toward the back seat. "You're crazy. Why would I try to kill anybody?"

"Good question," Tino said enthusiastically as he slapped the back of Merzone's head to keep him faced forward. "A little bird flew up to me yesterday and said you made a call to Pete Mastro. So please don't give me any crap that you don't know what I'm talking about.

"Tino please. I swear, it wasn't me."

"Ya know, Ralph," Tino said growing more irritated. "You're not smart enough to be a killer. So...why?"

"Tino, please. I've got a lot of money. I could make you a rich man."

"*I asked you why,*" Tino shouted. The force of the question caused Merzone to jump forward and raise his arms around his head to protect himself from being hit again.

"I didn't want it to all end," Merzone cried. "If Quinn didn't testify we might have had a chance to beat this. If I could have stopped him, then maybe Reno would have given me a piece of the business. I was sick of watching Sammy get all the action and all the time he's running his mouth about what he's doing with Reno. It was Sammy and his big mouth that ruined this for me. Traffarro was pushing Quinn to talk to the Feds. Traffarro was as guilty as Quinn. He wanted the old man's position in the Union and he got Quinn to talk to the Feds. I'm sorry Tino, but I had to do *something*. I promise I won't go near any of them again. I swear."

Tino slowly sat back in the seat and just stared at the back of Merzone's head. "I know," Tino said in a raspy whisper as he raised the Beretta and shot Merzone twice in the back of the head. "Fucking amateurs," He said with contempt, putting the Beretta back in its holster.

At 7:30 the next morning, Traffarro was having a cup of coffee and reading the newspaper at the Coffee Shop. He didn't pay any attention when the front door of the shop opened and hit the tiny bell that announced the comings and goings of the customers. A man strode quietly across the floor and stopped in front of Traffarro's table.

Traffarro slowly lowered his paper as he looked up and said calmly, " Hello, Tino."

"It was Ralph Merzone," Tino said. "It's been taken care of. Tell Quinn he can relax now."

Tino turned and walked out of the shop.

"Tino," Traffarro said and waited for Tino to turn around. "Thank you." Tino just raised one hand in casual acknowledgement and walked out the door.

Chapter Eighteen
Death and Betrayal

It wasn't too long before life returned to normal. Well, as normal as my life ever gets. But there was no doubt that life had been racing past us at ninety miles an hour. Rane vacated her apartment and moved in with me and we set a date to be married. The legal action started by Norris plodded along at the usual governmental pace. Ultimately, Renato Costa, Sammy Fontana, Vinny Maldanado, and several others were indicted by Norris. Douglas and Garcia took some much needed vacation time while Traffarro and Nicky quietly started to gather support for Traffarro's bid to take over after Costa went to jail. As you might expect, Massarro and Big Nappi turned their attention back to bribing politicians.

It was a nice period of peace and quiet. A trial date had been set for three months out. Business was good and Sammy hadn't been in the office since he was indicted. It was as if nothing had ever happened. I lazily reached across my desk and picked up the ringing phone.

"Quinn?" the voice said. "It's Anthony. Reno's dead."

"What?" I yelped. "What happened?" All of a sudden the memories of recent events came flooding back. My first thought was that someone had murdered Costa.

"It looks like a heart attack, but they won't know for sure until they do an autopsy."

"Jesus Christ! So what happens now?"

"I'll take over the Union until there's an election. I shouldn't have much trouble with that. I've been practically running it by myself for the past four years. I've made a lot of friends over the years and the old man was too busy fucking around to pay much attention to it. I expect the day after tomorrow they'll have the wake and probably bury him on Saturday. Whether you go to the wake or funeral is up to you."

"I doubt anyone will miss me if I'm not there," I said, shifting uncomfortably in my chair at the thought of seeing all of Costa's people at the funeral.

"Don't start feeling bad about what happened, Quinn," Traffarro said sensing my continued discomfort with testifying against Sammy and Costa. "Everyone except those assholes was behind you, and they still are. You made it possible for thousands of union member to get an even break. They'll never know what you did for them, but I do and I won't forget it."

I decided that going to the wake could cause a scene. There was no way I wanted to see Sammy and his crew. If they had their way, I'd be sharing the casket with Costa. I really didn't like Costa and hated what he stood for, so why be a hypocrite. Let the old man go to wherever he was headed in peace.

Norris wasn't surprised to hear that Costa had died. He was absolutely outraged! It was his obsession to put Costa in prison and now the old bastard had cheated him out of a victory. Norris actually sat and visualized the old man being led out of the court room, a broken man about to spend the rest of his life behind bars. He could feel the thrill of the victory and now it was ripped away. All he had left was Fontana and some bit players. He felt empty. How could a just God have denied him?

A week after Costa's death, Fontana's attorney started the negotiations with Norris on a plea bargain for his client. Norris almost didn't care. He put up a modest fight but settled for four years in Federal prison for Fontana. The others followed with similar sentences. It was over for them, but not for Norris. If he couldn't have Costa, he'd have the Union. He wanted to show that the Union was so filled with corruption it should be put under a Federal Trustee and that would effectively emasculate it. Cripple it bad enough, Norris thought and over time it will crumble under the weight of its ineffectiveness. All he would have to do was wait and keep the pressure on, Norris thought and sooner or later he'd have a victory. He wanted to ruin Costa, to crush him, but now, he'd settle for ruining the Union.

Traffarro was right in believing that he'd be elected. When the election was held, no one ran against him. One of the first things he did was to raise the retirement pay for the existing pensioners. It was something that hadn't been done in years and everyone applauded him for it. He successfully negotiated two major contracts by working closely with management. It meant solid gains for the members and although management signed the new contracts reluctantly, they were pleased with the new spirit of cooperation that Traffarro brought to the negotiations. As for me, I saw the amount of commissions coming to the firm plummet, but I understood that the old days were gone forever and was content to have at least some portion of the business. The one person that wasn't satisfied was Nicky Tagliano. He wanted Traffarro to appoint him as a trustee to the big pension fund and give him a preferred provider status for his dental business. With a pool of over forty thousand members it would guarantee that he could rapidly expand his business and make millions in the process.

Nicky had waited impatiently for Traffarro to give him what he wanted, but the irritation pushed him beyond the breaking point. He decided to go to Traffarro's office and settle the issue once and for all.

"Anthony," Nicky pleaded as he stood on front of Traffarro's desk. "I've been with you though all the bullshit. I brought you Quinn, helped get Connie a job, went with you all over the state to get support for the election. Through all of it, I was there. You got what you want now, for Christ's sake, give me what I deserve."

"You're crazy," Traffarro replied, jumping up from his chair. "The fucking Government is watching us so close I can't take a fucking crap without them knowing how many times I wiped my ass. If I give you preferred provider status they'll be crawling all over me. Then you want me to put you on the big fund. Who the fuck do I get rid of? Each one of the employer trustees has at least a thousand employees. You've got what...twenty-five? And you don't think fuckin' Norris is going to think that looks just a little suspicious. It doesn't make any difference if it's legal or not. What it looks like is irresponsible and that's all they need to bring in a Federal Trustee. When that happens you're out, I'm out, we're all out. I've got forty thousand members that finally stand a chance to have decent representation and you want me to piss all that away so you can open some more fucking stores?"

"No! I want you to do it because you fuckin' owe me."

"Look, Nicky," Traffarro said, letting out a big sigh and sitting back down in his chair in an attempt to try to calm things down. "I didn't say this would ever happen. You're the one who's come up with this idea. And yes, I feel like I owe you something and that's why I'm not saying it will never happen. I am saying it can't happen with the Feds breathing down my neck. All I'm asking you to do is be patient. Give it some time."

"Fine! When?"

"When?" Traffarro said in total exasperation. "How the fuck do I know when. When the Feds decide they don't want to tear this Union a new asshole. That's when!"

"You're fucking me, Anthony!" Nicky said as he pointed his finger at Traffarro. "You're fucking me just like you fucked Quinn."

"*Quinn*?" Traffarro said as the veins in his neck started to swell and turn a deep red. "Quinn nearly got killed...twice! How about you? Did I miss something? Did somebody shoot at you or try to blow your ass into the next century. I know...I must have missed it when someone put a shotgun to the back of your fucking head and tried to blow your brains all over a bar room wall. Quinn had to dance between Massarro and the Feds. Who the fuck did you have to dance with Nicky? Quinn wound up with a quarter of what he had and you know what? He's happy! He knows he could have lost all the business. Guess what? He hasn't come in here once and cried about how he got screwed."

"Fuck you, Anthony," Nicky shouted as he turned and stormed out of Traffarro's office.

Nicky had spent years cultivating his relationship with the Union and Traffarro. He always knew that Traffarro would be the man to take over after Costa was gone and he would be at the right hand of the new king. He would be the one people would have to come to get any favors. Nicky thought it was his time and he was due. He couldn't begin to understand why he should have to wait years to get what he wanted. Traffarro was living out his dream and there was no way he wanted to sit quietly on the side line waiting for Traffarro to get up the courage to give him what he deserved. After a few hours, Nicky decided to take a little trip with his newest girlfriend, Angie Cingerelli to get his mind off of Traffarro. A long weekend in Toronto would be just what the doctor ordered. The first thing he did when he arrived back in his office was to call Angie.

"Heyee, Angie," Nicky said in his most seductive voice. "How you doin'? I got a great idea. Why don't we spend a nice long weekend in Toronto? We could stay at the Hyatt, have some nice dinners, go to a show and maybe do some shopping for you. Ya know a nice new dress or two, maybe some jewelry, a little this a little that, bada-bing bada-boop. What da ya say? We'll drive up Friday morning."

"Sounds nice," She replied with a flirting laugh. "I'll call one of the girls at work and get someone to cover for me.

"Great! I'll pick you up around 10:30 on Friday morning," Nicky crooned into the phone. *Great*, he thought. *A nice piece of ass and a little trip out of this fucking city and I'll feel better. Maybe when I get back I'll sit down with Anthony and see how we can move things along.*

His next call was to his wife to tell her that he couldn't make his daughter's recital Friday night. Nicky knew exactly what to tell her. He had to drive to Toronto to close a deal on a new product line that would save him a fortune. The man was only going to be in Toronto Friday and Saturday before he flew back to Germany. He'd tell her how sorry he was and that he'd bring back something special for her and the kids. The business story always worked. *What could she say?* he thought. *I don't want your business to be successful so you can take care of the kids and me?*

It only took Nicky three hours to drive to Toronto and get a room at the Hyatt. A phone call later and he had tickets for a show Saturday night and an eight ball of cocaine and they all were cheerfully delivered to his hotel room.

Toronto is a beautiful city, somewhat like New York only clean and civilized. They left the hotel to walk around the city and do a little shopping. A couple of dresses and a beautiful watch later and Angie was floating in a sea of fairy tale dreams. The finishing touch was a dinner of coq au vin and a fine bottle of champagne with few lines of cocaine for dessert. Nicky knew that all the preparations were perfect and it was time to head back to the room for some late night activities.

Back in the room he poured them each a drink from the bar. He had no intention of drinking them but he wanted to make the anticipation last a few minutes longer. He placed the drinks on the table and unbuttoned his shirt. She stood up and slowly ran her fingers though the hair on his chest and gently kissed it. By this time, Angie was wound tighter than a two-dollar watch and would have made love to Ronald McDonald if he happened to stroll through the room. She stood back and unzipped her dress letting it fall to the floor. In Nicky's eyes, she was picture perfect. Angie had raven black hair, a very slender body, and small tight breasts that looked as if they had been formed in one of Madonna's metal stage bras. Angie stood there for a moment to let Nicky gaze at her body. All she had on were tiny black thong panties, her black stiletto heeled shoes, and a pair of thigh high nylons that clung to her silky legs like paint on a Picasso.

"Let's see what you have in here for me," she said with a coquettish smile as she undid his pants. "Ooohh! I must look *very* good to you." She grabbed him with her slender fingers as she slowly slid down to her knees.

Nicky didn't think about Traffarro much for two and a half days. Having all the cocaine, liquor, and sex he wanted, managed to keep him otherwise occupied. They packed up their things and started the drive back early Sunday morning. When they hit Customs at the border, the line was still short and they didn't expect any delays. The agent looked at Nicky's driver's license and asked the usual questions.

"How long have you been in Canada, Mr. Tagliano?" the agent asked politely, looking at the license and then back at Nicky.

"We came here Friday for some sightseeing," Nicky replied calmly.

"Do either of you have anything to declare?" the agent said as he handed the license back.

"No," Nicky said, flashing a big smile at the agent and putting his wallet back in his pocket.

"Please stay here for a moment. I'll be right back," the agent said, turning and walking to his booth. A few minutes later, the agent returned to Nicky's Corvette.

"Would you please back your car up and follow me. We'd like to conduct a random search of your vehicle, sir."

"What did we do wrong?" Nicky pleaded.

"Nothing, sir. This shouldn't take more than a few minutes. Please back the vehicle up and follow me."

Nicky backed the car up and crept along behind the agent to a covered area marked 'Inspection Area'. He was rapidly falling off the cliff of terror. When he put the rest of the cocaine in the glove compartment that morning, he never thought about being searched at the border. Now he thought his only hope would be if they just did a routine search of the luggage. His heart hit bottom when he saw the happy but determined German Shepherd emerge from the building tugging on his leash with anticipation. Angie and Nicky were instructed to take their luggage inside for inspection. Once inside the building, Nicky watched helplessly as the dog bounced into his car and almost immediately started to bark at the glove compartment. He knew it was pointless to run and lying about knowing that it was there was equally as hopeless.

"Would you like to tell me about this, Mr. Tagliano?" the agent said as he walked into the office holding the bag of cocaine in his extended hand.

"I know I'm not supposed to have that, but I swear to you I didn't buy it to sell to anyone," Nicky pleaded desperately.

"I'm sorry, Mr. Tagliano. You and the lady will have to wait here until the State Police arrive. You'll be taken to the police barracks and your car will be impounded. Transporting narcotics across the border into the United States is a major felony, Mr. Tagliano. You're looking at a lengthy jail sentence."

Nicky's head just fell forward as his entire world crashed around him. Everything he had accomplished throughout his life raced through his mind and the loss of all of it was more than he could bear. He and Angie waited for the police to arrive. Nicky told her he would take the blame for all of it and that she should say that she didn't know that it was in the car.

It was the middle of the afternoon when they arrived at the police barracks with their hands cuffed behind their backs. Angie had two bouts of sobbing on the way there. She was sure she'd be spending a long time in prison and the thought of coming out as an old woman with a record was tearing her up. What would her family think?

Nicky was put into a small room with a table and a chair on each side. He was told to wait for a detective from the Bureau of Criminal Investigation to arrive. Angie was put in another room to await the same fate. The twenty-minute wait seemed like days. Finally, a tall heavyset man in a suit came in and closed the door.

"Mr. Tagliano, my name is Lieutenant Michael Corrigan of the State BCI and you're in a world of shit my friend," the detective said as he sat down with a manila folder in his hand. "That's a sizable amount of cocaine you brought into the country. What were you planning to do with it?"

"I don't know. I guess I was planning to use it at some time in the future," Nicky replied, trying to get some moisture back in his mouth. He was so upset that it was almost impossible to speak. "I never had any intention of selling it or giving it to anyone. I swear."

"What about the lady? What's she got to do with this?"

"Nothing," Nicky said. "She didn't even know it was there."

"Smuggling cocaine into the country is a major Federal crime," the detective growled as he threw the folder down on the table. "You're looking at twenty-five years of Federal time my friend. You know what Federal time is? It means you don't get out in eight for good behavior like a State rap. You do the whole twenty-five and that's if you're lucky. The judge can give you life. Tell me Mr. Tagliano, how does spending the rest of your life in prison sound?"

The thought was beyond his comprehension. He couldn't imagine spending *any* time in prison much less the rest of his life. The word 'Federal' kept playing in his mind. He had seen the Feds work on the Union. Then it came to him.

"Look, I can give you something big if you get me out of this," Nicky said with as much enthusiasm as he could muster under the circumstances. "I can give you the head of a major labor Union and all the people involved with bribery and extortion. All you have to do is call the Federal Prosecutor. His name is Kevin Norris. He knows who I am and that I'm close to the Union and what's going on there. He'll tell you I can be a very valuable witness. But, you've got to cut me a deal."

'If you're wasting my time," the detective said as he pointed his finger at Nicky. "I'll make it my mission in life to see that you do time in the shittiest hole the judge can find. Now, what was this prosecutors name again and where is he?"

"Kevin Norris. He's the Federal Prosecutor for the Central District. I swear, I'm telling you the truth."

The detective grabbed the file off the table as he stood up and leered at Nicky before he left the room. He had one of the clerks look up Norris's phone number and sat down to give him a call. He didn't approach the call with much feeling. This wasn't the first time that some asshole sent him on a wild goose chase.

"Mr. Norris?" he said flatly. "This is Detective Michael Corrigan of the State BCI. We caught a Nicky Tagliano transporting cocaine across the Canadian border. He says he knows you and that he's willing to testify to the fact that some big Union official is guilty of bribery and extortion. He's looking to cut a deal. Does this ring any bells for you?"

"Oh, yeah," Norris said with a mix of curiosity and delight. "Where is he now?"

"I've got him locked in one of our interrogation rooms here in the police barracks about twenty miles south of the border. You want this guy?"

"Oh, I most certainly do, Detective," Norris felt like he'd been redeemed. Maybe God didn't hate him after all. What were the odds that Tagliano would be stupid enough to run drugs across the border and get caught? The border was as about as tight as a sieve and it had to be a stroke of providence that Tagliano would get caught in a random check. "If I get you the paper work to you immediately, when can you get Tagliano down here to the Federal Building?"

"Tomorrow morning, if everything's in order. What about the woman?"

"His wife?" Norris asked in a complete surprise.

"No. I'd say it was a girlfriend," Corrigan said as he opened the file. "It's one Angelina Cingerelli. She says she didn't know the drugs were in the vehicle and Tagliano corroborated her statement. Frankly, I think they're both lying through their teeth."

"I don't give a shit about her," Norris said in an irritated voice. "If you've got something on her, do whatever you want. If not, let her go. What I want is Tagliano and I want him as soon as you can get him here."

Nicky and Angie spent the night in jail and the next morning, after the paperwork cleared, they were put in an unmarked car for the drive back to the city. Corrigan felt he had enough on his plate and didn't really want to pursue her prosecution. He let her go with a strong lecture about the value of choosing her friends more wisely. Nicky's Corvette stayed impounded awaiting disposition.

Nicky walked into Norris's office feeling that he had a chance to get out of this without any jail time. *Fuck Traffarro*, he thought. *What had he ever done for him?* He figured he'd show Traffarro what it meant to fail to honor one's obligations. Once Norris signed the document releasing Nicky into his custody, Nicky finally got out of his handcuffs. Norris went behind his desk and pointed to a chair and told Nicky to sit down. Douglas and Garcia came into Norris's office and stood on either side of Nicky. Their standard play was to intimidate first and ask questions later.

"These two gentlemen are Special Agent Bill Douglas from the FBI and Agent Felix Garcia from Treasury. Well, Mr. Tagliano," Norris said in a very self-satisfied manner. "It looks like you've gotten yourself into quite a bit of trouble and you want me to get you out of it in exchange for what?"

"I can give you Anthony Traffarro and Parker Quinn," Nicky replied with pride. "I'll give you the payoffs, the bribes, the New Issue game, and anything else you want. They're running the same game as Costa and Merzone. But I want immunity from this drug thing."

"I can do that, Mr. Tagliano, but...it all depends on what you can give me and how much you cooperate with the investigation."

Norris proceeded to grill Nicky for more than two hours. It was easy for Nicky. All he had to do was remember how Costa and Merzone had worked their deal and substitute Traffarro and Quinn as the characters. He simply took the basic scenario and changed the times and places to fit the current players. None of it was true, but it didn't matter to Nicky. He was dedicated to getting his ass out of this mess and he would say or do anything. He even threw in Rane for good measure by telling a story about a phony bank loan scam they were developing to steal millions from the bank. He put his heart and soul into his story and had Norris literally sitting on the edge of his chair. Norris could taste blood and he was getting feverish at the anticipation of a real victory. Douglas and Garcia just stood back and listened with amused smiles on their faces.

"Okay, Mr. Tagliano," Norris finally said. "I'll get you out of your drug charge, but you'll have to testify under oath about what you just told me and you'll have to cooperate in *anyway* we deem necessary to make this case. Is that understood? You fuck up once my friend and so help me God; I'll personally put you away for the rest of our miserable fucking life. Is that clear?"

"Yeah, sure...I understand," Nicky said with as sigh of relief. If Norris wanted him to walk naked down Main Street, he would.

"I want you to go home and make up some story about where you've been. I'm sure that shouldn't be too hard for a man like you," Norris said sarcastically. "You don't tell anyone about our conversation. If anyone finds out about the drug bust you tell 'em it was all a misunderstanding and nobody charged you with anything. Is that clear?"

"Absolutely! I promise you, you won't regret this."

"Bullshit!" Norris shouted, jumping up from his chair. "I already regret it. What makes you think I like dealing with people like you. Every time I talk to one of you people, I have to take a shower to get the smell off. Now get the fuck out of my office and do what I told you."

Norris was right about one thing, it wouldn't take long for Nicky's drug bust to circulate around the Eastside. He might have been the Pavarotti of liars to his wife and friends, but Angie was a rank amateur. She'd been scared to death and when she had to explain her unexpected absence to her friends, she told them everything in abundant detail. Nicky was history as far as she was concerned. He might have been a gentleman in trying to save her, but he was an idiot for getting caught. This had been one experience she never wanted to revisit.

Traffarro couldn't believe the news when he heard it. How could Nicky possibly be that stupid? He wanted to help him get onto the board of trustees and to get his preferred provider status but that would take time. Now, Nicky had killed any possibility it would ever happen. Even if no charges were filed, the appearance of what had happened would never pass the Governments scrutiny. *What the fuck was he thinking*, Traffarro thought? He's got a family and he takes some broad to Canada for the weekend. If his wife bought into this, they deserved each other.

It was a quiet Wednesday and I hadn't gone out to lunch in over a week. Junior had closed the restaurant for a week after the bombing and I hadn't stopped by yet to see Junior's 'new look'. It was as good a reason as any to go to Salvatore's and see what the place looked like now. I was hoping Junior wasn't still angry with me for nearly causing his restaurant to burn down. When I arrived at the restaurant, I couldn't believe my eyes. Junior always did a good lunch business, but this saw was incredible. There were cars everywhere and I actually had to park half a block away. I walked in through the front door, which was something I hadn't done since the first time I came in. I made my way through the small crowd at the entrance and was stopped by—*a maitre-de*? Give me a break! What the hell had happened?

"Excuse me sir," the maitre-de said. "Do you have a reservation?"

"I just came by to see Junior," I replied with a bit of irritation. This used to be a great place to come, great food, good service, and of course verbal battles with Junior. Now it had become—what? *Trendy?*

"I'm terribly sorry sir, but Mr. Traffarro is presently occupied in the Cocktail Lounge," the maitre-de said with manners more polite than ever existed in this place.

"*Cocktail Lounge?*" I blurted out in amazement. "Yeah, right. Excuse me," I said as I pushed my way past the man. As I approached the bar, I saw Junior standing and talking to a couple seated at the bar—*in a suit?* I just stood there for a minute and tried to absorb what I was seeing. I would have taken any bet offered that I would ever see Junior Traffarro in a suit.

"Mr. Traffarro, I presume?" I said sarcastically, tapping junior on the shoulder.

"Quinn!" Junior exclaimed with a big smile on his face. "How good of you to stop by" Junior said in his best, though ridiculous English accent. "Please step over here. We must chat." He grabbed my arm and moved me to a vacant corner of the 'Cocktail Lounge'.

"Well," said I dryly. "I guess it's fair to say that you're not pissed at me any more for blowing up your restaurant."

"Pissed? How the fuck could I be pissed at the man who helped make me a fortune? Look at this place. I got more insurance money than I fuckin' hoped for. I painted the joint inside and out, got new tables and look—*new tablecloths!* Look at the new bar stools. *Real leather*! I got Ma in the kitchen with *three* assistants. She's so fuckin' busy she don't have time to piss me off. Ya gotta have reservations for lunch *and* dinner. The place is packed 'til ten at night. I'm makin' so much fuckin' money I can't hide it all. And—I have you to thank. Who would have fuckin' thought?"

"Yeah," I said flatly. "Who would've fuckin' thought? The renovations actually made this big a difference?"

"Oh fuck no." Junior said in a dismissive fashion. "The place is now a landmark. This is the place were "*the man was blown up*," Junior said as he held up his hands and made mock quotation marks with his fingers. "It's hotter than my ex-wife's wedding ring. We got real class now."

"I suppose this means I can't get a table for lunch?"

"Please! I'll just throw a couple of these fuckin' bums out. You can sit down whenever you want. Excuse me, Quinn. I think I see the mayor."

I decided to have a beer at the bar before I sat down. I saw a few of my wealthier clients sitting there waiting for a table. This place had come a long way since I first walked in and guys were diving out the windows thinking I was FBI. Now it was so upscale, even the Bureau couldn't get in without a reservation. I walked over to say hello to the clients. I was amused when I heard the woman say that she heard that the food was brought in from Italy. After a few minutes of conversation, I decided that I couldn't take much more of the continual adoration of Salvatore's. These people wouldn't have been caught dead in this place before it became the 'in place' to be. Junior found me a table within a few minutes and I was looking forward to a nice quiet lunch.

"Quinn," Junior said as he approached the table. "I forgot to ask you, if you heard about Nicky?"

"I know I haven't seen him in a while. What happened?"

"He got busted carrying coke across the border."

"What?" I said in a voice that jumped two octaves. "Where is he, in jail?"

"No, he's walking around like nothing happened. I don't know what's up, but I don't like what I'm seeing."

Bill Douglas's life was back to the hell he had gone through with Norris while he was investigating Costa and Merzone. Norris was hounding him to produce evidence to support Nicky's allegations. If he couldn't come up with some kind of hard documentation, he wouldn't be able to make his case and he swore he wouldn't be cheated out of his victory again. Breaking this Union was all he lived for and his obsession ran deeper than ever. He was pounding on Douglas daily to get something and he wasn't very particular about how. Finally, Douglas felt he had only one option and that was Nicky. He phoned Nicky and told him to meet him at the Sheraton downtown. He told Nicky that he needed some documentation from my office and that there was no way a judge would issue a search warrant on what they had so far. He wanted Nicky to break into the office and secure any relevant papers he could find. Go through the files and books and anything else you can find, he told Nicky. He instructed him to make copies right there in the office and bring everything to him. Nicky told Douglas that he knew a guy that could pick any lock, but he wanted Douglas to guarantee he would cover for him if he got caught. There was no way Nicky wanted to spend one more minute in jail. Douglas assured him he would protect him, but he knew that if Nicky got caught he'd be on his own. He almost laughed at the thought of Nicky explaining to a cop that the FBI had put him up to the break-in.

It was midnight when Nicky and his friend approached the outer door to the offices. It only took the man a few seconds to pick the lock and let Nicky in. He handed the man two hundred dollars and closed the door behind him. None of the interior offices were locked and he knew exactly were mine was because he had been there many times to see his 'friend'. Nicky started with the file cabinets. There was nothing there but personal client files and certainly nothing that would tie me to the Union. He rifled through my desk and found nothing. A sense of panic was starting to overtake him. He knew he couldn't go back to Douglas empty-handed. Nicky fell back into my chair and decided to think for a minute. While he sat in the chair, he played with his pen-sized flashlight, wiggling it back and forth between his fingers. He watched the light as it danced across the desk. The end of the arch the dancing light was making kept falling on the same book on the desk. It had a large label on the binding that read 'Institutional Accts.'. Nicky put the penlight in his mouth and reached for the book. When he opened it he found more than a hundred different union accounts. There were unions spread all over the country that had their pension funds managed by the same managers that ran the local Union's money. He knew he had hit pay dirt. Closing the book he went out into the hall to turn on the copier. *All I have to do was copy the pages and I'll have my deal guaranteed*, he thought. Page after page after page, he continued to copy until the copier suddenly stopped. "E" the light kept flashing. *What the fuck is* "E", he thought. He looked over the top of the machine with his light until it fell on a label with the meanings of the letter codes. "Error: Paper Jam", it read. Nicky groped all over the copier trying to find how to open it. "Son of a bitch," he said as he slammed the side of the machine with his hand. He could feel the fear start to build in his stomach. Maybe one of the secretaries would fix the machine in the morning and wouldn't pay any attention to whatever was stuck inside. Looking quickly around the hall, he realized he had spent quite a while in the office and the fear of being caught overwhelmed him. He quickly grabbed the copies from the machine and returned the book back to its former location on the desk. All he wanted to do now was get out of there without being noticed.

Nicky met Douglas the next morning at the hotel. As soon as he walked through the door, he handed the pile of copies to Douglas.

"What's this?" Douglas asked Nicky as he took the papers from Nicky.

"There's nearly a hundred different union accounts from all over the country in this pile," Nicky said, smiling with pride in his work. "That's how Quinn gets the money to pay Anthony. All these money managers feed their business to Quinn so he can payoff Anthony. This is bigger than I thought. They're all in it together. You ought to thank me. This is gonna make you guys famous."

Douglas just stood there and flipped through the pages. Electrician's Union, Carpenter's Union, Transportation Worker's Union. He couldn't believe all the accounts. They had to represent billions in pension fund money. *Maybe this deal with Tagliano wasn't such a bad thing after all,* he thought. Maybe he was wrong about me. He thought Tagliano was making up the whole story to save his sorry ass, but by the look of what was in his hands, he must have been wrong.

"I must admit, you did good. Now, why don't you take off and let me handle this."

I got to the office early as usual and was the first one in. I went to my office and grabbed a letter from the desk that I drafted late the day before. Making copies of correspondence wasn't only a good habit, it was regulation. I went to the copier and turned it on and waited for the warm-up light to turn green. What greeted me was "E". "Son of a bitch," I said, wondering who would leave the copier jammed and just wait for the next person to fix it. I reached my arms around both sides of the front of the copier and pulled the front down to reveal the machine inside. It took me a couple of minutes of turning some of the rollers by hand to finally free the offending piece of paper. The paper was crumpled like an accordion and the ink was smeared, but there was no mistaking what I held in my hand. At first, I didn't know what to make of it. I couldn't remember making a copy of this page and the more I thought about it the more I realized it couldn't have been me if for no other reason than the fact that I never would have left the copier jammed. Was one of the other guys planning to leave for another firm and copying my book in hopes of stealing the accounts later? I didn't dwell that theory too long. The brokers knew the type of accounts these were and none of them would ever believe they could steal this business. The fact of the matter was, that the business wasn't really even mine. It was a kind of compensation granted by the money managers to people that maintained key relationships with some of their largest clients. This was a reward for helping the manager keep the client. If you lose the client, you lose the commissions. It wasn't special treatment, it was an industry standard. I ran it over and over in my mind, but I just couldn't make the connection.

When Norris looked through the copies that Douglas brought him, he reacted as if he had just won the lottery. *It was all the same as before*, he thought. *Tagliano isn't lying.* Here was what he needed for the foundation of his case. Now that he knew what was in my books, he could go to the judge later and get a search warrant for documents from my office. In the meantime, he planned to use this to pressure me into cooperating for a reduced sentence.

"This is great, Bill," Norris said with excitement. "We've got the bastards dead to rights. I want you to have a talk with Quinn and see if you can get him to cooperate. Offer to reduce the sentence and see what happens. Quinn never had the stomach for any of this."

It was the middle of the afternoon when I got the call from Douglas. It came as a total surprise. I hadn't heard or seen Douglas in several months and the last person I expected to be calling me was Bill Douglas.

"Quinn? This is Bill Douglas," he began. "I'd like you to come down to the Sheraton to room 417. I've got a big account that I'd like you to handle."

"What the hell is this all about, Bill? Since when does the Federal Government give money to brokers to manage?"

"You've got a choice, Quinn," Douglas bellowed. "You can either come down here and talk to us, or we can come up there and pull you out of your office in front of all your employees. So, what's it gonna be?"

"Give me ten minutes," I said and slammed down the phone. That's just what these assholes want, I thought. They'd love to drag my ass out of here in handcuffs.

As I walked down the hall again, I could see that this time they had the common sense to leave the unmarked door open. I walked up to 417 and knocked. Douglas opened the door.

"Hello, Bill," I said with sarcastic cheeriness. "How've you been?"

"Get in here Quinn and sit down," Garcia shouted from the other side of the room as he pointed to a solitary chair.

Douglas stepped aside and swept his free hand through the air in a gesture that said, 'Please enter'. I walked in and looked around. I wasn't exactly sure what I expected to see other than a normal hotel room. I took a seat in the chair and folded his arms across my chest. Douglas sat down on the corner of the bed and Garcia just stood next to him and glowered. *Crap!* I thought. *Haven't we done this enough?* It was obvious they had planned the positioning of the players. I was seated decidedly lower than either of them.

"You're looking rather dapper today, Bill," I said. Douglas's attire was not what you would have expected on an FBI agent. He had on a blue double-breasted jacket with gray slacks, a light blue shirt with a white collar and a red silk tie. He looked more 'Yacht Club' than Bureau.

"You're going away for five to seven years, Quinn," Garcia said as he pointed his finger at Quinn.

"Bill, what the hell is he talking about," I said as I regained my composure. Even though I had been through this game before, having the Feds screaming your sentence in your face has a tendency to make you nervous and I was no exception. Without any charges, you don't know but what you just might have broken some obscure law. After all, I didn't always travel in the best of company. Maybe this had something to do with Massarro. Maybe I had violated some securities law, although the SEC doesn't usually start an investigation by bashing your brains in with some whacked-out Fed.

"Shut up!" Garcia screamed. "Don't talk to him. I'm the one who's gonna bust your ass. We know about the payoffs to Traffarro. We know all about the hundred plus union accounts you have and how you use them to generate commissions to bribe Traffarro.

We've got you on bribery and conspiracy and that's just for starters."

"Garcia, you're full of shit," I said calmly. "You want to know how I know you're full of shit? Well, I'll tell you. *Because it never fucking happened*!" I shouted back at Garcia with the same force.

Garcia lunged at me and came down with his hands on each side of my throat. "I'm gonna put your ass in jail for the rest of your fucking life you miserable prick," Garcia screamed as his face turned red with rage.

Douglas jumped from the bed and pulled Garcia off. "For Christ's sake Felix, go get a cup of coffee. I'll stay here and talk to Quinn."

Garcia stood in front of me for a moment before he turned and headed out of the room. He was proud of himself. He had played this game many times before and always got a charge out of scaring the shit out of people. I straightened my jacket as Douglas, slowly shaking his head, sat back down on the bed.

"I'm sorry about that, Quinn. Felix gets a little excited from time to time. But, he's right. We do know all about the kickbacks. I don't think you really know just how much trouble you're in here, Quinn. I don't know why, but I like you. You seem like a decent guy, so I had a long talk with Norris and I persuaded him to offer you a deal. If you wear a wire and can get Traffarro into a conversation about the pension fund and the payments you made to him, he's promised to go easy on you." Douglas paused and rubbed his forehead thoughtfully. "Listen to me Quinn, if I were you I'd take his deal. You're not the type that can do a long stretch in prison."

"Give me a break, Bill," I said somewhat amused. "Tell me you're not playing good cop, bad cop. I thought that crap was only in the movies."

Douglas, true to his roll, never showed any expression. "I'm serious, Quinn. We're making this a one-time offer. You walk out of this room and the deal's off. Don't ruin your life over somebody like Traffarro."

"I'll tell you what, Bill," I said as I got up from the chair. "Let me think about it and if I decide to wear a wire on Traffarro, I'm betting the deal's still good. So, why don't you give me twenty-four hours to think this over and I'll get back to you. Now, if you don't mind I'd like to leave before that lunatic comes back."

I was always calm in a crisis and this hadn't been any different. After the crisis, however, was a different story. When I got back to my car, I just put my head back and shouted, "Fuck!" I drove back to the office and called Mario Rizzelli. Even though I was sure I hadn't done anything wrong, I didn't want to face the Feds without an attorney. Being ballsy with these assholes was one thing, being stupid was another. When I got Rizzelli on the phone I told him I had to talk to him someplace safe. Rizzelli told me to meet him in the parking lot at the old Barrington Mill No.1 at six o'clock. He didn't want to take the chance the Feds had already tapped his phone.

I drove into the Barrington lot and arrived a little before six. It was completely empty. The mill hadn't operated in decades. I just looked at the huge vacant buildings. I had heard the stories about this place from Traffarro. Apparently old man Barrington killed himself. I wondered what could have been so bad that you killed yourself. What happened to the family? There weren't any Barringtons left in the city. I couldn't imagine how Barrington's wife and family must have felt when the old man died. There was no doubt in my mind how Rane would feel if I killed himself. She'd dig me up and shoot me again. As I contemplated the fate of the Barringtons, I saw a car driving into the lot. It pulled right up to me so that the driver's windows were next to each other.

It was Rizzelli and he wanted to know every detail about the day's events. He chuckled when I told him that Garcia had assaulted me. Then he thought for a moment and asked if I wanted to press charges. I laughed and told him about the 'good cop, bad cop' routine. When I told Rizzelli about the wire, Rizzelli wanted to know what I wanted to do.

"Mario," I said a bit irritated. "Even if I did what they said; I would never save my own ass by screwing over a friend. None of this shit they're talking about ever happened. How could I possibly wear a wire on Anthony? I'd rather go to jail."

"Okay, here's what I want you to do. First, you don't talk to the Feds any more. Talking to those assholes only makes things worse. I'll call Norris and tell him you've retained me to represent you and that you're not going to wear any wire. If he has anything he wants to say to you, he can do it through me. Secondly, I want you to act like everything you say, regardless of where you are, is being taped, because it probably will be. Third, call Anthony tonight and tell him you want to talk to him in private. He'll know what to do. Last, swear to me there aren't going to be any surprises. I can help you whether you did this or not, but I'll drop you like a fucking hot potato if you bullshit me."

"Mario, I swear on my kids. None of this crap is true."

Mario was a good attorney. He grew up in the old Italian ways and was not about to get weak-kneed in front of any Fed. His family had been connected to the mob in one way or the other for years and he was used to a life of fighting the government.

The drive home gave me a few minutes to think about the Union and everything that happened over the past two years. It was like quicksand. The more you fought the deeper you sank with a healthy dash of helplessness thrown in. When I finally reached the house, Rane was waiting. I arrived a lot later than usual and she suspected that something was wrong as soon as I walked through the door.

"Okay, what happened?" she said as soon as I sat down. If woman's intuition was valuable, Rane had a million dollars in her head.

I motioned to Rane to follow me. As I passed through the living room, I grabbed the remote and switched on the television and turned the volume up. Rane followed me upstairs to the bar and I poured us both a stiff drink. She was a little perplexed by my actions, but her prior experiences with me caused her to follow without a lot of questions.

"The Feds are after Anthony and me," I began after I took a long drink. "I got a call to go to the Sheraton today and had the pleasure of getting the third degree by two of the Government's finest. The first words out of their mouths were that I was going away for seven to ten years for bribery and conspiracy." I took another big swallow of bourbon. I knew I'd be able to get my arms around this, but at the moment a little liquid fortitude seemed to be appropriate.

"Parker, I have to ask this," Rane said in a soft voice. "Regardless of the answer, I'll stand with you though whatever happens, but I have to know. Did you do it?"

"*Fuck no! Of course not!*" I said with a wave of his hand. "Hell, I tried to give Anthony a few hundred for printing expenses for his election and he wouldn't take it. I couldn't pay Anthony ten cents if I wanted to. Get this. Those assholes want me to wear a wire and trap Anthony saying something about payoffs. Christ, I wouldn't do that to anyone even if I did do what they said. I still feel bad about testifying against Costa and Merzone, for Christ's sake and they *were* genuine assholes."

"So...now what?" Rane said with a feeling of dread in her heart.

"I've got to call Anthony and tell him what's going on," I said with a far away look. I've already spoken to Mario Rizzelli and he's going to represent me and get Frick and Frack, those two asshole Feds, off my back. We've got to watch what we say in the house or on the phones. I don't want to give these pricks anything they could twist out of context and hang me with. Trouble is this Norris is a psycho motherfucker who'll do anything to get the Union and us. I've heard the Feds will manufacture evidence if they want you bad enough. Look what they did to John Gotti. They couldn't beat his lawyer so they disqualified him."

My nerves were settling back to normal, but another drink seemed to fit the situation. I had to tell Rane something and for this, as much strength as I could pour was required. "I want to postpone our wedding until this mess is out of the way. I'm not going to marry you, Rane and then go to jail for seven years. I absolutely won't do it."

"Do you really think it'll make a difference to me if we're married and you're in jail?" Rane said as she put her hand on mine. "You think I'm gonna say, Gee, too bad Parker's in jail. I guess I'll go out and fuck another guy?"

"I would hope not. I'd hope you'd wait an appropriate mourning period. You know...a day or two at least before you spread those lovely legs of yours," I said jokingly. I knew this was a serious topic, but a little levity was in order. I was wrong.

"Ya know, Parker," she said with hurt and irritation in her voice. "Sometimes you can be a real shit. You think I only love you when things are going great? I don't know if you've noticed it or not, but things haven't been exactly a bed of roses since we started seeing each other," she said pointing to the bullet scar on her head.

"Rane," I said softly. "I love you more than you'll ever know and I don't want to put you in a bad place."

"You've already put me in a bad place you big jerk," she said with a little laugh. "You got me shot in the head. Did I pack my bags then? But...I'll tell you what. Out of respect for that oversized sense of honor that you have, I'll agree to postpone the wedding. However...if you *ever* try to postpone it again...so help me God, I'm gone! But it won't be until after I put a bullet in your head and I guarantee *mine* won't bounce off," she said as she swatted the side of my head.

"Yes, Miss Rane," I said holding my hands up in defense. "You da boss, Miss Rane." I leaned across the bar and gave her a big kiss. "Let me go call Anthony. The sooner we get all this crap behind us, the sooner we can get back to a normal life."

"Parker," she said. "I've got a feeling, that with you, this *is* normal."

I called Traffarro and we agreed to meet in the mall at the fountain in the center court. Anthony reasoned that all the noise from the falling water would make it impossible for the FBI to listen to our conversation. Traffarro was not the most demonstrative or emotional person that I had met, but it was obvious he was upset by my news. Traffarro knew that Norris was obsessed with ruining the Union and he expected him to make some kind of move against him, but this tactic came out of left field. Like me, Traffarro was worried that if Norris wanted him bad enough, he would do whatever he could to get him.

When I arrived at the fountain, I saw Traffarro making believe he was window-shopping. I laughed to myself as I thought I had better tell Traffarro that staring into the Victoria's Secrets window was not the best way to be inconspicuous. I figured I would just sit down and wait for Traffarro. It only took Traffarro a moment more before he turned around to scan the area and saw me sitting quietly by the fountain.

"What the fuck!" Traffarro said showing his obvious irritation. "Didn't you *see* me over there?"

"Of course, but I figured you needed to find the right bra so—."

"Just what I need, a fucking comedian," Traffarro said cutting me off. "So, tell me what happened."

I went through the whole experience for Traffarro. "I gotta tell ya Anthony, I thought all this shit was over. I knew Norris was watching you but I never figured it would play out this way."

"It shouldn't have. And it wouldn't have if it hadn't been for Nicky."

"Nicky?" I said surprised. "What the hell does Nicky have to do with this?"

"After you called me last night, I made a call to a cop friend in the department," Traffarro said. "He told me how Nicky got out of that drug bust. He told the cops he could give them the head of a major union on bribery and conspiracy. Nicky sold you and me out to save his own ass. He's already been to Norris. All he did was give him the Costa story and change the names. Norris's got such a hard-on for this Union that he bought it all and gave Nicky a pass on the drug thing."

"Anthony...Nicky and I were like brothers. We drank together, we played golf, and we chased broads together. I paused and reflected on all the time the two of us had spent together. "What am I saying? *You two were even closer!* "

"I know," Traffarro said sadly. "I'm godfather to one of his kids for Christ's sake. It's a sick fuckin' world we live in, Quinn." Traffarro was hurt as deeply as if his own son had died. He and Nicky had been the closest of friends for years. They were like family and to have this happen was truly like a death. His dearest friend had died and been replaced by someone he didn't even know. He would have given Nicky everything he wanted if only Nicky could have been more patient. If he could have waited a few years until the heat was off, they both could have had a great life. Now, the victories seemed hollow. All the years of planning were gone in one faithless act.

"I appreciate what you did about the wire. At least *you* honored our friendship."

"Anthony, please," I said as I put my hand on Traffarro's shoulder. "We haven't known each other very long, but we've been through a lot. You and Connie are like family. I would never do anything to hurt either one of you. You know that."

"Yeah, well thanks anyway. Look, Mario Rizzelli is a good attorney. He's also a good man and he knows how to handle pricks like Norris. Don't worry. We'll be fine. I've got a call into an attorney in Chicago that's done some work for the guys at the International. He's got a lot of juice. By the way, when are you and Rane supposed to get married?" Traffarro said as he tried to turn the conversation on a happier subject.

"I convinced her to postpone it until all this shakes out," I said as I took a deep breath. "She's not too happy about it, but I couldn't put her in that position. God forbid this thing doesn't go our way, I don't want her tied to me because she's married."

"Nicky even fucked that up. That cocksucker! Traffarro turned and motioned for us to leave the mall. He patted me on the back as he said, "You're right about the wedding. It's the right thing to do. Women think they know how they feel, but seven or more years is a long fucking time to ask a woman to wait."

Chapter Nineteen
The Plan

Norris had a plan to bring down Traffarro and the Union well before Nicky laid this gift in his lap. He had calculated that Traffarro would retain Rizzelli when Norris finally came after him. They had been friends and associates for a long time and Rizzelli was the one that Traffarro always turned to for legal advice. When the hammer fell, Norris was sure that it would be Mario Rizzelli that Traffarro would run to. Norris had learned that Rizzelli's secretary was an old friend of Sammy Merzone's wife. He had one of the guards at the Federal Correctional Facility in Lewisburg, Pennsylvania contact Merzone soon after his arrival. The guard told Merzone that he might be able to get some payback if he could get his wife to contact Rizzelli's secretary and have her pass on anything she heard or saw in Rizzelli's office regarding the Union. Once he went after Traffarro, Norris would have a pipeline directly to the defense. He'd be able to counter their every move. 'Attorney client privilege' was not in Norris's vocabulary, not when it meant he could bring down the one thing he hated more than anything else in the world ... Costa's Union.

It was 9:30 in the morning when Norris received his call from Rizzelli. "Mr. Norris," Rizzelli said dryly. Norris broke into a sly smile when he heard Rizzelli. The game was on and he was sure all his players were in place. He just wanted to hear those sweet words about Traffarro retaining Rizelli.

"I have been retained by Parker Quinn to represent him in your investigation into alleged bribery and conspiracy activities that you believe involve my client. I wish to inform you that my client has decided to reject your offer to reduce any potential charges against him in exchange for his cooperation to obtain statements from Mr. Traffarro using a wire. I would also like to advise you that in the future, if you want to contact my client for any reason that you are to do so through me. Do you have any questions, Mr. Norris?"

"No, thank you Mr. Rizzelli," Norris replied trying to contain his anger. "I'm sorry your client chose not to cooperate. He leaves me no choice but to prosecute him to the fullest extent of the law."

"Look, Norris," Rizzelli said with a touch of anger in his voice. "I know your reputation and how you get things done, but let me warn you. You try any of that bullshit in this case and so help me I'll have your ass in front of the Bar Association so fast you won't know what hit you. Good bye."

Norris slammed the phone down so hard that a glass of water on his desk fell over and landed in his lap. He jumped up from his desk and swore loud enough that it could have been heard throughout the building. *Who the hell do these fucking people think they are,* he thought to himself? *I'll humiliate that bastard Rizzelli and put Quinn and Traffarro away so long they'll be old men by the time they ever breathe a breath of free air.*

Fifteen minutes later, Norris's phone rang. The call would be another blow to Norris's soaring aspirations to ruin his opponents. Aside from Tagliano's statement and the account forms that he had in the file, Norris didn't have enough to convict anyone. The opposition was mounting their forces.

"Hello, Mr. Norris," the man on the phone said. "This is Saul Bergmann. I am with the firm of Bergmann, Stachel, Estes, and Yates here in Chicago. I represent Mr. Anthony Traffarro. Mr. Traffarro has advised me that he may be a target of an investigation by your office. First, Mr. Norris, is my client the target of any investigation?

"Yes. Your client is the subject of a Federal probe into corruption and racketeering."

"Then I'm sure you won't mind directing all your future contact with my client through my office." There was a long silence as Bergmann waited for a reply. "Mr. Norris? Is there a problem? I'll follow up our conversation with a letter. You'll find all the particulars there. I'm sure we'll speak again. Thank you."

I didn't see Traffarro again for ten days. Traffarro thought it would be best not to give the FBI anything to report back to Norris. He had hired one of the most powerful trial lawyers and someone who had a long history defending union officials. Bergmann joked with Traffarro and said that it would be refreshing to go to court with a client who was actually innocent for a change. He also told Traffarro that he shouldn't worry. Bergmann said that Norris didn't have much choice when Nicky came to him. If he ignored Nicky and his statement turned out to be true, then Norris would look like a fool. If he proceeds and gives Nicky a break and it's all phony, then maybe he would go back after Nicky and tack on a few more charges. He advised Traffarro that Norris was on a fishing expedition and once the trail came up dry, he'd drop the case. Had Bergmann been aware of Norris's mental state, he might not have been so cavalier about the subject.

I was in my office when Rizzelli called and asked me to come to his office as soon as possible. When I walked into Rizzelli's office I was surprised to see Cheryl Debret sitting behind a desk. Somehow, I knew the face, but couldn't place the name or how I knew her. Then in a flash it came to me. I hadn't seen Sammy Merzone's wife all that often, but when I did it was a safe bet that Cheryl Debret would be with her. I was in no mood to be going over old times with this woman and the subject they would likely be discussing wasn't one of my favorites. Keep it short and simple, I thought.

"Hey, Cheryl, how've you been?" I asked with polite enthusiasm. "Is Mario busy?"

"Hi. I'm good and yourself. Mario's on the phone. Why don't you have a seat? He shouldn't be long." Debret was solidly in the Merzone camp and the sight of me walking through the door filled her with anticipation. She was looking forward to the opportunity to help her old friends. Cheryl Debret couldn't give two shits about Rizzelli and his sacred relationship with his clients. She wanted revenge for her friends and was more than happy to help Norris put them away.

I was glad she didn't pursue the conversation any further. The truth was that neither of us had anything the other person wanted to hear. As far as I was concerned, the less said the better. It was about five minutes before she told me to go into Rizzelli's office.

"What's up, Mario," I asked as I walked into Rizzelli's office. "... or don't I want to know?"

"I got a call from your friend Norris," Rizzelli said sarcastically, reaching over his desk to shake my hand. "He wanted to know if you'd appear before the Grand Jury. I told him that if you were subpoenaed you'd plead the Fifth."

"*What*?" I shrieked. "Why the fuck would I plead the Fifth? Are you trying to hang a guilty sign around my neck? I don't have anything to hide and I'm sure as hell not afraid of Norris *or* the Grand Jury."

"Listen to me," Rizzelli said calmly, leaning forward and laying his arms on his desk. "Norris is searching for something to hang you and Anthony with. I don't know what he's got, but I'm not about to allow you to go in there and help him make his case. The Grand Jury is *his* playground. He gets the chance to throw up trial balloons and see if the Jury will bite. He gets to make his mistakes in the Grand Jury and there's no one to challenge him. If you go in there, you'll be doing him a big favor while at the same time shooting yourself in the foot."

"Did you tell Anthony about this?"

"No, not yet," Rizzelli replied.

"Well then, please do," I said emphatically, shifting my weight in the chair. I felt an overwhelming urge to hit something. My head turned slowly around as I looked for something to destroy. Fortunately, I couldn't find any good candidates. Thankfully that minute or two of contemplative destruction allowed my blood to come back from the boiling point. "I'm sorry, Mario but this is a team effort. I'm not going to do anything that's going to hurt Anthony and I respect your opinion, but I'd like to hear his thoughts on this. If everyone agrees that taking the Fifth is the right thing to do then fine, but I want everybody on the same page."

I left Rizzelli's office more than a little stunned. I thought that anyone who pleaded the Fifth must have something to hide and that was the one thing I didn't want to portray. It also bothered me that Traffarro hadn't been asked to appear before the Grand Jury. What did Norris think that I would go in there and crumble under the weight of his brilliant offense? Did Rizzelli think I really *did* have something to hide? I wasn't nervous about the outcome of the investigation. I had already made up my mind that if I went to prison, I could survive it because I knew I was innocent. I thought that going to prison because I was guilty was far worse. How could I face Rane if I had really done all the things that Norris was trying to pin on me? I would find some peace with whatever outcome developed, but I was getting really pissed about the process. I wasn't comfortable about not being in control and having my fate in the hands of some avenging lunatic like Norris really ticked me off.

Rizzelli did as he was told and discussed our conversation with Traffarro and he told Rizzelli that he wanted to talk to Saul

Bergmann. Traffarro knew Rizzelli was good but Bergmann was truly a master of the game.

"Basically Anthony, Mario's right," Bergmann said thoughtfully. "You never put your client before the Grand Jury and let the Prosecution have a free shot, but maybe in this case we get the free shot. How smart is this Quinn and how much do you trust him?

"I have no doubt about Quinn's intelligence," Traffarro replied earnestly. "He's been up against Norris before and he knows what to expect. I don't think Norris can trip him up and besides, Quinn really doesn't have anything to hide. As far as trust goes, Quinn's probably one of the most honorable men I've ever known and I'd trust him with my life."

"Good. Let's see if Mario can get Norris to fall for a general discussion in Norris's office," Bergmann said like the spider enticing the fly. "We might just be able to have Mr. Norris give up more than he gets. I think it would be better if I called Mario, Anthony. I want to be sure he understands the strategy and agrees. Remember, Quinn is still his client and he might not want to put him in harm's way."

Norris was completely surprised when Rizzelli called him. He viewed the offer as two shots for him to get at Quinn. He'd have the opportunity to question Quinn and get his reaction *before* he was actually in the Grand Jury room. If Quinn made one mistake, he'd beat him to death with it during the Grand Jury testimony and hopefully that might be enough to get Quinn to break and give up Traffarro. Maybe Rizzelli wasn't as smart as he thought. He never expected Rizzelli to give up his client. Norris reflected on the course of events. When he thought it would take years to get Traffarro and the Union, Tagliano fell into his lap. When Quinn screwed up his plan to eavesdrop on Traffarro's defense by having Cheryl Debret provide a blow by blow description of the defense's strategy,

Rizzelli gives up Quinn to be questioned. It must be his destiny to finally get some revenge on the Union.

I was in my office contemplating the coming events and I was finally satisfied. I was going to have the chance to face Norris and end this investigation once and for all. I couldn't imagine what Norris thought he had besides Nicky's unsubstantiated statement. He couldn't have any proof of something that never happened unless he was manufacturing his own evidence. I was a million miles away when Connie rang my office to tell me that Nicky was in the lobby and wanted to see me. Nicky hadn't been around in almost two months and all of a sudden he shows up? I just shook my head when I realized it hadn't been that long since I turned down the FBI's offer to wear a wire. I couldn't believe that the FBI and Norris were this stupid. Did they really think that I wouldn't put two and two together and have it add up to Nicky wearing a wire? Norris had to be getting desperate for him to try something this obvious. Well, at least this should be interesting.

When Nicky walked through the door to my office, I almost didn't recognize him. His face was drawn from an obvious weight loss and the wonderful tan skin he always seemed to have, now looked almost gray. I almost felt sorry for him. All of the shit he had gotten himself into had taken a huge toll on him. I thought Nicky should pose for a poster against crime. They could do a before and after comparison. *Here's Nicky Tagliano before he did something incredibly stupid and sold out his friends and here's Nicky after being a complete asshole.*

"Hey, Nicky," I said in a sympathetic voice. Regardless what this man was trying to do to me, we had been like brothers and I couldn't help but feel for him. I knew that if I had asked Nicky a year ago if he would ever sell out a friend to save his own ass, Nicky would probably have punched me in the face. But now...here he was wired and about to try his best to put me and Traffarro away for a long time.

"Come on in and sit down," I continued. "It's been a long time, Nicky."

"Yeah well, I've been real busy with the stores and what with Anthony only paying attention to the Union," he said with a voice of a man who had lost his soul. I watched as he fidgeted in his seat. "Well anyway, I just figured I should stop by and say hello. I wanted to talk to you about what's been going on. You know...with Anthony and you and the Union."

"How's Lorie and the kids?" I asked, partly because he cared, but mostly because I wanted to stretch this farce out a little. I realized that I could have some fun with Douglas and Garcia, who were probably sitting in a car outside the office listening to the conversation. If I ever had any feelings of friendship with Douglas they were long gone. If it wasn't so obviously illegal, I'd like to go out and shoot the two of them.

"She wants a divorce," Nicky said. The first thoughts that flashed into my mind were sympathy for the whole family. Those thoughts quickly turned to selective scorn as Nicky continued. "Connie's been talkin' to her. Tellin' her how I've been fuckin' around for years and she shouldn't stand for it. God damned fuckin' Traffarros! They're all out to fuck me over."

I couldn't believe what I was hearing. What fucking planet is this guy from, I thought? The fact that he got caught with drugs *and* another woman didn't mean anything to him? This was all Connie's and Anthony's fault? You have to be fucking kidding me! How is it possible, that one human being could screw up their life so obviously and completely and then blame everything on other people?

"You want to know what's going on with me and Anthony, Nicky?" I asked. "As far as I know, Anthony's helped out the retirees and got some damned good contracts signed. I've been fortunate to have been able to keep some of the commission business with the fund, but beyond that, Nicky I don't know what you're referring to." The whole dialog was a presentation for the assholes at the other end of the wire.

"Come on, Quinn," Nicky said, leaning forward and stretching out his hands in supplication. His nerves were starting to seep into his voice. "I know Anthony's got his fucking hand in the pension funds. He's getting paid off to make certain loans. You know that and you've been fuckin' paying him all along, too. Come on! All I wanted was for him to put me on one of the boards and he wouldn't do it. Why not? Are you two the only ones that get to play this fucking game? Anthony's living large and what the hell do you and I get? You get a few lousy fucking trades, which you gotta pay him for, and I get *nothing*! That's bullshit Quinn and you know it."

Nicky was obviously getting himself worked up. He couldn't get past the fact that what he wanted wasn't being delivered to him fast enough. Fine, I thought. You're pissed at Anthony, but what did I ever do to you to justify you trying to ruin my life. I could feel the sympathy I initially felt change to anger.

"Are you completely out of your mind? When someone asked Willie Sutton why he robbed banks, he said 'because that's where the money is'. I don't think old Willie said he robbed the banks that were surrounded by the fucking FBI, the Justice Department, the DOL and the local cops! Anthony's been trying to clean up the Union for years. He's done more for the members in the short time he's been there than the old man did in over a decade. Anthony's no idiot, Nicky. He knows the Feds are all over the Union and just waiting for the slightest reason to take it over. He's not about to do anything as ridiculous as what you're saying. And, what makes you think I'm paying money to Anthony?" I never forgot that the FBI was listening and I was careful about every word that I said. I wanted to make this as difficult as possible for them to ever consider using the tape I knew they were recording.

"Come on, Quinn," Nicky pleaded. "Anthony's been waiting for years to get on the same fucking gravy train that the old man was on. It's worth millions and he's gonna get his and you and I are gonna be left out. Maybe that doesn't piss you off, but it bugs the shit out of me. All I wanted to do was talk to you about it and see what you thought."

Now I was really getting pissed. This moron was insulting my intelligence. Why not be up front and call it what it is, I thought...a bullshit frame job.

"Look Nicky, I don't have the slightest clue what you're talking about. I'm sure, you could put every transaction that Anthony's done since he's been running the Union under a microscope and you wouldn't find anything. Do you know why I can say that with such confidence? Because I'm sure that asshole Norris and his two agency stooges have already done it." I was hoping Douglas would play the tape for Norris. I wanted him to know exactly what I thought of them. "If you want to talk about golf or your screwed up marriage, I'm all ears, but if you want to continue with this type of conversation...well, let's just say that I don't have the fucking time."

"I'm sorry you feel that way. I'd hoped we could do something for ourselves, but I guess not."

"Nicky, you were the closest friend I ever had," I said with a heavy heart. "I don't know what happened to you, but I'm sorry." I got up from my desk in an attempt to end the conversation. I walked over to Nicky and tried to give him a hug for old time's sake, but Nicky pushed me away as if I were on fire. The realization of what that meant, hit me almost immediately. Nicky was afraid I would feel the wire he had strapped to his body. I just shook my head and extended my hand. I had very mixed emotions about what had happened and I realized this would probably be the last time I would see Nicky. What a waste, I thought.

After Nicky left, I called Traffarro. I was sure that Douglas wouldn't let this fish off the hook with just one failed attempt. I guessed that Nicky would be on his way to Traffarro's office for another try to get Norris the evidence he so desperately desired and although I knew that Traffarro was smart enough to recognize the game that was being played, I didn't want to take any chances.

"Anthony, it's Quinn," I said. I wanted to be as cryptic as possible, but realized that it wouldn't do any good. The FBI would have a tape of the phone call and they'd certainly know why he was calling Traffarro. I wasn't sure what they could do with it, but at this point I really didn't care. "Our friend Mr. Tagliano was just here. He was asking me all kinds of questions about bribery and kickbacks. I told him I didn't have a clue what he was talking about. My guess is he's probably on his way over to you to have the same discussion."

"I understand. Thanks, Quinn."

I had a sense that Norris was getting desperate. I was sure now that Norris really didn't have anything because if he did, he wouldn't be trying such a ridiculous stunt as sending Nicky in wired. It was a few days later that I started to see the lengths that Norris would go to in an effort to make his case.

"Hi, Dad," the voice on the phone said. It was my daughter, Grace. She was going to college at Colgate University and was in her senior year. I admired her immensely. I had been tough on her when she was young and she took it in stride. I made her work when she was in high school and I made her work while she was in college. I believed it would give her a good foundation when she got out into the real world because the real world doesn't give a damn about who you are and whatever problems you might have. She had been a real hell raiser in high school. Never doing anything that any normal parent would be truly upset about, but she definitely kept me on the edge of my seat. As the official inventor of "Senior Skip Day", a day all the seniors were supposed to play hooky and go swimming, she held a special place in my heart. She'd been living with a young man, David Parnell, who also attended Colgate and I took it as a matter of course that they would be married soon after graduation.

"Dad? What's going on?" she said as more of a demand than a question. "Two FBI agents said that you were in some kind of trouble with the Union and the Government visited David and me. They hoped we could provide some information that might help you. Believe me Dad, I know they weren't there to help you. If there's one thing that you've taught me over the years, it's that the Government never knocks on your door to help you. They asked a million questions about stuff that I told them I knew nothing about. I told them you and I hadn't actually seen each other in a while and that I didn't know what they were talking about. I also got a call from, Mom. She said they went to see her too. What's up?"

"Everything and nothing, Honey," I said. I was getting very angry about what I considered to be harassment by Norris. "You remember Nicky Tagliano? He got caught with drugs coming across the Canadian border and to save his ass, he's cooked up some story about me paying off Anthony. Before you even ask...no, I didn't do it. The Federal Prosecutor's a real asshole and I think he believes that hassling you is going to make me confess or something. I'm sorry they bothered you Honey, but try to forget about it. It's really nothing."

"Dad, please," she said as if I had insulted her. "These people don't bother me. Actually, I thought it was pretty funny. It's not every kid on campus that has the FBI knocking on their door asking about their father. David kinda freaked out. He thought you might be some kind of gangster. I told him, Yeah right, my father, 'Public Enemy Number One'. Get real!"

"What did your mother say?"

"You know, Mom,"

Yeah, I thought. I could just imagine what she had told them and none of it would have been good. Luckily, Norris couldn't put me in jail because my ex-wife wanted to nail my hide to a barn door. The more I thought about Norris and his tactics the angrier I got. It wasn't going to be easy to sit down with Norris and have a conversation about all this and not jump across his desk and fucking kill the miserable prick. Little did I know, how right I would be. Norris was playing every dirty trick in the book and he wasn't finished. I met Mario Rizzelli outside of Norris's office at 10:00 the next morning.

"Quinn," Rizzelli said cheerily as he strode down the short hallway. "Are you ready to dance with the devil?" Rizzelli carried a briefcase large enough to hold a small child. Among the many things that were in there were items I had given him. I had provided an accounting of all my pay stubs, my bank deposits, a copy of all my checking account statements with a copy of each check for the last two years along with a copy of my brokerage accounts for the same period. If Norris could figure out how I could be paying Traffarro from the evidence that I was giving him, then more power to him, I thought.

"Nice analogy, Mario," I said dryly. There was not much that anyone could say to me about Norris that I'd find humorous. "You did bring the income accounting that I worked up?"

"Yup. Do me a favor, will you? Don't lose your temper in there and say anything that might make things worse. Norris's a vindictive prick and I don't want to provoke him. Okay?"

"No problem," I said holding my hands up in an act of surrender. "I'll be on my best behavior."

After a brief wait, we were shown into Norris's office. I wasn't entirely surprised to see Douglas and Garcia standing behind Norris's desk. It was faintly reminiscent of our little meeting at the Sheraton. As soon as I saw Garcia, my blood started a slow boil and I realized that my promise of good behavior was already in jeopardy.

"Please sit down," Norris said politely. "I want to express my gratitude to you, Mr. Quinn for coming in here today. Are you still willing to appear before the Grand Jury?"

"Yes," I said calmly. One thing I learned at my last Grand Jury appearance was to keep your answers short and to the point. The more you say to a Prosecutor, the more chance you give him to twist your words.

"Good. Why don't we get started then," Norris said enthusiastically.

"Before we do," Rizzelli interrupted. "My client has volunteered to provide you with a two year accounting of all of his personal finances. I have a copy here that I would like to give you," Rizzelli said as he reached into the cavernous briefcase. "I would also like to point out that my client is here voluntarily and desires to cooperate in this investigation in any way he can."

"How nice," Norris said sarcastically. "Now if there are no further interruptions...Let's start with something easy, shall we. Tell me Mr. Quinn, how is it that a broker like you in this little city has so many larger institutional accounts from all over the country." As Norris spoke, he dropped the copied files on his desk with great drama."

"Are you telling me that I have to be in a big city like New York or Chicago in order to do this type of business?" I wasn't sure, but I thought I had just been insulted.

"Come on, Mr. Quinn," Norris said as his voice got more sarcastic and louder. "You're a not so special broker in a small city that is getting business directed to him by some of the largest money managers in the country. What could somebody *like you* provide them that they couldn't get anywhere else?"

Now, I was sure! I *had* been insulted. "It's a common business practice in this industry Mr. Norris, that money managers direct some business to those people who bring them business. If the broker maintains the relationship between the money manager and the client, they are deemed worthy of being compensated. It happens all the time, *even* in cities like ours." My tone was that normally reserved for small children who might have difficulty grasping certain concepts. It was specifically designed to return the insult to Norris.

"Isn't it true, that the only reason these people deal with you is because they know you're paying off Anthony Traffarro?"

"Nnnnoooo," I said in my most condescending tone. "I just explained to you why I get any business at all from these people."

"Let's go to the subject of New Issues for a moment," Norris said as he tried to regain the upper hand. "Why is it that you gave Anthony Traffarro so many of these hot New Issues? Was it because you knew he wouldn't allow you to have all the Union's business if you didn't pay him somehow?"

"What the hell are you talking about," I said in absolute amazement. "I haven't given Anthony a single New Issue."

"Bullshit! We know all about it. You've been feeding him New Issues ever since he took over."

"You've got proof of that I suppose," I said smugly. The arrogant little prick was starting to really get under my skin, but I was determined to maintain my composure.

"Of course," Norris replied as he traded smug expressions with me.

"You're actually dumber than I thought, Norris" Fuck it, I thought. The gloves are off. "Mr. Traffarro's wife works for me,

Mr. Norris. But I suppose you already knew that. I suggest that you be a little more thorough in your investigations before you try to bluff. You see, in the securities industry, it's against the law for employees of a brokerage company to buy New Issues and the same goes for their immediate family. Traffarro's account carries a special code that won't allow the entry of any New Issue orders without setting off alarms. So you see, Mr. Norris I couldn't place a New Issue in his account even if I wanted to." I just sat back in my chair as Norris nervously shuffled some papers on his desk. It was clear to me that Norris was going to lose it pretty soon and there was nothing I wanted to do more than push the bastard over the edge.

"Tell me about your friendship with Tino Drazzetti. Is it your normal practice to make friends with killers?" Norris said as he gathered himself together.

"Mr. Drazzetti's wife works for me," I said calmly. "I needed somebody, she applied, and I hired her. I didn't know Mr. Drazzetti at the time I hired her, but if I did I would probably have hired her anyway. I don't think it's fair to blame someone's wife for the wrongs of her husband. As far as being friends with Mr. Drazzetti, we've met several times at company social events and I've seen him out once or twice at restaurants. I hardly call that a basis for calling us friends."

"Oh, really. Then please explain what you were doing going to a mob cookout with Tino Drazzetti?" Norris said as he once again fell back in his chair with a smug expression on his face.

How the hell did he know about that? I thought. The only people that new about that incident was Traffarro, Tino, and Mario Rizzelli when he had asked about any ties or meetings with mob figures that might be brought up by Norris. I told Rizzelli about my Massarro meeting and about the offer to go with Tino to the cookout. Thank God, Traffarro had persuaded me not to go. But...if only four people knew about it, who told Norris?

"I never went to any cookout with Tino Drazzetti," I said. My irritation was starting to show. It wasn't Norris's whining voice that was bothering me at this point. It was the fact that somebody was feeding Norris information and I couldn't imagine who.

"Mr. Quinn, are you ever going to give me an honest answer?"

"If I was actually there, you'd have pictures," I said as my blood started to boil. "I'm sure there were probably more FBI agents at this cookout you keep referring to than bad guys. You don't have any pictures of me at this meeting do you? I know you don't, because I wasn't there. I don't know why you persist in this fantasy world of yours, Norris. I've just shown you how it would be impossible for me to give New Issues to Mr. Traffarro and you have my personal financial records on your desk. Why don't you review them for God's sake and do a competent job before you make wild accusations? I couldn't pay Anthony Traffarro ten cents even if I wanted to because he wouldn't take it. Why would he do something like that with you people watching his every move? I'll bet you know every time he takes a dump, for Christ's sake."

"Why?" Norris said as he stuck his chin out and leered at me and proceeded to use the most contemptuous tone that I ever heard. "Because that's the way you people are. You think you can take your Unions and ruin honest employers who've worked their whole lives to build something, just so you and your greasy friends can steal it all away. You can't help yourselves. It's just the nature of the type of people you are. Costa did it and now Traffarro thinks he can do it too. Well, it's not going to happen, Mr. Quinn because I've dedicated my life to removing the cancer that your precious Union represents. I don't give a shit about your phony personal statements. I'm going to bury you." Norris's eyes were nearly jumping out of their sockets and he was extending his body to such an extent that he was almost lying across his desk.

Rizzelli was thrown back in his chair by of Norris's actions. He sat with his mouth open unable to believe what he was seeing. This was unlike anything he had witnessed before. This man was obviously deranged. He was too overwhelmed by Norris's vehemence to notice that I had jumped out of my chair and was almost at Norris's desk. He bolted for me like a NFL linebacker. The last thing he wanted was for his client to wind up in jail for assaulting a Federal Prosecutor. He managed to get to me just as I was about to reach for Norris's throat.

"For God's sake, Quinn don't!" Rizzelli said as he tried to wrestle me off Norris's desk. "This isn't the way to handle this!"

"This guy's an incompetent idiot," I shouted as I allowed Rizzelli to hold me back.

Rizzelli stood as a weak defense in front of me. I was a head taller and outweighed him by a good fifty pounds. Norris had fallen back in his chair stone faced by the realization that the man who had just charged him could have inflicted serious harm. Douglas and Garcia were simply standing quietly behind Norris and looking at each other with smiles on their faces. Each was trying to decide whether it was Norris or me that was most insane. After a moment they nodded knowingly at each other...definitely, Norris!

"Mr. Norris," Rizzelli shouted. "My client came here voluntarily to answer your questions. He did not come here to be harassed and insulted. If you still wish to call my client before the Grand Jury, please contact me with the time of appearance. This session is over." Rizzelli turned me toward the door and gave me a small shove.

We didn't speak to each other until we got into the elevator. As we stood in the elevator with the thousand-mile stare most people get while riding between floors, I gazed lazily upward and said, "Well, that went well."

"*Well?*" Rizzelli said in exasperation. "It was a fucking disaster. I thought you were gonna kill him."

"Nnnnoooo," I said slowly. "I never intended to lay a hand on the miserable prick. It was just that...he was stickin' that God damned ferret face of his out with that fucking look of satisfaction," I said as I turned to Rizzelli in frustration. "I wanted to choke the livin' shit out of the little weasel, but I knew if I touched the little fruit those two apes behind him would have clubbed me to death before they threw my ass in jail."

"Oh, shit!" Rizzelli exclaimed. "I forgot my brief case."

"Well, I'd go back with you, but I'm afraid that if I saw Norris again I might not be so nice this time."

Rizzelli and I parted company in the lobby, but I didn't get to the front door before I remembered the question about the cookout. I wanted to address this issue as soon as possible and decided to wait for Rizzelli to come back down. I leaned against one of the marble columns that graced the ornate lobby and with my arms folded across my chest I waited patiently in the lobby for Rizzelli's return. A moment later the elevator doors opened to reveal Douglas and Garcia. As they strolled through the lobby, Douglas turned and saw me casually leaning on the pillar. Douglas just turned his gaze back to the floor and with a broad smile simply shook his head. I think he was pretty sure that I hadn't done anything wrong. Under different circumstances we might have been friends, but he had a job to do and he was too close to retirement to challenge a maniac like Norris.

I watched as Douglas and Garcia exited the building. When I turned my head back toward the elevators, Rizzelli was almost at my side.

"Problem?" Rizzelli asked.

"Yeah," I said dryly. "There were only four people that knew about the trip that I didn't take with Tino. There was Anthony and Tino, and I know they wouldn't get within five miles of Norris if they had any choice. Then there was you and me...and I know *I* didn't talk to Norris or anyone else about it. That leaves you, Mario. But......I don't think it was you because I can't figure out what you'd have to gain. So I kept thinking, who would want to supply information to Norris? Sammy Merzone? Sure, but he's in the can. But...his wife isn't and I'm sure she has no great love for Anthony or me. That led me to Cheryl Debret, who's stuck tighter to Merzone's wife than two coats of paint. You've got a leak in your office, my friend."

"I can't believe that. Even if Cheryl were stupid enough to do something like that, I can't believe Norris would take the chance of being caught pulling such a stunt. They'd disbar him for Christ's sake."

"Take a reality check, Mario!" I said not believing that Rizzelli could be this naïve. "The man's a certifiable nut-fuck! Norris had to figure that when the shit hit the fan, that Anthony would come to you for help. He got to Cheryl Debret long before he made his play. Only it didn't work out the way he planned and when I went to you after my little dance at the Sheraton, it screwed up Norris's plan. But Norris, being the crazy bastard he is, figured as long as he had Cheryl in place he might as well use her to find out whatever he could. He might have thought that you and Bergmann would have some conferences and he could find out what we were planning. Frankly Mario, I don't really give a shit whether you believe it or not and from now on, no more meetings in your office. No more conversations on the office phone and I don't want you leaving my file in your office when you're not there.

"All right, all right," Rizzelli said as he held up his hand to hold me off. "I think you're wrong, but it doesn't pay to be careless.

Now, do you think you can stay out of trouble for a few days 'til we see what Norris's next move is gonna be. Christ, bad shit follows you like the plague, Quinn," Rizzelli said as he turned and walked away. I know he didn't want to believe me, but everything I said made sense. How the hell was he going to run his office if he thought there was a spy in his midst? This was turning out to be one of the dirtiest cases Rizzelli had ever seen.

When Rizzelli arrived back at his office, he couldn't help but take a long look at Cheryl Debret as he walked past her desk just outside his office door. The seed had been planted and there was nothing he could do to change that. My argument was too compelling to ignore. Rizzelli was deep in thought when Cheryl broke his concentration.

"How'd it go?" she asked.

"Fine," he said. The answer was far shorter than he would normally have given, but the doubts were making him careful. He knew that this was a situation that couldn't last. The question was what to do about it. The answer to his problem was in his next phone call.

"Mario, this is Saul Bergmann," the voice on the phone said cheerily. "How'd the meeting with Norris go?"

"You mean before or after Quinn tried to kill Norris?"

"I take it that Mr. Norris and Mr. Quinn are not the best of friends." Saul Bergmann had seen more than one of his clients try to kill a Prosecutor and he didn't mean it in the figurative sense.

An idea came to Rizzelli as he looked at the open door to his office. "Norris didn't have anything to surprise us, Saul. We had an absolute answer for every charge he had." Rizzelli hesitated for a moment. "Listen Saul, I think the integrity of my office has been compromised. There seems to be confidential information getting to Norris. I really don't want to discuss this here. Why don't I fill Anthony in and he can give you an overview."

"You don't have to elaborate, but I take it that someone in your office might be playing for the opposition."

"I think so," Rizzelli said as he once again looked at his door.

Cheryl slowly put the receiver back down after she saw Rizzelli's phone light go out. She felt her mouth go dry and her lips started to tingle with fear when she heard Rizzelli's conversation. She knew enough about the law to know that she could be charged with conspiracy. But what really scared her was the Union's ties to the mob and they don't look very kindly on people who rat them out. She may have been a good friend to Sammy Merzone's wife, but this was starting to look very dangerous. If she stayed where she was she was certain Norris would keep squeezing her for information. The whole situation was starting to develop into a hurricane of terrifying thoughts in her mind. She knew she had to get out of the office so she could think.

"Mario?" she said as she walked into his office. "I'm not feeling very well. Would it be okay if I went home? I really feel sick."

"Of course, Cheryl," Rizzelli said with false concern. Now he knew. The question was what to do about it. He couldn't just fire her on the suspicion that she was giving Norris privileged information and he couldn't let her stay and compromise his office.

When I got home I was surprised to find Rane waiting. She was sitting on the couch reading the newspaper. It was getting to be an unfortunate habit that the Union and all of its problems were common fodder for the paper's canons. "What's up? How come you're home so early?" I said as I walked into the living room.

"It was a light day and I wanted to see how things went for you today," Rane said, her voice reflecting her concern. "Did you play nice with your friends?" she said in a lighter tone.

"Well, let's see," I said as I stroked my chin with my fingers. "Norris asked me a lot of stupid questions that I had all the answers for and then I tried to kill him in his office."

"*What*! Please tell me you're kidding."

"No," I said calmly. "He really pissed me off so I tried to climb over his desk and choke the little shit. But don't worry. Mario's a lot quicker than he looks. He managed to get to me before I could get my hands on Norris's neck. After that we left.

Rane just stared at me for a moment. "I've said it before and I'll say it again. You never cease to amaze me. Talk about wanting to be a fly on the wall. I really wish I had seen that. So what now? Don't tell me you managed to avoid the original charges but now your going to jail for assault?"

"Nah. Mario called me about twenty minutes ago to tell me that I've got to appear before the Grand Jury on Friday. Unless this guy's gonna pull a rabbit out of his hat, I can't imagine what the hell he's gonna ask me that's new. But I promise Honey, when I'm in front of the Grand Jury I'll behave myself."

"Yeah, right," she said as she went back to reading the newspaper.

Chapter Twenty
Death and Redemption

Rizzelli insisted that he be out in the hall while I was appearing before the Grand Jury. I think Rizzelli was more concerned about the possibility for another physical assault on Norris and that Rizzelli just wanted to be there to bail me out when I got my ass thrown in jail. I was actually looking forward to the hearing. I couldn't believe that Norris would produce anything new and I sensed that the whole ordeal was going to be ending soon. I promised Rane that I would be my 'normal cheery self,' and that I'd dazzle the jury with charm. It was going to be a pleasure to show the eighteen jury members what a complete asshole Norris was.

As I walked down the hall, I saw Rizzelli dutifully sitting outside the jury room. I just shook my head. Poor, Mario, I thought. His secretary is a spy and he thinks his job is to keep me from killing Norris.

"Don't even say it, Mario. I promised Rane and now I'll promise you. I will not cause any problems today." I raised my hand as if he were swearing an oath. "Okay?"

Rizzelli never had a chance to respond before the court clerk came out to get me. When I followed the clerk into the room I looked around. Same set-up just a different jury, I thought. After I was sworn in, I turned and looked at the same chair I sat in before. For an instant, the memories of the previous Grand Jury visit raced through my mind. I didn't have much time to reflect as I saw Norris approaching me.

"Hello, Mr. Norris," I said with a broad smile. Norris never acknowledged my greeting, but rather just stood there and looked at me with a smirk on his face.

"You understand that you are a target of this investigation and that you have appeared here today of your own free will. I would also like to remind you that you still have the right to invoke the protection afforded you under the Fifth Amendment of the Constitution," Norris began.

Norris casually walked toward the jury as he prepared to deliver his next question. "Mr. Quinn, please tell the jury about your relationship with Anthony Traffarro."

On and on he went, asking the same questions he had asked me in his office. The only difference was that he broke them up into little bits and pieces and mixed them all up. One minute it was New Issues and the next minute it was payoffs. Then it was back to New Issues. I knew he was desperately trying to find a conflict in my testimony, but it's hard to trip up a person when they're telling the truth and they have nothing to hide. Finally, I couldn't take it any longer. Norris got into such a complex issue and it took him nearly three minutes to outline his question. It was time to have some fun.

"I'm sorry Mr. Norris, but could you please repeat the question," I asked as politely as possible. Then I just sat there pretending to be intent on listening to every word while Norris went through the entire question again. I was sitting there wondering, how many times could I get this asshole to repeat the same question? Norris finally finished.

"I'm sorry Mr. Norris, but I still don't understand your question. Could you possibly rephrase it please?"

Norris thought for a moment and proceeded to restate his question, only this time it took him twice as long. I appeared to hang on his every word, but once again I was contemplating how far I could push Norris. When Norris finished the question, I was ready for his response.

"Mr. Norris," I said slowly. "This must not be a very good day for me, but none of what you said makes any sense to me and I'm afraid that I'm more confused now than I was when you first asked this question. Would you like to take another attempt? I do apologize." I said it with such sweetness that the jury in unison turned and looked at Norris to see if he could help this poor man. Norris stood there a stared at me. Gradually, the edge of one side of his mouth started to turn up in a scowling grin as he realized what I had done.

"No, Mr. Quinn. I think we can let this one pass."

Norris walked over to his table to collect himself. I was waiting patiently for the next question when a woman walked into the room with a piece of paper. I recognized her as Norris's secretary. She walked over to Norris and said a few words before she handed him the message. I was surprised to see Norris read the message and then slump down into his chair. He stayed there for quite awhile before he got up and addressed me and the jury.

"Ladies and gentlemen, I have no further questions of this witness. Mr. Quinn you may leave. Ladies and gentlemen of the jury you are excused," Norris said in a hollow voice. Whatever was in the message had affected Norris deeply.

It wasn't until the next day that I figured out the apparent contents of the message. I got a call from Traffarro who told me to go out and buy a newspaper and read the article on page two

Lucille Barrington Norris die yesterday in Boston of an apparent heart attack, she was sixty eight, I read on. *She was the loving daughter of Russell Barrington who had built an empire in the textile industry. He had taken his own life after his business collapsed.* The connection didn't immediately jump out at me until I had read a bit further. *Mrs. Norris is survived by her husband*

Charles and her two daughters Mary and Susan and her son Kevin Norris who is a Federal Prosecutor. I couldn't believe what I was reading. Barrington? Norris? I had heard the stories about the Barringtons. When Costa was in his early twenties, he had worked for Barrington. Labor unrest in Barrington Mills was the start of Costa's beginning in the labor movement and the Union he formed. Costa's power grew and he ultimately destroyed Barrington. Russell Barrington supposedly killed himself over the shame of losing his fortune. His daughter Lucille was the one who found him lying across his desk with his brains blown out. The experience was so traumatic for her that she didn't utter another word for months. Mrs. Barrington's grief turned to revenge and she tried for the rest of her life to get at Costa, who she considered the cause of the family's heartache. The more I looked at the paper and thought about the connection the more I realized that I must be a witness to a family's legacy of revenge. It was a revenge that had been passed down from mother to daughter and then to her son Kevin. No wonder Norris is a raving lunatic, I thought. He had been raised to hate Costa and the Union and spent his whole life trying to get the revenge that his whole family sought.

Norris left the Grand Jury and stormed down the hall to his office clutching the message in his hand. His mind was drowning in an ocean of pain and anger. He had spent his entire life focused on one purpose, the destruction of Renato Costa and his damned Union. Norris never considered what he would do with his life after the success or failure of his quest. The hate had been placed so deep in his psyche that it consumed his life, leaving little room for anything else. Douglas was sitting in his office when Norris charged past. He got up immediately and followed Norris down the hall trying to express his sympathies to the man who seemed oblivious to the world around him. Norris threw open the door to his office with such force that the glass in the door shattered. Norris stood bent over with his hands on his desk and his head slowly shaking back and forth. Then with one sweep of his arm, he flung everything on the desk across the room.

"My mother spent her *whole life* wanting revenge for the death of her father," Norris wailed. "She *never* had time for me *or* my father. It was always about Costa, Costa, Costa! How he ruined our family. How the Union had destroyed her life. The one thing that I could have given her that would have meant something was Costa and his damned Union. This wasn't what I wanted to do, it was what I *had* to do." Norris said as he finally looked up at Douglas with a face that begged for understanding. "*I had to do it!* What do I do now?" Norris said as he walked slowly out of his office. "I'm driving to Boston. I'll call you"

"For God's sake, Kevin! You can't drive anywhere in your state of mind. Let me drive you."

"No. I'll drive myself. I need to be alone so I can think." Norris didn't even go home to pack. He just got into his car and started driving.

This was not the condition to be in when driving on the interstate at seventy five miles an hour in the pouring rain. Half way to Boston, Kevin Norris lost control of his car and was killed.

It would be a month before a replacement for Norris finally arrived in the city. He carefully reviewed the evidence and testimony relating to the charges against Traffarro and I. Ultimately, he decided to dismiss the Grand Jury without any attempt to move for an indictment. Traffarro pressed Saul Bergmann to get a letter from the Government that clearly stated that there was no evidence of wrong doing by Traffarro in the investigation. When the new Prosecutor reviewed the files again, he found suspicious references to a Cheryl Debret, who he discovered was in the employment of a defense attorney. It seemed to him the lesser of two evils was to write Traffarro his letter and make the whole thing go away.

Traffarro said that this was the only letter of its kind ever issued by the Government to a union leader. But it was a very empty victory for him. Nicky's betrayal had wounded him deeply.

Nicky Tagliano's divorce forced the sale of his business. He was so despised by the community he had grown up in that he moved away. Nobody knew where he went and for the most part, no one cared. He had twisted the honor that this community held in such high regard to suit his own purpose. The revenge he used to rationalize the betrayal of his friends to save himself resulted in a prison sentence of a different kind.

Bill Douglas retired after twenty-five years with the Bureau. He left the area for Florida after two winters of freezing his ass off and started a security consulting firm that serviced some of the biggest companies in the state.

Rane and I finally got married. We became close friends with Anthony and Connie and great number of the people in the Italian community. These were ties that would last for the rest of our lives and included Tino Drazzetti and Rocco Massarro. I was very much in love and had the close family I had searched for my whole life. Finally, I found a place were I belonged.

15571717R00137

Made in the USA
Lexington, KY
08 June 2012